Read

Bone to Pick

"*Bone to Pick* is a great mystery that is sure to pull readers in from the beginning."

—Top 2 Bottom Reviews

"TA Moore brings readers a solid, well written, suspenseful mystery in *Bone to Pick*. The plot is multi-layered and peppered with suspicious characters who had me fooled almost to the very end."

—The Novel Approach

Liar, Liar

"I highly recommend this story to everyone in the mood for something tense, action packed, and oddly romantic."

—Love Bites

"*Liar, Liar* is a great suspense with some twisty moments and really fun characters. I can definitely recommend this one, particularly if you are fan of romantic suspense and like your heroes a little bit outside the box."

—Joyfully Jay

Dog Days

"Wow. *Dog Days* turned out to be even more than I expected... Trust me when I say you won't regret reading this... not if you love twists, turns, and horror."

—Rainbow Book Reviews

By TA MOORE

Bone to Pick
Dog Days
Liar, Liar
Wanted – Bad Boyfriend

Published by DREAMSPINNER PRESS
www.dreamspinnerpress.com

Wanted –
BAD BOYFRIEND

TA MOORE

DREAMSPINNER PRESS

Published by
DREAMSPINNER PRESS

5032 Capital Circle SW, Suite 2, PMB# 279,
Tallahassee, FL 32305-7886 USA
www.dreamspinnerpress.com

Wanted – Bad Boyfriend
© 2018 TA Moore.

Cover Art
© 2018 Reece Notley.
reece@vitaenoir.com
Cover content is for illustrative purposes only and any person depicted on the cover is a model.

Mass Market Paperback ISBN: 978-1-64108-010-1
Trade Paperback ISBN: 978-1-64080-538-5
Digital ISBN: 978-1-64080-260-5
Library of Congress Control Number: 2017917047
Mass Market Paperback published August 2018
v. 1.0

Printed in the United States of America
∞
This paper meets the requirements of
ANSI/NISO Z39.48-1992 (Permanence of Paper).

As always, I would never have gotten here without the support of my mum and the "go on and do it" poking from The Five. Love you all!

CHAPTER ONE

"You know, my nephew's gay. Maybe if you hire him to do some work in the garden, they could... run into each other?"

THE GRANSHIRE Hotel brooded elegantly over some of Ceremony Island's most stunning vistas. At the back the cliffs dropped down to the deep, white-sand crescent of the bay, where brightly colored boats rocked at anchor a few miles out. At the front the moorland rolled down, all heather and wildflowers, until it reached the straight, stone-built walls that fenced off the farmland. A small herd of deer sometimes roamed across the land.

The *Tatler* had named it one of the top ten destination-wedding locations in the UK. Wedding parties arrived from around the world. It wasn't cheap, and it wasn't easy to reach. Even UK couples had a long drive over rutted coastal roads and had to take a ferry over the stretch of Irish sea. But couples in search of the perfect wedding seemed to think it was worth it.

It wasn't just the aged stone hall or posing on the elegant stairway with its black oak railings carved to look like twisted briars. They wanted the trip down to the fairy caves on the beach, the congratulatory pint of Guinness in the traditional country pub with the brasses behind the bar, and the "something old" picked out of the trinket shop in the hollowed-out fisherman's cottage on the beach—or any number of the other Instagrammable moments the island could provide.

Couples who came to Ceremony wanted a well-chronicled fairy tale or a rom-com, and as the Granshire's wedding planner, it was Nate Moffatt's job to make sure they got it—even on days when the last thing he wanted to think about was anybody's happily ever after.

"Shoes?" he asked as he leaned in through the doors to the Granshire's bar.

The bar was an expanse of sea-bleached wood and polished metal surfaces that usually looked like it was ready for a magazine spread. It was covered in the detritus of the previous evening's wedding party, with crumpled confetti swept into multicolored drifts in the corners and glasses sticky with the dregs of fruity cocktails on every flat surface.

A skeleton staff of the bar crew were already making inroads on the cleanup, yawning as they dragged bags of rubbish behind them. They paused long enough to shrug their "no ideas" Nate's way. He made a mental note to up the usual "thanks for a good job" gratuity he'd send down.

Technically he didn't need to. Some couples wanted to hire a marquee or get married in the old distillery, which meant hiring on extra staff, but the newly minted Sanders had just gone with the hotel package. So the staff were included. Still, in Nate's experience it was always better to have a reputation as a good person to work for—for that one event when you had to ask them to dress up like the Mad Hatter and serve Long Island iced teas into the a.m.

Nate left the staff to get on with clearing the glasses and picked his way through the tables to the bar. He leaned over the bar and whistled sharply between his teeth to catch the bar manager's attention.

"Bride's shoes?" he asked. "One of a kind. Designer. Look like every other pair of sparkly silver Cinderella slippers you've ever seen?"

Max tossed two empty bottles of prosecco into the recycling and raised his eyebrows at Nate. "Somebody woke up pissy," he said. The short, stylishly scruffy man was the son of the hotel's owner and Nate's best friend since they were two awkward gay kids trying to work out why more girls seemed to like them than boys did. It turned out that if you were best mates with the other queer kid in your small, islander class of twenty... that could be your gay quota until you graduated. "I haven't seen any shoes. I found one of the bridesmaids sleeping it off in the toilet, though, if that helps."

It was hard to resist Max's smirk. Despite his sour mood, Nate caught the corners of his mouth twitching up in a return grin.

No matter how Grimm's-fairy-tale pretty the weddings looked, the aftermaths were always a bit more like something out of the original stories—full of regrets, secrets to keep, and sometimes blood on the floor. Mostly vomit, but sometimes blood.

"As of midnight yesterday, the bridesmaids were back on their own time and not my problem," Nate said.

"You could check the gardens," Max suggested as he lifted the pot of coffee from the machine and poured Nate a cup. He didn't need to ask if Nate wanted it. The answer was always yes. "I saw some of the wedding party dancing out there."

Nate lifted the cup and took a scalding sip. There were bottles of syrup lined up on the wall, everything from basic bitch vanilla to cheesecake, but those were for people who drank coffee to enjoy it. This was maintenance coffee—hot, strong, and thick enough to stand a spoon upright in.

When he looked up, Max had taken a break from clearing the bar and was leaning on it instead. His arms were crossed, and he raised his eyebrows expectantly. "So? Long night why you're such a cranky git this morning?"

It had been, but Nate didn't think Max was wasting a suggestive leer on a 3:00 a.m. escort to her suite for the groom's tiddly and depressed mother. That left....

Nate hissed out a sigh through clenched teeth. The morning seemed determined to just get on his last nerve. "I take it you're the one who gave the groom's brother my number?"

Max's leer deepened. "Yeah, you owe me one. He still back at yours?"

"No."

The leer collapsed. "Didn't he call you?" Max asked. He sounded genuinely surprised. "I can't believe it. He seemed really into you, said you were a silver fox."

Nate glanced past Max into the mirror behind the bar and self-consciously brushed gray-streaked brown curls back from his forehead. He was thirty-seven. That was too young to be a silver fox, even if he had been going gray since before he was twenty.

"He called."

Texted actually. Nate wondered dryly if his mild offense at that meant he should accept that he was older than he felt.

Max looked at him quizzically. "And? He thought you were hot. He called. You hooked up—"

"I didn't answer him," Nate said flatly. "I was in the middle of running a wedding. I didn't have time to hook up with a random stranger."

Instead of picking up on the prickle of irritation underlying Nate's voice and backing off, Max made a rude noise. "It never stopped you before. I remember back in Durham, when you were volunteering at the book festival. One night you hooked up with three different blokes between talks and readings, including one of the authors. Still got everyone to fill in your satisfaction survey at the end."

Nate had to admit, that *had* been a good night. Of course his years in Durham had been full of good nights. Even if he ended up never using that English Lit degree for anything but impressing boys who liked sonnets. Ceremony wasn't Durham, though, and Nate wasn't twenty anymore.

"That was over a decade ago," Nate said. "And I was a horny idiot."

"Happy, though," Max pointed out. He flashed the grin that had gotten more than a few men to follow him for a quick tumble. And the numbers had increased recently. Max wasn't handsome. There was too much nose and too much jaw, and his hair was too thick for styling, but he had that gloss of growing up wealthy and sure of himself. It had gotten Nate into more trouble than he could easily list over the years, since the first time a ten-year-old Maxwell had poked him in the ribs, grinned, and suggested they do something stupid. "C'mon, Nate. I know your ex did a number on you, but—"

It was the wrong thing to say. It was pretty much always the wrong thing to say.

"Fuck you, Max."

He put the half-finished cup of coffee neatly down on the counter and stalked out. The bar staff gave each other "this is awkward" grimaces as he passed them. Nate scored out the mental note he'd made about their gratuity, even though he knew he'd back down on that before HR drew up their paychecks.

"Nate," Max called after him. "Hold on, okay? I didn't mean to…. Shit."

The doors into the gardens swung shut behind Nate and cut off anything else Max wanted to say.

It would be fine. Later on Max would apologize and stand Nate one of the crappy, local craft beers he insisted on stocking. Nate would forgive him, because it wasn't as though bringing up an ex was a good reason to properly fall out with someone. And he might not be a silver fox yet, but he was definitely too old to make a new best friend.

It wasn't even Max that Nate was angry at anyhow. Or his ex. Despite what everyone seemed to think, he wasn't pining for that asshole like some Cookson romance heroine.

He walked through the hotel's small, elegant rose garden. The bride's shoes were sitting on the edge of the fountain, sparkly silver and damp from dew. Nate left them there for a second and walked to the edge of the garden so he could look over the wall.

The view crashed straight down gray cliffs dotted with seagulls to the decorative, deceptive white slice of sandy beach far below. It was only the start of May and a few sunbathing bodies decorated the sand, while out in the bay, someone was trying to drag a sodden parasail out of the waves. Nate leaned his elbows on the stone, rubbed his eyes, and waited for the hot bubble of anger to sink back into the pit of his stomach.

He spent most of his days planning other people's weddings. There was the occasional festival and the village fair, but it was mostly weddings. He listened to meet-cute stories, wrangled bridesmaids, vetted speeches, and occasionally pulled off the impossible. To his clients he was charming, supportive, and made sure that the couple got the day they'd dreamed about.

But the happiest day of his client's life was just another Tuesday for him. When he went home, he wanted to take his suit off, eat leftover pizza, watch *Fortitude* or something equally miserable, and be a grumpy, single bastard in peace.

It wasn't too much to ask.

Or he didn't think so. Everyone else in his life seemed to think differently. His friends kept trying to set him up on blind dates—or blind fucks in Max's case—and since her cancer diagnosis, his mother was obsessed with the idea that she was going to die before he found someone… and that he'd then die alone and be eaten by cats.

"DO YOU even have a cat?" Max asked.

It was eight hours later. Max was forgiven, Mary Sanders nee Black had her shoes back, and the beer tasted just as bad as Nate had expected. He slouched down on the sofa in Max's office, one leg swung up over the worn leather arm.

"No." Nate took a second sip of the beer, which claimed to be cranberry and rosehip flavored, in case the taste grew on you. If it did, it hadn't so far.

Max kicked back in his office chair and put his feet up on the desk. A footstool was pretty much all he'd ever used the desk for. It wasn't that he was lazy, but he'd never reacted well to being put somewhere and told to stay there. He couldn't even talk on the phone unless he was moving, pacing out his conversations in laps of the bar. Why his dad had insisted on the office and then complained that Max was never in it, was beyond Nate.

"So," Max said. He scratched his jaw with the base of his beer. "Does your mum think you're going to turn into a crazy cat lady from loneliness? Or are cats just going to be drawn to your corpse from across the island once you've karked it?"

Nate shrugged. "No idea." He kicked his foot absently, and his heel bounced off the side of the sofa. "Look, I knew it wouldn't be easy having her come to live with me while she recuperated. But I thought it would be endless cups of tea and her constantly asking me 'who's that, then?' in the middle of TV shows— not her obsessing about me getting married before she dies, which is apparently going to be any day now."

That creased Max's face into a frown, and he straightened up. The chair creaked under him as he shifted his weight. "Is she okay?" He sounded worried. "If Ally's not feeling well, we should get her back to the hospital."

Nate decided to blame the beer for the bad taste in the back of his throat. They weren't kids anymore, and it was petty to be jealous that, in a lot of ways, Max got on better with Nate's mother than he did. It wasn't that Nate and his mum didn't love each other—most of the time—it was just that Ally Moffatt and Max Saint John had all that "free-spirit, difficult relationships with their dads, think they know best for Nate thing" in common.

"Mum's fine," Nate said. "That's the problem. Her brain used to be full of doctor's appointments and drug regimes. Now she doesn't have to worry about that, so she's packed the space with paranoia and matchmaking."

Max looked like that reassurance hadn't put his mind entirely at ease, but he let it go. He gestured with the beer.

"C'mon, though. It's not like she's trying to make you marry a woman, and, I don't know, study to be a divorce lawyer," Max said. "She just wants you to be happy, and it's not like you are."

"I'm happy." Nate tossed his hands in the air in frustration. Beer splashed out of the bottle and onto his wrist. It stained the cuff of his shirt, which only put him in a better mood, dammit. "I'm thrilled. I'm fucking ecstatic."

"Yeah." Max rocked back in the chair and folded his arms over his stomach with the bottle balanced on his belt buckle. His eyes glittered over his hook of a nose. "You really sound it."

Nate rolled his eyes. "Okay. Not right now. Generally I'm *fine*. Right now, I'm just okay with my own company, you know?"

"You mean wanking?"

"No."

Max snorted his opinion. Nate ignored him and took another swig of beer. The taste was not getting any better the more time it spent on his tongue.

And yeah, he wanked. It wasn't like he'd signed up for celibacy—although with his mother living there it felt like it sometimes—but that wasn't the point. There *wasn't* a point. Despite what people seemed to think, he hadn't made any big decision about locking his balls away and joining the monkhood.

"Why is it always me, anyhow?" Nate asked. "How come no one is after you to settle down and adopt some deserving little buggers to carry on the family name?"

Max winced and crossed himself with the bottle. His eyes flicked piously upward. "He's joking. Don't listen." He looked back at Nate. "Besides, the last guy my family met was twenty years younger than me, a semiprofessional fire-eater, and stole ten grand from me on his way out the door. My dad lives in fear of me getting attached to the losers I bang."

"Did you ever get that money back?"

"Nope," Max said. He scrubbed his hand through his hair, which was a feat considering how dense it was. "Never saw it or my dad's respect again. The things that guy could do with his mouth, though? Worth it."

Both of them knew that was a lie. They sat out the slightly uncomfortable opportunity to address it, letting the seconds drag out as they shifted and sighed and picked at the label of their beers. Then Max dragged his smirk back out from where it had sunk and made a crack about hot mouths. It was easy to fill the air with banter. They'd had thirty years of practice, and it left plenty of Nate's brain to mull over his new idea.

He'd never had a really *bad* boyfriend. Yeah, Jamie had been a dick at the end, but that had just been... shitty boyfriend behavior. Not country-song bad. Maybe what Nate needed was for people to realize there were worse things for him than watching too much TV.

"Want another beer?" Max licked the last drips from the lip of the bottle.

Nate glanced at his. Somehow he'd managed to accidentally drink most of it. Only a third was left behind the murky orange glass.

"No. I still have to drive home." He set the bottle down on Max's unused desk, next to his friend's kicked-up boots. "Also this tastes like shit."

"Yeah. The rosehips added something weird to the profile." Max swung his feet down, stood up, and stretched until things in his spine popped. He slung an arm around Nate's shoulder and dragged him into a rough hug. "You know, if you don't like me picking your dates? There's a whole bar full of people that will be checking out in a couple of days. And they already have a room booked."

Nate snorted and slung a reciprocal arm around Max's neck. Twenty years on from the day it happened, and it still made him feel smug that he was taller.

"I have a big wedding party coming in next week. I want to get an early, sober start," he said. "Besides, Mum would worry."

Max laughed, told him to give Ally his love, and waved him off through the bar. On his way out through the hotel, nodding goodbye to the receptionist on duty as he crossed the marble-tiled entry, Nate wondered where he could find a bad boyfriend at short notice on an island.

Of course, when he put it like that, there was really only one choice.

CHAPTER TWO

"If he doesn't have something to hide, then why doesn't he come out and say we're wrong about him being a criminal?"

"FISH SUPPER, chicken nuggets, and a curry!" Gennie the barmaid yelled out as she shoved the plates onto the bar.

A man looked up from one of the coin-sized round tables that filled the space between the booths and the bar. He had two whining, wilting children with him, and the harried look of a man who hadn't thought through what a weekend away with the kids would be like. He lifted his hand hopefully. Gennie gave the plates a shove toward the edge of the bar.

The guy sighed and got up, jabbed a finger at the kids, and squeezed his way to the bar. No one moved their chair for him. He reached the bar and fumbled at the plates as he tried to balance all three. Flynn propped himself up on his elbow and watched the man struggle.

The curry was the guy's second mistake. The first was not going to the Fox and Swan. The Hairy Dog was the local pub. The food was cheaper, the atmosphere less friendly.

Gennie finished pulling Flynn's beer. Froth dribbled down over her heavily-ringed fingers as she shoved it toward him.

"Three thirty," she said. "Want me to start a tab?"

Flynn passed her a five instead. His father had drunk there all his life. When he died, his tab was thirty pounds, and the pub had wiped it in honor of him.

The beleaguered dad finally made it back to his table. Most of the food was still on the plates. The chicken dippers that had hit the floor were already being cleaned up by the pub dog, who'd been a sheepdog in Flynn's dad's day and was a lanky spaniel now.

"Mum said—" the pouting little girl started.

"Well, this is Dad's weekend." He tucked the napkin into her collar. "And on Dad's weekend, we have chips."

Poor bugger.

Flynn picked up the beer, the glass slippery under his fingers, and sucked the foam off the surface. His shoulder protested the movement. Some idiots had decided to go skinny-dipping off the bay, not realizing how quickly the weather went from balmy to Baltic once it started to get dark. The rescue ended with Flynn dunked in the freezing water as one of the idiots panicked when he was yanking them out.

The chill had sunk into his bones, and once the adrenaline wore off, his shoulder hurt. It was the sort of ache that smugly promised it was going to grow up to be a throb.

He was getting too old to be crawling up cliffs and diving into the Irish Sea. Twenty years earlier he'd have hauled himself back out of the water laughing. Fuck, twenty years earlier he'd have been the idiot pruning up his balls by skinny-dipping.

Yeah, he thought sourly as he drained the beer, but what else was he going to do? There weren't a lot of options for a guy with his background. If there had been, he wouldn't be propping up the same bar as his dad, would he?

"Well, I tell you what, Katie, I wouldn't want him rescuing me. He'd have your wallet out of the water before you."

It was the familiarity that caught his ear.

Flynn twisted around and leaned back against the counter with both his elbows braced behind him. He glanced around until he saw the two women at the end of the bar. Both were perched on stools, their heads tilted together over tall, lipstick-stained glasses of coke and something boozy. Chewed lemon slices lay on the side of the coasters. He vaguely recognized both. It was a small island.

"That's a best-case scenario, Fi. My sister's lad Ben and him used to be mates. What Ben says about what he got up to over on the mainland? Doesn't bear repeating."

She stopped and took a slurped drink of her coke and whatever-it-was for punctuation.

It was nothing new. The beer tasted sour on Flynn's tongue all of a sudden. He left the pint sitting, pushed himself upright, and headed for the door.

Fi saw him coming, nudged her friend, and arched her eyebrows meaningfully. Before the woman could turn around, Flynn leaned in over her shoulder.

"Aw, go on, Katie. Repeat it," he drawled. The low rasp of his voice in her ear, all growl and yeast, made Katie pull herself up straight and offended. "You know you want to."

He winked at Fi and left them to sit and stew as he ducked out through the old black-wood main door. It was still summer—the season held on until the start of October—but Flynn could feel the chill creeping in.

His Land Rover was parked on the pavement outside the bar. Mud was splattered up the sides from the tire well to the back windows. Flynn hadn't bothered to lock it. It wasn't that there was no crime on the island—there were a lot of drugs, fights, bruises doled out behind closed doors—but if you stole a car, there was nothing to do with it but drive it to the other side of the island. If you stole Flynn's car, you could drive the thing into the sea, and it would just have to be towed out and dried out. It was twenty years old, and there wasn't much to it other than a heavy metal chassis and a red diesel-stained engine.

Flynn scrambled up into the driver's seat and started the car. The heavy growl of the engine kicking to life rattled up through his bones. He jolted down off the pavement, one hand on the wheel as he headed out of town.

He passed the turnoff up to the Granshire halfway back to his house. They'd strung up old coach lanterns to illuminate the sight—brass and glass and class. Those got stolen pretty regularly.

Two turns and a sheep blocking the road for five minutes later, he saw the pale pillar of the old lighthouse appear on the headland. It stuck up like a defiant white finger at the Granshire, who'd tried to buy it after it was decommissioned.

But some old entailment on the property gave the lighthouse keeper first refusal and a generous discount. Flynn's dad had still been in debt until the day he died. After the funeral, before the dirt had even settled, Teddy Saint John tried to buy it again, and Flynn had told him where to stick his offer. Ceremony might need the Saint Johns' money and the posh bastards who came to the Granshire to get wed, fed, and off their head on expensive island whiskey, but no one liked them.

Besides, Flynn had been pissed at the world then—more pissed—and it was satisfying to have someone to aim that at.

He turned off the road and onto the rutted dirt track that led up to the lighthouse. The Land Rover jolted and juddered up the hill to the roughly flattened square of dirt and paving stones he used as a drive. There was another car already parked there, a sleek gray sports car covered in a fresh layer of dust and dirt, and at the top of the stairs to the lighthouse, Flynn could see a bright ember glowing against the dark. The firefly flicker of it rose and fell as he parked and got out of the car.

"I told you," Flynn said as he climbed up the mossy concrete steps. "I'm not interested in renting my place out."

Nate Moffatt exhaled a cloud of pale smoke into the air. He was sitting cross-legged on the old black

painted bench next to the door. It wasn't his space, but
that didn't seem to bother him. Like a cat, he assumed
that he improved whatever area he was in.

Flynn disagreed with him on principle. He was
too pretty to agree with. It would just encourage him.

"That's not why I'm here," Nate said. He took another drag on the cigarette and flicked the butt away
from him. It arched toward the cliff edge in a trail of
short-lived sparks, and Nate crooked the corner of his
mouth in a wry smile. "I wanted to ask a favor."

"A favor?" Flynn hooked his thumbs into the
pockets of his jeans and raised his eyebrows curiously.
"A favor is what has Saint John's errand boy hanging
out up here at this time of night?"

The "errand boy" crack curdled the smile at the
edges, but it hung on.

"Well, I did try and catch you earlier. But you're
a hard man to pin down," Nate said. "And yeah, just
a favor."

"Well, I don't wanna do that either." That killed
the smile. Flynn ignored the flick of disappointment he felt and nudged Nate out of the way with
his shoulder as he stepped past him. Unlike his car,
he locked the heavy black door of the lighthouse. It
took an old-fashioned, long-shafted key that rattled in
the wrought-iron mechanism, and the hinges resisted
opening for a second.

Long enough for Nate to slip in, "It will *really*
piss off Max."

The hook caught. Flynn braced his hand on the
door, his tanned, scarred fingers against the dark wood,
and huffed out his irritation. He glanced sidelong at

Nate, who had his crooked smile back and added the expectant quirk of a dark, manicured eyebrow to it.

Goddammit. He could resist anything but pettiness and pretty men. Now there they both were in one well-dressed package.

Flynn put his shoulder into it and shoved the door. It swung back until the iron-shod corner of it caught in the sandy rut a century of use had ground into the floor. Flynn jerked his thumb inside.

"I'm not promising anything," he growled.

"Wouldn't ask you to."

Nate ducked past him into the lighthouse and did a half turn on his heel as he checked out the rough plaster curves of the walls and the bare-bones spiral staircase that dominated the room. He looked interested, maybe approving, and Flynn bit his tongue on the unfamiliar urge to explain why he'd done something.

For a second, Flynn wondered if he'd made a mistake. He knew the type of man Nate was. He'd met them before. Nate would ask for an inch, take a mile, and make you feel like he'd done you a favor. Except he was already in, and Flynn might as well listen. He could always toss him out on his ear later if he felt like it.

"The favor?" he said.

Nate ran his fingers up the squared-off rod of metal that served as the banister. "I like this," he said. "Very utilitarian."

"I thought that was bad?"

"Depends on the context. This context? It works."

Nate gave the stairs a last, absent rub, and Flynn forced down his dick's urge to make something of that and turned back around. Nate flashed him a grin that was all practiced charm. "I'll have a coffee, if you're having one."

"I'm not."

"Tea?"

"Favor."

There was a pause. Nate took a deep breath and bounced nervously on the balls of his feet. He gestured with his hands as he talked, each sentence punctuated with a jabbed finger or spread palm. "I do want to rent something. Not the lighthouse, though." He brought his palms together and made his index fingers into a gun that pointed at Flynn's chest. "I want to rent you."

Flynn's dick was all in, but his common sense thought it was time to chuck him out. Flynn compromised with "Fuck off."

He shed his jacket, hung it up on the back of the door, and went into the galley kitchen he'd squeezed into the old tool shed during renovation. It was tiled black and white because that had been cheaper at B&Q, and it was spotlessly clean because he didn't use it that much.

There was half a takeout carton of vindaloo and rice in the fridge. He tipped it into a white bowl and put it into the microwave. When he looked around, Nate was leaning against the doorframe. His arms were folded, and his soft pink shirt was pulled tightly over his chest. Flynn spent a second trying to pretend that he was surprised Nate hadn't fucked off.

"I could eat." When Flynn narrowed his eyes at him, Nate rubbed the back of his neck. He shrugged one shoulder. "Just let me explain. Then you can chuck me out on my ass if you want."

The ping of the microwave interrupted them. Behind the smoked glass, the curry bubbled enthusiastically. What the hell. The joy of reheating was that you could always reheat again.

"I'm not feeding you," he said. It was his turn to cross his arms and lean his hip against the scarred wood countertop. His shoulder whined at the stress on it, but he let it. "But go on. Spit it out."

Nate blinked. Maybe he hadn't expected it to be that easy.

"Everyone thinks I need a boyfriend," he said. "So I thought I'd get one—a really bad one, or at least the worst one I can find at short notice on an island."

"And you immediately thought of me," Flynn said. And he'd thought the posh boy trying to buy his ass was insulting. Showed what he knew. "What? The island's child molester died finally?"

CHAPTER THREE

"Have you thought about Tinder? Online dating is how all the boys do it these days."

ALL RIGHT. Nate could hear it. Said out loud, standing in Flynn's own kitchen, that did sound worse than it had in Nate's head.

"Okay, I can see that sounds a bit offensive." He drew the words out carefully. "But hear me out."

Flynn scowled at him. He drew his dark, heavy brows down to shadow his chilly, sea-gray eyes, but he waited. That was great. It meant he was open to discussion, which was more than Flynn had ever been about the idea of renting the lighthouse out as a honeymoon suite.

Of course it also meant that Nate had to find a way to put his plan that didn't sound like it was "my loved ones would rather I die alone than date you."

Since that was the plan, it wouldn't be easy. Nate bit his lower lip and tried to think of a less abrasive way to explain that.

"You going to say anything?" Flynn asked. "Or just stand there looking pretty?"

"Would that work?" Nate asked.

Flynn looked him up and down, from his hair to the sneakers that he was, one day, going to replace with grown-up shoes. The slow, unabashed study flushed a dull heat under Nate's skin, and he shifted uncomfortably. It might have been the wrong tack to flirt with Flynn. He seemed the type to take things too literally, and the whole point of being there was to put a temporary pin in Nate's love life, not complicate things by noticing that Flynn actually looked sexier with a lean jaw and crow's feet weathered into pale skin than he had when he was young, meaty, and St. Tropez amber. Of course, Nate had a wholly inappropriate crush on him back then too.

A sly little voice that he hadn't heard for a while nudged his brain suggestively and reminded him that fifteen and twenty was inappropriate. Thirty-seven and forty-three was—

"No. You're not that pretty," Flynn said flatly and interrupted Nate's train of thought before it could get away with him. "Look. I don't see any way you're going to convince me to play your bit of rough because you don't have the balls to tell people to fuck off. So either come up with something good or get out of my house so I can eat my dinner."

Usually Nate didn't have a problem coming up with a convincing line. He routinely talked fathers of brides into putting down a large and nonrefundable deposit at the Granshire. He convinced brides to com-promise on having owls fly in and drop the rings into the couple's waiting hands. He cozened Mr. Saint John into putting on his Irish and making an appearance at the occasional wedding. This time he had nothing.

He wished he hadn't used the "pissing off Max" angle to get through the door. If he'd thought about how bad the whole "I want to rent you" thing was go-ing to sound, he'd have kept that in reserve. Instead all he had was a couple of flaccid rejoinders scraped from the bottom of the barrel. Since he was pretty sure "I'll pay you" would make things worse, that left him only one.

"Have you got anything better to do?" he asked.

There was a pause as Flynn stared at him. "I work for the Emergency Services," he finally said, each word stated slowly as though Nate might misunder-stand. "I save people's lives."

"I'm sure that's very rewarding. It's not like you can plan your Friday night around someone falling down a hole, though."

"You'd be surprised," Flynn muttered. He popped the door of the microwave open and pulled out the bowl of curry and rice. The heat made him juggle it from hand to hand. "If I wanted to party on a weekend, I'd still live in London."

From what Nate had heard, that wasn't an op-tion. But he let the statement pass unchallenged and stepped out of the way to let Flynn get a fork out of the drawer.

"And if you wanted to be a hermit, you'd have moved to a smaller island," Nate countered. "Come on. You go out with me for a couple of weeks, get to go to a bunch of events and be a dick to Max. Where's the downside?"

Flynn pointed the fork at him. "Do you want me to list them? For a start, it's not dating. It's being paraded around downtown while you ring a bell and shout 'bad boyfriend' like I'm some sort of relationship leper. I have to lie to everyone. I have to pretend that I want to bang you." That stung. Nate swallowed the bitter pill and pretended it was sugar. If nothing else it undercut the distracting awareness of Flynn's broad, muscled frame. "Besides, despite what you think, not everyone on this island hates me. I'd like to keep it that way. You need anything more?"

The answer would probably have been "not really," since that had been a pretty comprehensive list. Flynn took a pointed step toward the door, but Nate held his ground and blocked the way.

"C'mon, Flynn," he said. "You know you've got a reputation around the island. Nobody thinks you're a danger to the sheep, but nobody's granny is trying to set you up either."

"Move."

Nate backed out of the kitchen into the big white round of the main room. He was briefly distracted by the space. The lighthouse really would be ideal for some of his couples—an indulgent, one-night stay, honeymoon getaway. Even if the rent went straight into Flynn's pocket, the word-of-mouth would be great.

He dragged his mind back onto topic as Flynn kicked a chair out and sat down at the stripped-pine table. It wasn't going nearly as well as he'd imagined.

"I don't want you to steal my life savings and release a sex video online." It was probably a push to sit down, so Nate leaned on the squared-off back of the chair opposite Flynn. He tapped his fingers on the wood. "Just be yourself. That'll get up Max's nose, and I'm sure one of my mum's friends will fill her in on what bad news you're meant to be. We 'break up' and they get off my back without me having to—"

"Talk to them?"

"Fight with them."

Flynn shoved a forkful of rice and curry into his mouth. He wiped his mouth on the back of his hand, sat back, and hooked his arm over the chair. The sleeve of his T-shirt crawled up his bicep and flashed a blurred tangle of faded black ink lines that curled around his bicep.

"You asked me to hear you out. I did. I'm not interested in playing your bit of rough. Time to go, Mr. Moffatt."

Nate started to argue but caught himself. The point was to dodge dating, not skip straight to the resentment and bartering aisle of a shitty relationship. Besides, under the chill dose of Flynn's contempt, it was possible it wasn't such a great idea. Even if none of the stories about Flynn Delaney and why he'd come back to the island last year after nearly twenty years on the mainland were true? He was still a miserable bastard. Nate wanted to date again one day. Someday. A couple of months of Flynn and he'd get Wi-Fi put into the old hermit's cave on the beach.

The ache in his balls snorted at that for a lie, but he stuck to it.

"Yes, it is." He pushed himself up off the chair. "Sorry to take up your time."

He got a grunt from Flynn for that. On his way out the door, Nate stopped and spun around. Rejection was never nice, even if it was for a fake relationship designed to go wrong, and it was instinct to gloss it over.

That was something he'd learned from Max's dad. Teddy Saint John never failed. He just succeeded sideways.

"By the way," he said. "Now that I've finally seen the inside of this place? It would be perfect as part of one of the Granshire's wedding packages. I'll drop you down a proposal."

"Don't."

"It's a couple of bits of paper." Nate rolled his eyes. "Read it or burn it. It's up to you. Good night, Mr. Delaney."

Outside, with the door closed behind him, he let some of the facade slip. The night air was cool against his hot face as he stalked down the slippery steps to his car.

That was humiliating. He felt like an idiot. He felt like the fifteen-year-old kid he used to be, all sweaty from a crush and rejection. The only difference was that teenage Nate thought he'd eventually grow out of it. Instead he was a stone's throw from forty, with burning ears and a deep-seated desire to eat a whole bag of Mars Minis.

At least there was slightly more dignity in driving off in a car, rather than trying to make a brooding exit on a BMX.

"YOU SHOULD eat breakfast," Ally said. "It's the most important meal of the day."

Nate grabbed a slice of toast from the rack and shoved it in his mouth. He tore the corner off and chewed it while he pulled the carafe off the coffee machine and filled his travel mug.

"There." He took a swig of coffee to wash away the dry toast crumbs and bent down to kiss his mother's cheek. "Happy?"

She *tched* at him and pointedly added a cup of nuts and dried berries to her breakfast. The spoon clinked self-righteously against the china as she stirred the roughage into her yogurt.

"That's not breakfast," she said. "That's a recipe for an ulcer."

"You used to eat Tayto Cheese and Onion Crisps for breakfast," Nate pointed out. "You said it was two of your five a day."

Ally spread her hands. "And I got cancer," she pointed out. As if that were the "I win" clause to every argument they had from then on. It kind of was, even with her hair growing back in baby-fuzz curls. "Eat some yogurt. Or we have granola."

"No time," Nate said. It was technically true. He had a "crack of the morning" meeting with Teddy, and then he had to get to the ferry to meet the head of a charity that wanted to hold a fundraiser there. But even if he had the morning free, he wouldn't eat the granola. Ally ordered it from some artisan farmer's website, and it was flavored with fennel and green tea. At least the toast—although it had been carved off some sprouted-wheat probiotic sourdough loaf—was burned enough that it only tasted crisp. "And I have a bride coming in this week with her family to finalize the plans."

That distracted Ally from force-feeding him something healthy. She perked up over her green tea and demanded details. Nate filled her in as he added cream to his coffee and cinnamon sugar to his toast and got his suit jacket on.

His mother was a wedding fanatic, and he learned his skills by osmosis when he was growing up. From celebrity wedding pictures in glossy magazines to organizing them for her friends, Ally loved it all. She didn't believe in marriage, but who could object to a three-tiered cake and a poufy dress?

"Snorkeling?" Ally scoffed. "You want to talk them into doing that after the wedding. A bride's feet get uncomfortable enough without getting them cut up from rocks."

Nate grinned. "Already on it." He buttoned his jacket and turned to face her, arms spread to give her the full effect. "How do I look?"

"Very handsome," she said. "You always do. That's why it's such a shame—"

"Mum."

"—that I'm the only one who gets to appreciate it. You spend every day making people happy. When are you going to spend some time *being* happy?"

"I'm happy."

"Happy people don't eat all the Mars bars."

Nate bit his tongue on an answer. In the month since she'd gotten the all clear, Ally had bounced back from the bag of bones she'd been. She was eating, exercising, and cheerfully going to all her physio appointments. Nate felt like one harsh word might undo all that. He still snapped sometimes, but he always felt like crap afterward.

He forced a breath out through clenched teeth and shook his head.

"I'm fine." He picked up her crutches from where they leaned against the sink and carried them around to her. "What are you up to today?"

"Nothing much." She took the crutches and slid her arms into the cuffs. The jersey sleeves of her pajamas bunched up as she put her weight on the metal to stand. One leg of the pajama bottoms ended in a slipper. The other flapped empty from just below Ally's knee. "Yoga this morning. This afternoon I'm going into the office to talk about when I'm going back."

Nate frowned. "Isn't that too soon? You're barely back on your feet."

"Foot."

"Mum."

She wrinkled her nose at him and wobbled sideways to jab him with her elbow. "Stop being so serious, sweetheart. I'm not dead, so all that's left is getting on with living. After all, one of us has to."

Last jab of the morning delivered, Ally hopped her way determinedly out of the room. Nate pulled a sour face at her back and raked his fingers through his hair. He cupped the back of his skull and looked up at the ceiling for a second.

"Your idea," he reminded himself.

He let go of his hair and checked his reflection on the way down the hall. His haircut was expensive enough that he could do pretty much anything to it and come out the other end still looking expensively tousled. Even grabbing handfuls of it in frustration just took a quick ruffle to get the curls flopped the right way again.

"I'm going now, Mum." He stopped outside her door. "Don't push yourself too hard. Okay?"

The only answer he got was an inarticulate rude noise. He got his coat from the rack at the bottom of the stairs and shrugged it on as he headed out the front door.

Sometimes he wasn't sure if his mother living with him was turning him into a fifteen-year-old version of himself or a forty-year-old version of her. He spent his time either rolling his eyes with teenage angst at her fussing, or nagging her while she threw herself into a second lease on life as though she were a girly version of Max.

The thought made him snort as he unlocked the car, and the noise earned him a suspicious glare from Mrs. Saunders next door as she stepped over the threshold in slippers and a housecoat to wrestle her bin over the threshold. He nodded to her politely, and she puffed herself up like an affronted pigeon and disappeared back inside. The door slammed behind her.

She'd never liked him. Nate wasn't sure if it was because he was gay, because he was relatively young to own a house on Ceremony where property was sell-your-kidneys expensive, or because he worked at the Granshire. It could be all three, he supposed.

He folded himself into the car and was about to pull away from the curb when his phone rang. Nate sighed and grabbed it without even looking at the screen. He assumed it was Max with one of his usual last-minute plans that he wanted Nate to "just run by" his father.

Turned out, it wasn't Max.

"I'll play your bad boy," Flynn said. In the background of the call Nate could hear gulls and the grate of metal. "On one condition."

A very dirty scenario flashed through Nate's mind—fairly dirty, anyhow. It was all sweat and aches and stickiness. He blinked and glanced out the window at Mrs. Saunders's house, as though she might somehow sense the gay was rising. The curtains twitched closed as he watched, so maybe she could.

"What condition?" Hopefully the crack in his voice would pass unremarked due to the hour. "I'm not dressing up as a dirty mascot or dancing anywhere."

The laugh that rattled down the line was rough as a stray cat's purr. Nate shifted on the leather seat and tugged at the leg of his trousers.

"Maybe you need better friends. If I do this, you quit trying to get me to shill for the Granshire—no proposals, no links to Airbnb, no offers, nothing. If Teddy Saint John wants my lighthouse, he can come down and do his own begging. It will make it more fun to tell him to piss off."

Nate considered his long-held idea of being able to offer couples the cliffside dwelling for romantic, storm-swept evenings. It would have been great, but he had to admit he didn't have any real hope that Flynn was going to suddenly agree.

"I can do that," he said. "So…."

"So I'll pick you up for a date," Flynn said. "Text me where and when."

He hung up. Nate caught himself scowling at the disconnected phone and grimaced into a reluctant smile. Well, he said he wanted a bad boyfriend. It looked like Flynn was just getting a head start on that.

The window for getting to the Granshire in time for a coffee and recap of his notes was closing, but Nate just sat with his hands on the wheel and frowned out the windshield at the street.

It had just occurred to him that if it went wrong—

He shook his head impatiently and dislodged the thought before he could spiral into unrealistic disaster scenarios. The idea wasn't going to go wrong. It was too simple to go wrong. He would go on a couple of dates, everyone would make dismayed noises, and then it would be over.

It was foolproof.

And he was going to be late. Or at least not as early as he'd like.

CHAPTER FOUR

"I heard that he snitched on the Russian Mob. They killed his partner, and now he's on the run. Well, that's what I heard."

FLYNN TOSSED his phone—one generation old, five generations worth of battered—onto the scarred old desk that was shoved into a corner of the office. It bounced off the six weeks of receipts and paperwork that he was almost definitely going to get around to.

Not yet, though. Maybe that excuse was why he'd agreed to Nate's ridiculous idea.

He remembered Nate in his house, all expensive suit, bitten-lip smile, and hair that managed to look like he'd just rolled out of bed. No surprise there. He hadn't been able to get Nathan Moffat out of his brain all week. The man was good-looking enough to be fantasy fodder just walking down the street, never

mind in Flynn's living room, making proposals that
could have done with being a little more indecent.

So yeah, it might not be entirely down to wanting
to avoid admin.

The office door opened, and Kenny stuck his head
in. There was a smear of oil running from his pierced
eyebrow up into his buzz-cut, bleached-out hair.

"Boss?" He jerked his thumb back over his shoulder into the garage and pulled a face. "Mr. Park is
here. He wants to talk to you."

What that actually meant was "Mr. Park wants to
complain."

"Tell him I'll be right there." While Kenny ducked
back out to do that, Flynn had a quick shuffle through
the paperwork for Park's invoice. It was folded in
half under a letter from his old captain that he hadn't
gotten around to reading yet. And for some reason, it
was stuck together with a Post-it he'd written a phone
number on. The number didn't ring a bell, so he tossed
it. Then he folded the invoice up and tucked it into a
pocket on his thigh.

Mr. Park stood in front of the main doors of the
garage, his feet shoulder-width apart and braced as
though he intended to prevent anyone else from coming in. At his feet a scruffy black-and-white collie
looked vaguely embarrassed to be there.

"Mr. Park," Flynn said. "Come to settle up?"

Outrage puffed Park up, and a red flush crept from
under his collar and over his face.

"Settle up?" he blustered as he wagged a gnarled
hand in Flynn's direction. "You're trying to rip me
off, Flynn Delaney. Your pa must be turning. In. His.
Grave."

Probably like a top. Not only was Flynn still fucking men, he was going on a date with someone who worked for Teddy Saint John. Even if he'd been cheating Park, which he wasn't, it wasn't going to add a revolution.

"I'm not ripping you off, Mr. Park," Flynn said. He crossed his arms and leaned against the bumper of the Volvo he'd been working on. It creaked under him. "Your tractor needed work. I did the work. Now you have to pay."

"Well, I talked to my son, and he went on the internet. Apparently all that was wrong with the tractor was a blockage in the filter inlet. I could have fixed it myself."

"If that had been what was wrong, you could have," Flynn said. "The lift pump was cracked and sucking air, and there was a carbon buildup on the injectors. I told you that, and what it would cost, when I called you to ask if you wanted to go ahead with the fix."

"Well, my son says that—"

"Then you should have gotten your son to fix the tractor," Flynn said brusquely. "I said what was wrong with it, and I fixed it. Now you have to pay up."

"I still think you're charging too much. Sixty pounds an hour for your time? What's so valuable about your time? I pay blokes to work the fields eight pounds an hour, and they work a bloody sight harder than you do."

Flynn rolled his head to the side. The crack of the vertebra in his neck sounded painfully loud as it settled between his ears.

"I guess if *they* had the keys to your tractor, they could ask for more," he said. "Either pay up or I'll go in and take the pump back out."

"I'll pay for parts," Park said. He pulled the invoice Flynn had sent him out of his pocket and ripped it up. "And half the hours you're billing for."

Bits of paper floated down to the oil-greasy floor. The collie dropped its nose to sniff curiously at one. Flynn waited out the drift and then took the other copy of the invoice out of his pocket. If Park had been one of the old hill farmers, the ones still trying to crawl out from under the dead sheep left after the last bad winter, he'd have given a discount.

But Frank Park was not hurting. He'd had enough grant money to build wind farms and turn old crofter cottages into B&Bs. A bill for a broken tractor wouldn't break the bank.

Park balled the invoice up in his fist. For a second he looked like he was going to throw it. Then he depuffed and sourly shoved it into his pocket.

"Fine," he snapped. "I'll pay you, but only because you'd probably send your heavies round to my farm if I didn't. I won't be using your garage again, I can tell you that. Twenty years I've been coming here, since your pa opened it, and now you've lost my business."

Flynn scratched his jaw. His nails scraped through the short scruff of stubble.

"I can give you the number of a good garage on the mainland," he said. "Don't know what the ferry would charge for a tractor, though."

Park glared at him, and the muscles in his jaw bunched as he ground his grudge between his teeth, but he wrestled his wallet out of his pocket. While he stalked over to Kenny and shoved a credit card at him, Flynn scratched the collie's ears. It wagged its tail and stirred up the bits of paper.

Payment completed, Park snatched the keys out of Kenny's extended hand.

"I'll send one of the boys down to get the tractor." He gave Flynn a black glare on his way out. "It better not be damaged."

The collie sat for one more ear ruffle and then scrambled after its master.

"That is one angry man," Kenny said as he tore the receipt off the machine. He absently scratched his eyebrow piercing and cocked his head. "Am I your heavy, by the way, because I'm not sure I'm up to it."

Flynn's palm was coated with dog hair and dirt. He wiped it on his thigh. Irritation was a sour taste in the back of his throat. He should be used to the rubbish some people came out with.

"Get back to your job, Kenny."

Flynn got to work on a Volkswagen that needed new points and the oil changed. He was elbow deep in it when his pager went off in his hip pocket, and he left a chunk of his palm on the engine as he pushed himself from under the hood.

"Kenny, I have to go."

He stripped out of his overalls, down to jeans and a grubby gray T-shirt with a rip in the sleeve, and checked the pager. Kenny rolled out from under the truck and propped himself up on his elbow.

"Someone hurt?" he asked.

"Accident down at Dog Crap Beach," Flynn answered curtly, using the derogatory local nickname for the stretch of public coastline. "I'll call if I need you to lock up."

He grabbed his keys and jogged outside to the Land Rover. It usually took fifteen minutes to get to the beach from the outskirts of town. With the justification of an emergency call and a few rat runs through housing developments, he could make it in ten.

THE SALT water was frigid against Flynn's thighs as he splashed out into the tide, his balls clenched as if that would help them hide from the bite of the waves. The water hit his groin—it shocked a gasp from his gut up to his throat—and then his stomach.

The Jet Ski bobbed up and down as the sea pushed it toward the shore, the custom Union Jack paint job torn up along the side where it had cracked against the rocks at the mouth of the bay. The driver floated along in its wake, and his one-handed attempts to paddle turned his body in slow circles. Blood ribbons trailed behind him.

"Hey, heard someone took a spill," Flynn said. He caught the guy and steadied him. "That you?"

Panic hitched the guy's chest as he grabbed frantically at Flynn's arm. His teeth were chattering with a mixture of panic and cold, but practice helped Flynn translate.

"Fuck. I hit the wall." The guy stopped for a second to grab a breath, his eyes squeezed shut from pain as he breathed in. "Oh fuck, mate. I think I'm hurt."

Flynn ran a professional eye down the man's limply floating body.

"Yeah, you look a bit banged up there."

The damage was bad enough to make Flynn wince in sympathy, but not bad enough to make him panic. The neoprene wet suit was torn where the guy hit the rocks. It had peeled away from his skin like a steamed shrimp shell, but it gave enough protection that he was scraped up instead of shredded. He had raw abrasions down the ribs on his left side and his thigh, and unless he started the day with his nose on his cheek that was going to take some rebuilding.

His right arm was bashed up too, probably from an attempt to protect himself from the impact. The intact neoprene made it hard to tell, but it was either broken or dislocated. Flynn would have put his money on both. That was probably the worst, depending on how much water he'd swallowed.

"Don't worry," Flynn reassured him. "We'll get you out of this. What's your name?"

He had to ask again, and it took two blinks and a hard swallow before he got an answer. That was more worrying than the scrapes and cuts.

"Mark. Mark Jameson," the man finally got out.

Mark's skin was pale and clammy-looking. Flynn glanced over his shoulder. The ambulance had pulled up in the parking lot at the top of the beach, blue lights flashing over the cab, and the other member of the rescue service on duty had made it into the surf. Jessie waded toward Flynn and dragged the basket stretcher along behind her.

"Okay, Mark, we're going to get you back on land," Flynn said. "First, though, we have to get you onto the stretcher. That's going to hurt a bit."

"It already hurts."

"It's going to hurt a bit more," Flynn said. He'd never seen the point of lying to people.

Jessica let go of her side of the stretcher and moved around to the bottom. She had to lean into the water a bit as the tide got stronger.

"On three," Flynn said. He kept one hand under Mark's shoulder and moved to the side. The movement made the water feel even colder. Out of the corner of his eye, he could see one of the bystanders had waded out to corral the Jet Ski and drag it back up to the beach. "One. Two. Three."

Flynn ducked down slightly, the sand wet and loose under his feet, and steadied Mark's body as Jessie dunked the stretcher under the water. The hard edge of it caught Flynn in the thigh, and he let Mark's weight sink down to meet the plastic bed.

The slight motion made Mark yelp. Between the shock and the cold, he couldn't go any paler, but he managed to look a bit more green around the gills.

"There we go," Flynn said. "Now we just have to get you back up onto the beach, and you'll be off to the clinic."

He kept up a confident, reassuring narration as they floated the stretcher back toward the beach. The paramedics were waiting for them at the ambulance, their sleeves rolled back as though it were warm up there.

Bastards.

Halfway back to shore they had to take the weight of the stretcher out of the water. Flynn adjusted his grip, the pull of it tight across his shoulders, and put the extra bit of push into his stride as they hit the wet, grasping sand at the water's edge.

Mark groaned, and the muscles in his jaw stood out under his pallid skin as he tried to choke the noise back. With his good hand, he clutched the side of the stretcher and squeezed until the tendons stood out on his wrist.

The people watching from the beach scattered to let them through. Most of them craned their necks to get a good view of Mark's battered body. A couple of them held their phones up to film it and turned their bodies to follow them to the cracked concrete ramp up to the road where the paramedics were waiting to take over.

"Contusions and abrasions to his left side and face," Flynn reported as they handed Mark over. "Right arm is broken, dislocated, or both. May have inhaled water."

"Thanks, Flynn. He was in the water." The lead paramedic, a square, dour-looking man with thin, mouse-colored hair, sneered. "We could have diagnosed that."

His partner gave Flynn an apologetic shrug, and then they hauled Mark up the ramp to the waiting bus.

"Dickhead," Jessie said. She sat down in the sand, collecting it with her wet ass, and pulled her foot onto her knee. Her heel was bleeding, and she pulled a ceramic-sharp bit of shell from the wound. She flicked it up the beach and tilted her head back, with one eye closed against the sun. "Tell me something, Flynn. Is any of the gossip going around about you true?"

He smirked down at her.

"None of it," he told her. A beat passed, and he shrugged. "Although of course that is what I'd say, right?"

She laughed, and he hauled her back onto her feet. The Cornish blonde had started as a lifeguard on the beach—a summer job while she studied law—but for two years she'd been there during the summer and then flown off to Australia to work in the winter. Flynn wasn't sure if she was ever going to finish her degree.

"See you at the pub tonight?" she asked as they headed back to their cars. "We can pick up tourists."

Flynn was about to shrug a *maybe* that he could ease into a *no* before five o'clock swung around, when he remembered he had an actual excuse.

"Actually I'm kind of dating someone," he said.

Jessie raised her eyebrows at him. "Huh?" she said and jabbed her bony little fist against his shoulder. "Good for you. It's been... a while... since you and what's-his-name called it quits."

"Kier."

Jessie shrugged a freckled shoulder. "I could have you told you, man," she said. "Long-distance relationships never work. Love 'em and leave 'em. That's my motto."

"He lives twenty miles away."

"Yeah, but in islander miles? That's long distance," Jessie said. "Well, feel free to bring your new man along tonight. I'd love to meet him."

Flynn grunted his answer, refusing to commit one way or the other, and waved her off as she put-putted her ridiculous, zombie-themed scooter out of the parking lot. Once she was gone, he poked absently at the emotional socket where Kier had been. It didn't hurt anymore, and that kind of pissed him off.

The last thing he wanted to admit was that Kier had had a point about how quickly they'd get over each other.

He grabbed his phone to text Kenny and let him know he was on his way back. Halfway through the *get off your ass*, his pager went off again and jittered along the plastic on the dashboard of the car.

Flynn stretched forward and grabbed it. He cursed as he saw the letters scroll over the screen. Another emergency callout, this time up in the hills. It was going to be one of those days.

THE TEXT from Nate had said to meet in the Granshire bar at eight.

Flynn was late. He would have had an apology ready, even though the delay bought him time to scrub off the sweat and the salt, but he was supposed to be a bad date. Might as well start as he meant to go on.

He squeezed through the glitzy crowd who packed the bar, and bodies bumped against him as they moved desultorily to the music blasted through the speakers. It wasn't quite dancing—that could have messed up their hair or spilled the drink—just movement between the knees and elbows.

Nate wasn't at the bar. Max was. The heir apparent to the hotel did a brisk business in prep-school charm and gaudily colored cocktails from behind the bar. He traded a bottle of beer for a slip of paper that he glanced at and grinned and then tucked into the pocket of his shirt.

When the cocky little bugger gave Flynn that look, he'd been fifteen with a fake ID that said he was twenty, and if Flynn had been a bit more drunk, he might have bought it. His whole life could have been fucked because one horny teenager fancied him. Yet somehow, for turning him over to his dad, Flynn was painted as the dickhead in Max's mind.

Through the gently moving tide of bodies, Flynn caught Max's eye. He tugged the corner of his mouth up in a smirk and tilted his chin down. A scowl chased the smug off Max's face, and he glared for a second, until an importuning customer managed to snag his attention. While he dealt with them, Flynn went looking for Nate.

It didn't take him long. The man stood out in a crowd.

He was out in the garden, having a smoke between the rosebushes. His lean, long-legged body was propped against a trellis, and his head dipped back as he languidly exhaled smoke up into the air. He'd traded the usual suit for a low-V-necked blue T-shirt and tailored black trousers, cuffed up at the bottom to flash the star on his gray Converse sneakers. Even they looked expensive—straight out of the box, as though they still had the tread on the bottom.

It was a good thing it wasn't a real date, because Nate was not Flynn's usual sort of bloke. He liked rough hands and worn jeans, cheap aftershave, and that fuzz of stubble at the back of a shorn head—not designer clothes and stupid curls.

Mind you, apparently his dick was all for designer clothes and curls. He swallowed the dry heat in his mouth and let himself out of the bar. The air outside was a cool relief after the body-heat temperature inside. The sound of the door closing behind Flynn made Nate glance up. Surprise flickered over his smooth, open face, and then a flash of appreciation dragged his eyes down and up in a quick once-over.

"About time," he said. "I was starting to think you'd stood me up."

Gravel crunched under Flynn's boots as he crossed the garden. He reached around and pushed his hands into the back pockets of his jeans—it could have been to see the way Nate watched the roll of his shoulders under his shirt.

"Maybe I should have. You wanted a bad date."

Nate tucked the corner of his mouth up wryly. "I want people to think I'm better off single. Not that I'm such a sad sack I'm making up boyfriends and somehow still expecting them to turn up."

"Fair point," Flynn said. He gestured to the wall around the garden, Nate followed him, and they sat down. The moonlight gave the sheer drop down to the sea a soft edge, blurred the sharp edges of the rock, and warmed the restless gray of the ocean. He leaned over, plucked the cigarette from Nate's fingers, and let it drop into the dark. "So what next?"

CHAPTER FIVE

"Do you think there's something wrong with him? His age? And doesn't have anyone? Seems a bit odd, doesn't it?"

NATE BIT his tongue against the first retort that came to mind. The whole idea was supposed to cut down on the people criticizing his bad habits, not to add one more. He resisted the urge to light up again. Technically he was trying to quit.

"After your call this morning, I drew up a plan." He absently rubbed his earlobe—an old tell. "Despite what it must look like, I don't want to lie to anyone. Not more than I have to. If my plan goes to schedule, we'll just have to stage a few scenes to make the impression we want, and then we let people make their own assumptions. Even the breakup can be—"

Flynn leaned into his space and put a big, scar-knuckled hand on Nate's shoulder. Heat scalded Nate's cheekbones. It wasn't just the hand on his shoulder. Flynn scrubbed up nice. He'd been hot the night before in ratty jeans and a baggy old T-shirt. Dressed up in a fitted wool sweater and skinny black jeans, with a scruff of salt-and-pepper stubble on his jaw?

Oh my God.

If it had been a real date, Nate would have forgiven him for being late. Forgiven him hard, a snickering part of his brain added, and maybe twice. Not helpful.

"Or we could just wing it." Flynn tightened his fingers on Nate's shoulder, and a jolt of awareness went straight down his spine and… elsewhere. That wasn't particularly helpful either, Nate thought dryly. A slow, cocky smirk lifted one side of Flynn's mouth and created a fan of sun-caused wrinkles around his pale eyes. "Trust me. I'm good at that."

Flynn smelled of woody cologne and orangey soap over salt and oil, and his breath was warm against Nate's jaw. That definitely wasn't part of Nate's plan—not for another few weeks, once he and Flynn had a better working relationship—but what the hell.

He hooked his hand in the waistband of Flynn's jeans, the denim and metal rough against his skin, and tugged him forward an inch to close the gap. It should have been a shit kiss, one of those "Okay, we'll write this one off and try again without the pressure later" kisses. Awkward, uncertain, with Nate's breath smoky and Flynn's lips chapped with salt.

Instead it felt like something Nate didn't know he'd been waiting for.

In the back of his mind, Nate could hear the murmur and chat of the party in the bar, and the laughter sounded sharp on the cool night air. He could also feel the smooth heat of Flynn's skin against his fingers and the soft prickle of his body hair. That kind of distracted him.

"Fuck me, Nate, you won't believe who fucking turned—"As Nate pulled back from Flynn's kiss, Max's voice cracked with disbelief. "What the *fuck* are you doing, Nate? Are you drunk?"

Flynn winked at Nate. "See?" he mouthed.

Oh. So that was what winging it looked like. Nate wasn't entirely sure how he felt about that, other than impressed with Flynn's ability to improvise, so he put a pin in it for later. He had a fake relationship to sell to his best friend.

He turned to face Max and felt a pinch of guilt when he saw the mixture of confusion and betrayal on his friend's open, tanned face. Max had always been there for Nate. They'd gotten drunk together over shit boyfriends and spent their rent money on designer shirts together—although that last was more of a problem for Nate than Max. And even if his grudge against Flynn was ridiculous, it was real. Maybe Nate was going too far. Or would be. He could still call it off.

"I know you told me you had a date, but I assumed you were just lying to look less of a sad sack," Max spluttered. He jabbed a finger at Flynn. "Not that you'd lost your mind. You do know who this is?"

Nate clenched his jaw so tightly that it ached. Okay. So he wasn't calling it off.

"Of course I know who he is."

"Of course you do," Max said. "He wears overalls with his name on them, after all."

Flynn snorted and gave Max's clothes a long look. "As opposed to a polo shirt with my dad's name on it?" Flynn leaned in and brushed a stubble-rough kiss over Nate's cheek. "I'm going to go get a drink. Come find me when you two work it out."

He stood up, smirked down at Max, and sauntered back toward the bar. Somehow even his shoulders looked smug as he left.

"Arrogant prick," Max muttered.

"You didn't exactly make him welcome."

"Because he's not?" The upward slide of Max's voice turned the statement into a question. A sarcastic one. "I mean, you remember what that asshole did? He humiliated me, made me look like a complete tit in front of the whole island."

Yes, he had. Or that was Max's story. It wasn't a lie—exactly—but it wasn't the truth—exactly— either. Nate had always just gone along with Max's interpretation because it was easier than having an argument.

Nate had enough self-awareness to identify the similarity between that and his current situation. He didn't need the memory of Flynn raising one dark eyebrow, although his brain apparently felt he did. He didn't care. His brain could raise all the judgy eyebrows it wanted, it wasn't worth poking that nest of hornets. Max was still his best friend, and in a couple of months, Nate would only see Flynn if he needed his car tuned up.

"That was twenty years ago," Nate said. "We've all grown up a bit since then."

"Speak for yourself."

Max dropped down onto the wall next to Nate and glared at the glass door to the bar as though he could pick Flynn's back out from all the other bodies in there. After a second he sighed and took a swig of beer. He shook his head in bewilderment.

"He's really your date? The one you thought stood you up?"

"Yeah," Nate said. Despite the fact that it was the reaction he wanted his "relationship" to elicit, he felt a vague defensiveness. "Not his fault. He got called out."

Max gave him a familiar eye roll. That was usually Nate's expression when Max made excuses for his latest romantic screwup. On balance it was more fun from the other side.

"So what?" Max asked. "A hot, twentysomething groomsman isn't good enough for you, but the island's washed-up mechanic is your dream guy? What is it? You're hot for the smell of Deep Heat?"

Nate gave him a skeptical look. "He's five years older than me."

"Hard years," Max muttered. He subsided under Nate's scowl and switched to a different line of complaint. "I heard he had a wife and kid back on the mainland. Total closet case."

It wasn't like Nate could argue that point. Nobody knew much about what Flynn had gotten up to after he left the island. His dad hadn't been a man to boast or complain about his kid. Flynn was even less inclined to talk about himself. Still—Nate licked his lips absently and tasted the kiss—it obviously wasn't a problem anymore.

"Ugh," Max interrupted his brief reverie. He wrinkled his upper lip at Nate. "Stop looking so smug.

I'll puke. Come on, Nate. A couple of days ago you were all 'respect mah celibacy,' and now you're dating *him*. What's going on?"

"I'd been trying to convince him to rent out the lighthouse. He won't, but then he called up and asked me out. And, I mean, you and Mum have been at me to get off the sofa and go on a date. So I said yes."

Max slung an arm around Nate's shoulders and pulled him into a rough, conciliatory hug. "You poor, stupid bastard." He ruffled Nate's hair with one hand. "You can do better. Let me hook you up. You know I can. The groomsman might have been a mistake, but I thought you just needed to, ah, drain the swamp."

"I hooked myself up, and I like him. So give over." Nate shoved an elbow into Max's ribs and squirmed out of the hug. "I don't judge who you date."

Max leaned back and screwed his face up skeptically.

"Really?"

"Not until after," Nate said. His stomach hurt. It was either the lying or Max's pushiness. Either way, he still stuck his hand out to his friend. Sometimes Max sucked, but so did Nate sometimes—less often, in his opinion, but still. "Come on. It's not like I've invited him to Christmas dinner."

"You better not. I've told you, my dad is between girlfriends. There's every chance him and Ally will hook up."

Max grabbed Nate's hand and hauled him up off the wall.

"Are we not a bit old for this *Parent Trap* shit?" Nate asked.

"Depends. Lindsey Lohan version, or Hayley Mills?"

"And you say Flynn is old?"

Max laughed and then looked as though he resented it. He sniffed the air and wrinkled his nose.

"Ugh. Does he smoke?" he asked. "I smell cigarettes."

Nate cleared his throat guiltily. "Do you? I don't, umm… smell it." He shrugged. "I suppose he might."

"I guess there's no need to worry about this being long-term then, since he's going to die young. Relatively young." Max shook his head in disgust as he waved his hands in wide, frustrated gestures. "Does he know how dangerous smoking is? For him, and for everyone around him. And around you, after Ally's cancer."

"I guess some people just can't kick their bad habits," Nate said.

"Yeah, well," Max muttered as he headed back into the bar, "some people should try."

Nate rubbed his earlobe miserably and tried not to think about how much he wanted another cigarette as he followed Max inside. Like he said, they took it in turns to suck a bit.

MAX MADE peace with a wide grin and an offering of two bottles of beer. A drunken thistle decorated the label, and it boasted notes of raisin and, for some god-awful reason, rubber.

"Sorry about before." He set the bottles down in front of Flynn. "I guess it was just a surprise. I didn't know that Nate was into… well, you."

Flynn leaned back on his stool with his elbow braced behind him. He shrugged and tossed a peanut in his mouth. "I am a hot piece of ass."

"Yeah, that's probably the Deep Heat," Max said. He stopped and glanced at Nate, his mouth twisted in a quick, apologetic grimace. "I'll leave you two to enjoy your date."

He restrained himself from hooking air quotes around the last word, but Nate could still hear it in his voice. "Thanks," he said dryly.

Max gave him a minimalist shrug. "I better get back to work." He slapped Nate on the shoulder on the way past. "I'll see you tomorrow."

"He might be a bit late," Flynn warned, his voice licked with something dark and suggestive.

Max laughed.

"I'm never late," Nate explained. "He's been late on purpose to everything since he was ten, and to make up for it, I'm pathologically punctual."

Flynn caught Nate's wrist and tugged him a step closer. "You've not dated me before."

"You're that good?"

He ran a callused hand up Nate's arm and back down again in an idle, skin-prickling caress. His mouth curved in a slow, intent smile that crinkled the corners of his eyes. A spark of humor was caught in the gray. "Naw. But I don't have a clock in the lighthouse."

It wasn't that funny. Somehow it still cracked Nate up. He laughed until he had to lean against the bar and blink the tears out of his eyes. Over the years, between him and Max, they'd called Flynn a lot of things, but neither of them had ever thought he might be funny.

"Sorry about Max," he said once he got his snickers under control. "He means... well, to be honest, he just doesn't like you."

"Yeah. It's mutual." Flynn picked up the beer by the neck of the bottle and tilted it so he could regard the label dubiously. His eyebrows rose. "He knows I'm driving, right?"

"I don't think you can get drunk on these."

"Nonalcoholic?" Flynn took a swig and nearly choked on it. He managed not to spit it out, but his face twisted unhappily as he swallowed.

"No, it's just rank," Nate said. He took both bottles and slid them down the bar. "We have distilleries making good gin and passable whiskey, but Max somehow finds the farmers making beer in the pig shed."

He leaned over the bar and craned his neck until he caught the eye of one of the staff. The dark young man paused in the middle of pouring a beer and held up a finger in a promise to be there in a minute. It took a second, but a glossy man on the other side of the bar was already complaining about people who jumped the line.

"So, save anyone today?" Nate asked as he dropped back onto his heels.

Flynn scratched the stubble on his jaw. "Nothing quite that bad," he said. "I pulled a guy with a broken arm out of the sea, and then some local kid got stuck on the cliff going after gull eggs."

It sounded better than Nate's day. He'd failed to put Teddy off his latest crazy plan and had to provide an increasingly soggy shoulder to a bride whose groom had stood her up. Not at the altar—he still planned to be there—but work commitments meant she had to ride the ferry over without him. Not the start to her fairy-tale week that either she or Nate had planned.

"I used to do that," Nate said. "Go after gull eggs, I mean, not rescue people."

Flynn looked Nate up and down, from knees to curls. "Can't imagine you scrambling up and down the rocks."

"I wanted to impress boys, and I wasn't good at sports," Nate said. "Stealing bird's eggs was the only other option."

"How'd that work out?"

"Not as well as you'd think," Nate said with a solemn nod.

The barman, beer drawn, brought them two artisan, hand-squeezed pink lemonades from behind the bar. It was what Nate usually drank when he was working a late-night party. People celebrating could be quite pushy about someone joining them for a drink, and the tart, cloudy liquid could pass as something boozy. Nate absently thanked the guy and shoved one glass toward Flynn.

"I never got an egg," he admitted. "Or a date."

"Not sure that getting an egg would have helped the dating thing," Flynn said. "Growing up hot was probably the better choice for you."

It wasn't *that* good a line, just like it hadn't been that good a joke earlier, but Nate still felt his ears flush hot at the compliment. He smirked and leaned against the bar.

"After turning gray before I was twenty, I needed a win," he said. "Leaving the island helped a lot too. The gay guys here were either too young, too old, or Max."

They both looked down the bar to where Max was juggling cocktail shakers for a clutch of drunk ladies who were all wearing pastel variations of the same floral dress.

"I can see how that would put you off," Flynn deadpanned. He took a gulp of his lemonade and made a face as the sour taste hit the back of his tongue. "So how many of these dates do you think it will take before we can wrap this up?"

Back when it first went viral, Nate had done the ice-bucket challenge. It felt a lot like this. He coughed to buy himself a second and wondered when it had slipped his mind that it wasn't a date and they weren't flirting. The lemonade should have given that away.

"I think Max is already on board with us breaking up," he said. "So hopefully not too many."

They toasted to it with a clink of glass. The lemonade tasted even more bitter than usual. Nate put the tumbler down and nudged it away from him.

Maybe the bar had gotten a bad bottle of grenadine.

CHAPTER SIX

"You know I don't gossip, but... he's in debt to his eyeballs, apparently. Owns nothing. It's all in hock to some Irish crime lord. I mean, I hate gossip, but if it's true, we need to know."

FLYNN WOKE up from a sweaty dream where he had to rescue Nate from an endless granite cliff. He had a hard-on and a sharp feeling of relief that his brain had stuck adult Nate on the cliff. It could have been worse. He peeled the sheet off his damp skin and tossed it off the bed to crumple on the floor. The morning sunlight poured in through the windows and bathed the heavy sprawl of his body from the shoulders down. His dick curved up toward his stomach, a taut rise of hard flesh. A slick of precome shone on the head of it like spit from an eager mouth.

He groaned low in his chest as he recalled a dream fragment in vivid, unrealistic color. The granite was sharp against Flynn's hands as Nate freed his dick between the jockstrap webbing of the rappelling harness and purred his gratitude for the rescue around a mouthful of proud flesh.

Health and Safety would definitely not approve.

Flynn snorted to himself and reached down to shackle one hand around his dick. He squeezed roughly at the base of it and felt the familiar throb in his balls that balanced on the border between pleasure and frustration. It leached out into surrounding muscle, and a heavy ache pulled tightly in his stomach and thighs.

He dragged his hand up his dick in a slow, smooth motion. The fine skin wrinkled under his grip and slid against the shaft underneath. Pleasure ran darkly and slowly along his nerves, like warm honey. He chewed on his lower lip and shifted on the bed to spread his thighs.

A quick glance at the clock confirmed he needed to get to work soon. The garage wouldn't open itself. He tilted his head back into the pillows, the line of his neck pulled tight, and stared at the ceiling while he pumped his hand along his dick in brisk, businesslike strokes.

All he needed was the mechanical relief—not to complicate his life by thinking too fucking much about things.

Pleasure and pressure built in his balls and tucked them up tightly against his groin. He lifted his knee and braced his foot against the mattress, and his breath hissed between his teeth in quick, hard bursts, in time with his hand on his dick.

Despite his best intentions, he couldn't stop his brain from wandering. His surefire, get-off-quickly wank imagery—Brad Pitt, half-remembered porn scenes, that bloke he used to work with who had the ridiculously distracting mouth—kept slipping. Instead he imagined manicured hands that always had faded ink notes scribbled on the palms, narrow, elegant features with a sly, foxy grin, and how *soft* he imagined Nate's expensively cut, glossy curls would be against his thighs.

A guttural noise dragged itself out of Flynn's chest. He chewed his lower lip and let go of his dick long enough to spit in his palm. The wet slick made it easier to stroke faster and to pretend he wasn't just touching himself.

He flexed his free hand against the sheets and twisted his fingers in them as he pretended it was a handful of gray and brown curls—the heat of a wet, eager mouth instead of his palm, the satin pressure of a clever tongue against the head of his cock instead of the rough pass of his thumb.

He already knew how soft Nate's mouth was and that his breath tasted of smoke and traces of mint.

Flynn twisted his hand roughly along his dick, from the base to the head, and swiped his thumb over the tender skin again. He could feel the clench of it down his dick, from the point of contact to the heavy sway of his balls. The dream image of Nate, his mouth wrapped lewdly around Flynn's hard dick and his hands hooked into the black webbing of the harness, flipped face up in his mind again. Then his body took over, and he didn't need anything to finish, other than the rough, final jerk of his hand.

Come puddled wet and sticky on his fingers and his stomach and matted in the grizzled hair that ran down to his groin.

Flynn let his hand slide away from his dick. It flopped over the flushed and tingling skin of his hip. He wiped his hand on his thigh and folded his arms behind his head. His body felt like a rag that enjoyed being wrung out.

What the hell.

Until a few nights before, Nate Moffatt was just another of the Granshire's midtier dogsbodies. A hot one—Flynn had been disinterested, not blind—but not that special. Then he charmed his way through the door, and Flynn's dick jolted to attention when Nate tried to rent him. Apparently snobby and desperate turned Flynn on.

So, fine. He'd agreed to the stupid plan with half an eye on a no-strings-attached fling. He didn't sign up for erotic dreams and invasive wank fantasies. None of it was going to end well, and he didn't intend to make it worse by getting attached.

The alarm went off, and he sighed and rolled out of bed. Gravity promptly reminded him that, no matter what he got up to daydreams, he wasn't in his twenties anymore and he hadn't taken good care of himself when he was. Things clicked when he stretched—a snap, crackle and pop of worn joints and sore muscles—and there were aches that he knew from experience would still be there when he rolled back into bed that night.

Sooner or later he was going to have to admit that he was getting too old for the rescue services. He'd been saying that for years, though. Flynn snorted at himself and headed into the bathroom. It was tucked into the curved space behind the bed, where glass bricks and a tiled, sunken floor prevented the bedroom from flooding.

He flicked the water on and stood under the hot, high-pressure stream until the warmth soaked through his skin and down to his bones.

BEFORE WORK he swung by the lifeguard station to deliver a bacon sandwich and a cup of coffee to Jessie. She was sitting on the stone walkway, her bare feet half-buried in the sand as she watched someone canter a horse up the field. Polarized, pink-lensed sunglasses hid her eyes from view, but there was a clammy undertone to her usually tanned skin.

"Hungover?" he asked.

She held her hands out for the bounty and made grabby gestures with her fingers. Flynn handed them over. She put the wrapped sandwich in her lap and cradled the cup in both hands so she could inhale the smell of hot coffee and caramel.

"No." Jessie took a drink of the coffee and, apparently revived enough, pushed her glasses up on top of her head. She leaned back, braced her weight on her free arm, and squinted up at him. The corners of her mouth tilted in a satisfied smile. "Damn, I love bridesmaids. There's always one down to fuck and they're gone in a week."

Flynn sat down next to her, leaned forward, and braced his elbows on his knees. The horse danced skittishly in the tide, and its hooves kicked up sprays of sand and water. "One of these days, you're going to wake up married."

The answer was a wet raspberry. Jessie swigged back another mouthful of coffee and set it aside as she unwrapped her sandwich. A glob of butter-laced brown sauce escaped the crust and landed on her knee. She swiped it off with her thumb and licked it clean.

"Maybe you should be the one worried about that." She took a bite of her breakfast and smirked at him around the mouthful of food. "You're the one dating the wedding planner."

Of course. Everything that happened on the island eventually became fodder. Flynn scratched his jaw. He hadn't bothered to shave, and his nails rasped through the short bristles.

"One date." He shrugged and stole Jessie's coffee back from her. It was too sweet for him, but the caffeine hit was welcome. "I think he's more into me than I am him."

That was a lie, but Jessie's snort of disbelief was hardly necessary.

"Are you blind?" she asked. "Nathan Moffatt is hot as fuck."

"You're a lesbian."

"Yeah, I'm not a *blind* lesbian." Jessie waved what was left of her breakfast at him. A bit of bacon flew out and landed on the sand. The seagulls were slacking. "He is a very attractive man. If he had a clone who was a lady and had his fashion sense, ten out of ten would bang."

"I didn't say I wouldn't bang him," Flynn said. "Just not that interested in conversation the morning after."

Jessie finished eating and wiped her hands on her legs. "Who is?"

"He likes to talk."

Of course Flynn hadn't minded talking that much either. He'd managed to get under Max Saint John's overprivileged skin *and* made Nate flush red twice. After a couple of years of casual hookups, where "Wanna fuck?" passed as sweet talk, it was good to know he could still flirt.

"In that case I'd only nine out of ten bang his lady clone." Jessie balled her wrapper up tightly and shoved it into the empty cup. "Met Office says the weather is going to take a turn this afternoon. We might get the tail end of it."

Flynn nodded. "Most of the tourists will come in on their own when it starts getting chilly. Just keep an eye out for any thrill seekers. You still going over to the mainland tomorrow?"

Jessie nodded and shoved one hand through her hair, obviously forgetting about her sunglasses. She rescued them from her salt-tangled curls and popped them back on her nose. "If I don't hand in my request by tomorrow, I won't get another extension. If you need me, though...."

"No. Davey can handle the beach for the day," he said. "I'll let the rest of Rescue know we'll be shorthanded down here, so they'll shake a leg if we get a call."

Down by the water, the horse stopped, lifted its tail, and ignored the riding boots in its ribs as it took a copious crap on the sand. Flynn and Jessie watched it in silence, and Jessie's mouth screwed farther to the side in distaste.

"Good thing you're not hungover," Flynn said and slapped her shoulder companionably as he stood up.

She made a disgusted sound, and he took the rubbish-stuffed cup with him as he left, and tossed it into the metal-grill bin at the entrance to the parking lot.

THE LITTLE blue Chevy was nearly twenty years old, and the only time it was ever used was when Maud got her nephew to drive it down for its inspection. Flynn hooked up the exhaust emissions test and stepped back to let it run. Then he picked up a mug of tea from the worktable and took a drink. It was cold.

He grimaced around the bitter taste of tannin and put it back down. If the day went true to form, he'd finish the mug, one grimaced taste at a time, before the end of the day.

The emissions were okay. Brakes were good. He just really needed to change the rear tires and one windshield wiper.

He reached in through the driver's side window and stretched down to pop the hood. It sprang open, and he went around to check the oil. The engine smelled of petrol, motor grease, and—weirdly enough—cat piss. Flynn supposed one of the barn cats had decided the perpetually parked car was a fancy litter box.

The low growl of an engine as it cut off caught his attention, followed by the distinctively smooth click of a well-hung car door closing.

"If you wanna take a seat, I'll be with you in a minute," Flynn said. "I'm nearly done."

"I can wait," Nate said.

Flynn had good nerves. So instead of whacking his head against metal, the muscles across his shoulders and down his back just clenched. He wiped the dipstick on his sleeve, adding another grimy stripe to the dozens already there, and slotted it back into place.

"I wasn't expecting to see you so soon." He unhooked the stand and let the hood clang back down into place. "Bad boys like to keep guys waiting. I figured I wouldn't call for at least a week."

Nate perched on the arm of the battered old sofa instead of sitting down. His foot, still wearing his Converse sneakers, kicked an idle tattoo against the worn tweed but stopped abruptly when he saw Flynn in his grubby old overalls.

It didn't look like he minded the view.

"Actually," he said, "that's what jerks do. It's an easy mistake to make."

Flynn grabbed a damp rag and wiped his hands on it. "So I know that people are gossiping about us. Your plan working?"

A flicker of something that looked a lot like annoyance passed over Nate's face. It pinched his mouth and the corners of his eyes, and then it was gone. He started to swing his foot again as he nodded.

"It got up Max's nose," he said. "Not far enough, though. He thinks you're a really delayed rebound. He's already lined up a list of possible replacements."

Old scars stood out on Flynn's knuckles as his hands tightened around the rag. The flash of temper startled him. It was as old as the scars, but there wasn't a lot that triggered it these days.

"Huh." He forced his hand to relax and shoved the oily rag in his pocket. "You sure he doesn't fancy you himself?"

Nate snorted at that idea, although Flynn wasn't sure he should dismiss it so quickly. Max seemed to be really involved in what his best friend was doing with his penis.

"Anyhow, I'm taking some clients to lunch at the Tax Shelter tomorrow," Nate said. "I thought you could come along and be a buffer between the mothers."

"Why would I want to?"

"You probably eat, and it'll give you a chance to change out of that."

He did an up-and-down finger wiggle at Flynn's grease-stained overalls and battered boots. Flynn raised his eyebrows and spread his arms, hands turned palm up in appeal.

"What? You don't like this?"

Nate pursed his lips and tilted his head to the side so he could take a good look as he thought about it. The tips of his ears flushed, and he shrugged.

"I never said that." He stood up and swiped lint off his trousers with a quick pass of his hand. "Just that I'm pretty sure the Tax Shelter has a dress code. You know, no oil stains, no steel-toe caps, no utility belts."

"I'm a mechanic, not Batman."

Nate grinned with that foxy flash of charm. "I'm going to chauffeur them down from the Granshire. If you want to come, we'll be at the Tax Shelter about one. I've booked a table for six under Moffatt."

"Six?" Flynn popped the fasteners on his overalls and pulled his arms free of the baggy sleeves. "Progressive wedding."

Nate laughed and walked backward toward the door with his hands held up in mock dread.

"I wish," he said. "Parents."

He tossed a wave over his shoulder on his way through the door. It swung shut behind him. The bell over it rattled tinnily. Flynn picked up his mug of tea as he wondered whether he should go or not.

It wasn't as if it had somehow turned into a good idea since the clarity of his morning wank. Flynn grimaced and looked down into the mug. The tea had not gotten any warmer.

CHAPTER SEVEN

"I wanted to introduce you to my friend Barry. I think you'll have so much in common. You're both gay, after all."

KATIE MCCREARY was smaller than she looked on screen. As a lesser McQueen on *Hollyoaks* she'd tottered over the screen in sky-high heels and masses of back-combed bright red hair. In the passenger seat of one of the Granshire's company cars—Nate loved his sports car, but it was barely suitable for island roads, never mind transporting one bride and two bickering mothers—she had none of that distinctive bolshiness, and the setter-red hair had been bleached nearly white for the big day. Concealer and some very expensive foundation had smudged away the evidence of her crying fit, but she was still downcast and reserved—unlike her mother in the back seat.

Fiona McCreary's sunny ebullience didn't leave any room for niggling doubts about why a bridegroom might suddenly be plagued with tardiness. Her glass was neither half-empty nor half-full. It was waiting for a refill of champagne.

"Such a gorgeous island," she trilled from behind Nate. He felt the seat jerk back as she grabbed hold of it to peer out his window at the angled fields. "Even the sheep look clean."

"For God's sake."

Sheila Ferguson was probably a lovely woman, but when Katie's character was killed on *Hollyoaks*? Sheila would have been rooting for the strangler. She mostly kept her opinions to snorts and muttered asides she could deny, but it wasn't hard to pick up on.

"Such a shame my Billy couldn't come with us today," Fiona sighed as she sat back. "He really wants to have a better look at the island."

Nate glanced briefly away from the winding road to flash her a smile in the rearview mirror.

"I'm sure he's having fun playing golf with Mr. Saint John, but I can arrange for a—"

His offer of a tour was interrupted by Sheila. "I thought he was sort of a baronet or something?" She sounded sharp and faintly accusatory, as though she'd caught him out.

"He is," Nate said. "But he thinks Sir Saint John sounds a bit daft for day-to-day."

Sheila sniffed, clearly disappointed. Out of the corner of his eye, Nate saw Katie roll her eyes. She pulled her sunglasses out of her cleavage and slid them on. Then she twisted her hands together in her lap and picked fretfully at her nails. Shreds of pale pink nail polish clung to the tattered denim of her jeans.

It was a couple of weeks before her wedding. Her nails would have time to grow back. That was assuming her groom didn't do anything to put her on edge.

"Of course you'll remember Star, Katie," he said. "She's the baker we picked out for your cake. Well, she's also the co-owner of this restaurant. The food's good, but the desserts are out of this world."

Katie huffed out a sigh. "I might just start with cake. Then more cake. And if she could put some cake in a glass, that would be perfect."

"What, you don't want them to pour wine over the cake?" Sheila asked with a fake-sounding chuckle. "Or have you sworn off after last night?"

Nate caught himself leaning on the accelerator with a heavy foot. He lifted it and tapped the brakes to slow the car down—just in time to hit a cattle grid and rattle across it. In the back both Fiona and Sheila huffed in displeasure. It was the first thing they'd agreed on all day.

"If you keep an eye out on the passenger side," he said, "you might see one of the local stags in the next stretch."

Even Sheila turned her head to search for that, and they spent the next stretch of road craning their necks and gasping in excitement as Fiona pointed out the deer loitering at the top of the hill. Nate hoped they wouldn't have venison on the menu at the Tax Shelter. Few people relished the realization that the Bambi they'd been *oohing* and *ahhing* over could well become bangers on someone's plate.

By the time they got to the restaurant and found a space to park, Nate hoped Flynn was there, even if only for someone to complain to.

He wasn't.

Nate swallowed his disappointment and got everyone seated. He dragged Star out of the kitchen in her chef's whites with her fingers stained with food dyes, to claim she was delighted to see Katie again.

"This is going to be my favorite cake ever," Star said earnestly. "It's just so perfect, and I love raspberry."

Sheila, it turned out, didn't. That wasn't a surprise.

Still, even she had to grudgingly admit that the Tax Shelter was "lovely." It was all bleached pale wood and beaten-copper highlights. The tables were covered with long sheets of acrylic printed with views from the various scenic outlooks on the island. Their table was a row of narrow brick houses, each with a door of a different color.

"I actually live…." Nate ran his finger along the table and nudged the salt and pepper out of the way. He tapped a bright green door. "Right there. Although we've repainted all the doors since this was taken."

Katie peered over the top of her menu at the picture. "Do you all have to agree?" she asked.

"Oh yeah." Nate rolled his eyes. "It's a whole thing. Last time we painted, two old fishermen nearly came to blows over whether the blue should be cornflower or robin's egg."

They hadn't actually cared. The argument had been over which of them got red that year. By the time it got to the shades of blue, they dug in their heels for the sake of it. If Nate hadn't already been gray, that month would have done it.

Still, it made Katie laugh. Even Sheila cracked a brief smile.

A waiter brought over a stack of menus and a bottle of champagne "on the house." The Granshire actually kept a case there, just so the couple felt celebrated. Nate popped the cork and poured glasses for them all. Fiona giggled when the bubbles overflowed the glass. Sheila primmed her lips in disapproval but let him dole out a half measure for her.

"To Katie and Bradley," Nate said. He bypassed direct mention of the wedding. Even if Sheila did leave the "Katie" out of her return toast, it was ignorable, especially when it was half drowned under Fiona's enthusiastic reply.

They agreed on coffee and settled down to peer over the menu. No venison sausages, thankfully. Nate had just decided to indulge in the most stickily indulgent thing on the menu—without dwelling on why— when Katie raised her faded eyebrows and peered over his shoulder.

"I take it that's who the extra seat is for?" she said.

Nate twisted around. Their waiter was taking Flynn on a winding route through the tables. He'd lost the overalls. The jeans and black T-shirt underneath weren't quite as nice as his clothes of the night before, but they'd definitely do.

A low mutter of disapproval spread from table to table. The diners eyed Flynn's back with a mixture of curiosity and dislike. He wasn't a popular man on the island.

"Yes. He is. I'll just be a minute, Katie."

He stood up as Flynn edged by Dottie Tancredi and her giant, suspiciously snoring purse. She scooted her chair away and glared at his back.

"I wasn't sure you'd make it."

"And stand you up?" Flynn asked. His mouth twitched with a flicker of dry humor. "That'd make me a pretty bad boyfriend, wouldn't it?"

He reached out, curled his hand around Nate's neck, his fingers warm and rough against the skin, and brushed a kiss over Nate's mouth. It was a light skim of lips, a hint of tea and peppermint on Flynn's breath, not some passionate dip and smooch, but Nate still caught himself leaning into the kiss with his hand curled around Flynn's arm as though he could pull him close.

Curiosity, he told himself. There had been a sweaty teenage time when "How does Flynn Delaney kiss?" was a question that occupied a lot of Nate's idle hours. Just after "How does Brad Pitt kiss?" and "Would my mum hate me if she knew?"

Since he'd probably never get a chance to kiss Flynn again once the "leave me alone" clause was invoked, he might as well get his answers—even if it was only a show kiss. But the kiss lingered longer than was really necessary for a "hello," and they were in a public place. After a second, Flynn drew back and Nate let him. His fingers slid down Flynn's arm—all hard muscle and warm skin.

"Flynn, this is Katie McCreary, her mother, Fiona, and her 'mother-in-law to be', Sheila," Nate said. "This is my boyfriend, Flynn."

The lie slid easily off his tongue. It felt strange, as though he half expected someone to burst out laughing and call him a liar. And he enjoyed saying it too much.

"Nice to meet you," Flynn said. He leaned over the table and clasped Katie's bitten-nailed hand in his. "Congratulations, Katie."

She went a little pink around the nose and giggled her thank-you as Nate slid back into his seat. It was good to know that he wasn't the only one who found that low rasp... distracting.

Flynn sat down next to Nate, bumped their knees together under the table, and glanced over the menu. Once their companions were distracted with arguing over the merits of their favorite dishes, he leaned in. He slung his arm over the back of the chair and cupped Nate's shoulder.

"So, do you want me to eat with my mouth open and hit on the waiter?" he asked in a whisper.

An image flashed through Nate's mind—the waiter bent over the bar while Flynn growled dirty talk in his ear. It was ridiculous, but it still generated a jab of sour envy that made him choke on his coffee.

He muttered an excuse about it being hotter than he thought, set the cup back down in its saucer, and picked up the napkin to wipe his lips.

Before he could hiss out a denial, Flynn chuckled darkly and scraped a stubble-rough kiss over his cheek.

"Don't choke. I'll be on my best behavior," he promised.

"If you want a reward, I can get a crate of Max's beer," Nate told him.

That got a whole laugh out of Flynn, and Katie glanced away from the debate about whether she could eat a rib and still lace her dress. She glanced at Nate curiously with big blue eyes.

"Max?" she said. "The bar manager?"

"Yes," Nate said. "Max is an old friend of mine, and—"

"And despite the good taste he shows in friends," Flynn said as he ruffled Nate's hair, "he's got god-awful taste in beer. I'd rather be nose deep in silage than drink some of his brews, and I've *been* nose deep in silage."

Katie leaned her elbows on the table and cupped her chin in her hands. "I just don't know what to ask about first," she said with laughter in her voice.

"I do," Fiona said. "Is Max cute?"

"Mum! Dad's just at the hotel."

"I can look," Fiona sniffed. "It's a free country."

Sheila ignored them, although, from the twitch at the corner of her mouth, it wasn't easy.

"Are you a farmer, then, Flynn?" she asked. "It's hard work."

"It is," Flynn said. His mouth slanted up in a self-mocking grin. "Too hard for me. I'm a mechanic."

Sheila added two cubes of sugar to her coffee and stirred enthusiastically. "Still hard work," she said as she set the spoon neatly on the saucer. "My late husband used to work at the Honda plant in Swindon. That's where we met. Don't know what he'd think of this place."

It wasn't clear if she was talking about the restaurant or Ceremony as a whole.

"Well, if he's anything like me," Flynn said, "he'd think that they charge way too much. And since I'm not paying, I'll be having the steak."

Sheila laughed. Apparently there was one thing on Ceremony that she liked, and it was Flynn. Before the conversation could go on, the waiter came over. Nate noticed that he had a rather weak chin, but the earlier flash of jealousy was apparently still hanging around.

"Can I take your order?" he asked.

Flynn ordered the steak, and so did Sheila, with a conspiratorial smirk over the table as she did so. It was fine by Nate. A steak was a small price to pay to keep her in a good mood.

Well, not a "small" price in the Tax Shelter, but acceptable.

Nate actually relaxed—a bit. Flynn left his arm hooked over the back of his chair, and it was warm against Nate's shoulders. Snippets of disapproving commentary slipped past the general chatter of restaurant service and caught his ear.

"…just out in public like that. Like they have no…."

"…Flynn Delaney and the Moffatt boy. And his poor mother practically on her death bed…."

"…apparently he was fired for taking bribes…."

"…maybe he's paying him…."

Nate resisted the urge to turn and find the source of that last murmur, just to ask who she thought was paying.

"It was lovely to meet you, Flynn," Sheila said as they left the restaurant with neat pink cardboard boxes of leftover dessert. She held out a hand with a narrow gold ring on it. When Flynn took it, she hung on and leaned in to murmur, "You're definitely not what I was expecting."

One of them should have been insulted. Nate had a feeling it was probably him. The storm had rolled in while they were eating, but it hadn't broken yet.

It brooded overhead in heavy black clots of cloud. A damp wind chilled the nape of Nate's neck and his fingers.

They were waiting for Katie and Fiona, the latter of whom kept escaping back into the kitchens to try and cozen a sample of the surprise wedding cake.

"I'll go wait in the car," Sheila said. She gave Nate a tight fold of the lips that was almost a genuine smile. "Give you two a minute. Besides, I'm not driving in the back seat with *her* after the amount of champagne she drank."

Almost genuine.

Nate sighed and handed the keys over. With a last nod to Flynn, Sheila walked briskly across the parking lot as the wind tugged at her trouser legs.

"I gotta tell you." Flynn hooked his arm around Nate's shoulder and rubbed a rough cheek against his jaw. "Pretty sure she thinks I'm slumming it with you."

"I'm not in her good books," Nate admitted. He faked a smile and a wave when Sheila looked back at them. "Could be worse, though. She could be my mother-in-law."

Flynn laughed and pushed himself upright, but he left his hand on Nate's shoulder. "So, was this actually part of your twelve-point plan?" he asked. "Or did you just want backup at the table?"

"It might have been a bit of both," Nate admitted. "Sorry. If we were really dating, I'd definitely make it up to you."

Flynn *huh'd* and grazed his thumb over Nate's throat. "And since we're not really dating?"

Once he had time to think about it, Nate was sure he'd come up with a lot of very smooth, confident

responses to that question—responses that an adult of
nearly forty would say when hit with a hammer of lust
to the balls. Since he didn't have that time, he had to
just go with what felt right.

"How about you get to keep the macarons?" He
shoved the small box of leftover confectionary into
Flynn's hands. Bad enough, from the slightly confused expression on Flynn's face, but then apparently
he had to keep talking. "My treat."

Flynn looked down, and his eyebrows hitched up
a skeptical inch.

"Thanks." He sounded as dry as sand. "Appreciate it."

Before Nate could think of anything else to say,
Katie guided a tipsy Fiona out through the doors. They
were both in giggling good humor. It was probably for
the best. Nate wasn't sure he could fumble the moment any more, but he didn't want to test it.

"I'll call you," he said.

Flynn hefted the pink box at him. "I'll be eating
cake. Katie, I hope your wedding goes well."

He turned and left. The huge, ugly Land Rover he
drove was unmissable.

"That is one hot man," Fiona said. She blinked
when Katie squeaked out a mortified "Mum!" "What?
I'm married. He's gay. Doesn't mean I'm blind, or that
he's not hot as hell."

"Sorry," Katie mouthed at Nate. Then she added
aloud, "We should probably get back to the hotel. I
want to try and call Bradley, let him know how things
are going. He's worried about whether his mum likes
'all this fancy stuff.'"

"What does she like?" Fiona asked. "Not even champagne. Who doesn't like free champagne?"

She followed the question up with a bout of the giggles that nearly knocked her and Katie over.

Nate gave a last rueful look after Flynn. With a sigh he abandoned the cake-box question and caught Fiona's arm to prop her up.

"Let's get you back to the hotel," he said.

The storm broke halfway across the parking lot. The rain bounced off the tarmac and puddled in the dips and hollows. Even the last half-run steps it took to get to the car were enough to leave them drenched and sober up Fiona a bit.

"Oh," she gasped with dramatic disappointment. "My cake got wet."

Nate knew how she felt—more or less.

CHAPTER EIGHT

"And after everything he put his dad through, you'd think he'd be ashamed to show his face."

IT HAD been nearly a week and the phone hadn't rung. Flynn had eaten all the macarons. He slouched in the battered black leather recliner while the rain pelted the side of the lighthouse, and he wondered if he'd finally ducked his head underwater one too many times. When someone bargained down from sex to an offer of leftover cake, it was a pretty good bet that, no matter how sweet they kissed or how hot their ears got, they weren't interested.

Even if he had been, did Flynn really want to play the bit of rough for real? Nate hadn't been wrong about what people on Ceremony thought about him. Some places might have seen him as the Prodigal Son when he came back, but all people on the island saw was that he hadn't had any choice.

He came back because he had to bury his father, and he stayed because he'd gotten into the habit of not leaving.

You're never going to leave. The echo of that last big fight with Kier, the one that turned out to be their last fight, bounced around Flynn's skull. *You still think you're that rebellious kid who left with the one-way ferry ticket and his black leather jacket, but you're not. You're too old for that fucking jacket. Too old for that fucking attitude. You need to come to terms with that and with whatever issues you have with your father.*

The memory of that cutting judgment made Flynn recoil, just like he had during the original argument. He was no longer a twenty-year-old—with a belly full of resentment for the island and a wrinkled envelope of cash in his back pocket—but that didn't mean anything. Working men's clothes and a tab at the bar wasn't for him. He could still leave.

Nate wouldn't, though. He was one of the Granshire boys. His friendship with Max tied him to the Saint John family as tightly as any that had the name—tighter than blood. Hell, there'd been enough mutterings back in the day that the name was all that Nate lacked. His mother had never told anyone who his father was, and the one time someone threw the gossip in Teddy's face, he didn't take it well.

Flynn absently ran his tongue over the back of his teeth as though the hot penny taste of blood were still fresh in his mouth.

A quick fuck might be fun, but it wasn't going to happen. Anything else wouldn't work. Yet—he picked up his phone and glanced at the screen—he was still waiting on the call like a teenager.

Idiot.

The abrupt buzz of a vibrating alert made him fumble the phone. He stared at it for a second, but it was still black and quiet. It wasn't the phone, and it wasn't Nate. Flynn grabbed his pager. It was the Royal National Lifeboat Institution, or RNLI, an emergency call for the lifeboat volunteers.

"Fuck," he muttered.

He lurched up out of the recliner and grabbed his jacket—the same battered black leather one that Kier so hated—and ran for the door. The rain hit him like needles as he stepped outside. It was in his ears and chilly down the back of his neck. He skidded precariously down the worn steps, which were more treacherous than usual in the rain, and got into his Land Rover.

The stopwatch in his brain ticked down. Five minutes to get to the RNLI station, eight minutes till they launched the lifeboat. It was an easier run from the garage, but if he scrambled, he could make it.

Four minutes.

FLYNN SAW Nate's car parked by the side of the marina as he swung into the parking lot. The glossy hunter-green paint job shed water like a duck. It occurred to him that Nate might be one of the new trainees, but it didn't take him long to dismiss that out of hand. As much as he liked Nate's lean elegance and nice hands, the idea of the man clinging to the side of a lifeboat was ridiculous.

There wasn't any more time to waste on Nate. He parked and jumped out of the Land Rover, and his jeans quickly soaked to midcalf as he ran through the puddles. Inside, Albert, the stocky, gingery coxswain, shoved his gear at him and ordered him onto the boat.

Flynn quickly stripped down to his T-shirt and underwear. After all the years he'd spent doing that, he didn't have much body modesty left. He wore boxers to spare the blushes of the trainees—that, and sometimes you ended up squeezing your junk into someone else's undersuit.

He stamped his feet into the bright yellow rubber boots and yanked the diagonal zipper closed across his body. Sweat broke on him almost immediately and was trapped inside the muggy environs of the suit. It wouldn't take long to change that.

"Oh God!" A shrill, terrified voice sliced through the low, businesslike mutter of noise in the boathouse. "I can't believe this is happening. Oh God."

He grabbed his life jacket and glanced around as he squirmed into it. At the doorway to the boathouse, Nate, still in his suit, held back a sobbing platinum blonde who was struggling to run to the lifeboat. One of the volunteers was trying to calm her down. It wasn't working.

The dawdling bridegroom, Flynn recalled abruptly. Nate had said, at some point during the awkward lunch, that maybe the happy couple could come back the next weekend. Maybe the poor bastard was running late again. What was his name? Brian? Bradley?

"Ready to go?" Albert grabbed the straps of the lifejacket and yanked on it hard enough to make Flynn stagger. Once he was sure Flynn was properly geared up, Albert shoved him toward the boat and grabbed spotty Deano Mac to adjust his cowl before he got drenched.

"I swear to God I know that lass," Deano said as they scrambled into position. "She's an actress or something."

"She's not your business," Albert snapped. "Focus on the job, Deano."

The minute the boat hit the open sea, Flynn completely forgot about sweating. It was always wet, but the spray the wind blew into his face felt like ice. His nose was numb, and his cheeks ached as he yelled information back to Albert.

It didn't take long to see the boat—or rather, to see an oily cloud of smoke being shredded by the rain. Flynn twisted around with one hand still locked on the anchor rope, and gestured for Albert to turn. Albert ducked his stubbled chin in acknowledgment and angled the lifeboat to the left. As they got close enough to see the details of the accident—a smoldering engine, a hard list to the left, and two shuddering, drenched men in their shirtsleeves—he cut the engine.

"You guys all right?" Flynn asked, his voice raised to be heard over the wind. "You hurt?"

One of the two men looked vaguely familiar. He was gray-haired and expensively tanned, instead of just weathered. Flynn couldn't place his name, so he was probably a blow-in instead of a local, but he'd seen him around. The other man had to be Katie's fiancé. He had buzz-cut short hair and a broad, earnest face that looked a bit blue at the moment.

"Just cold," he stammered out.

"You must be Bradley. I've met your bride-to-be." Flynn grabbed a mooring line from the bottom of the boat. He tossed one end of it to Deano, who grabbed it and hooked it to a cleat while Flynn fastened his end.

"So come clean—is this just your way of getting out of the doghouse for missing last week?"

Bradley chattered out a laugh and grabbed the loop Flynn tossed him. "I w... wish it was th... that easy."

"I don't know what happened," the graying owner of the boat said as he grabbed at the plaited cord. It slipped through his numb fingers, and he grabbed it again. "The boat was fine on the way over. I only had it serviced at the start of summer."

Between Deano and Flynn, they pulled the motorboat over to their rubber flank. Flynn kept a wary eye on the smoking engine. It was just belching oil, but it still made the back of his neck itch. They got both men off the boat and roughly wrapped them in crinkly silver foil blankets.

"I feel like an idiot," Bradley muttered. Despite his complaints, his cold-raw hands, scalded pink like they'd been burned, clutched the blanket up under his chin. "I didn't run a mara... marathon."

The chattering teeth and shivering were a good sign. They were cold, but not hypothermic.

Deano hopped onto the listing boat, arms out for balance, and bridled it so they could tow it back to shore. It was probably the engine pump, but Flynn didn't do boats, so he didn't have to worry.

"Don't you give me a sho... shot of whiskey?" Bradley asked. He wiped snot off his nose onto the back of his hand. "Warm us up?"

"That's a St. Bernard." Flynn clapped him on the shoulder. "We just give you a lecture on boat safety and a cup of hot soup when we get back."

From beneath the silver hood he'd constructed for himself, the owner of the boat snorted. "When *I* get back, I'm calling my lawyer. I'm goin... going to sue."

Flynn was glad he only dealt with cars and farm machinery.

"I'd drink the soup first," he advised.

Deano jumped back onto the lifeboat. Cocky little shit. His foot slipped on the wet rubber, and the wind gave him a shove. He nearly pitched over backward into the sea, but Flynn grabbed his lifejacket and hauled him back upright.

"Thanks," Deano panted. He slid down into position and wiped his face. "That woulda been shit."

The dip wouldn't have killed him—it was a squall, not a gale—but it wouldn't have been pleasant. He'd have been a damn long time living it down too.

"All secure?" Flynn checked. He got a nod in answer and twisted around to gesture to Albert to take them back in.

EVERYONE HAD gone. The boathouse was quiet, and the soup was slowly congealing in the cup that Flynn had been given. It was always chicken soup. Five different boathouses over the years, and the support staff always thought chicken soup was the best choice.

Flynn sat in the empty locker room and waited to feel like getting up. He braced his elbows on his knees and folded his hands behind his neck to rub slowly at the too-tight muscles. The cold had worked into his bones, and the fact that it had been an easy rescue had left an excess of adrenaline going sour in his muscles.

"Getting too old for this," he muttered aloud to the empty room. The words echoed off the tiles. It was just a shame he never remembered his age before he piled on the lifeboat.

He scrubbed his hand through his hair. It was halfway dry and stiff with salt.

"Flynn?"

He looked around through the crook of his arm and saw Nate lean in around the door. His nose wrinkled briefly at the smell—rubber, salt, and sweat—and then he eased the rest of the way into the locker room. The rubber soles of his sneakers scuffed on the tiles as he walked hesitantly.

"You okay?"

"Fine." Flynn straightened up. He was wryly aware that he'd probably have said the same thing if his knee were held on by shredded ligaments and hope. Pride was a brutal thing. He sucked in his stomach and reached for his sweater. "What are you still doing here?"

Nate pushed wet hair back from his forehead with an absent swipe of his hand. "Everyone's left. I sent Katie and Bradley back to the Granshire in a taxi."

"He should go to the hospital."

It probably wasn't necessary, but better safe than sorry.

"Teddy called out his doctor to check him over." Nate shoved his hands in his pockets and rocked on the balls of his feet. "That was—"

"Stupid," Flynn said flatly. The flash of anger caught him by surprise. He dragged his sweater on and blocked out his too-pretty fake boyfriend with wool. His mood was still there when he pulled it down over his head. "What the fuck were you thinking, sending some asshole in a motorboat out into that?"

He jerked his thumb seaward. The wind was still howling outside, although the rain had eased off to a stinging drizzle as they dragged the lifeboat back in.

Nate looked surprised for a second and then rallied indignantly. "Bradley was running late again. He missed the ferry. It wasn't even that bad when Tomas left. It was a bit of spitting rain and a brisk breeze. There was no way to know that the weather was going to get worse, or that something was going to go wrong with the boat."

Flynn stood up and glared down at Nate. "What do you think would have happened if something had happened to Bradley? You think Teddy Saint John would have had your back when the lawyers came calling?"

God knew, better men than Teddy had left Flynn swinging in the wind when the shit hit the fan.

"It was no different to putting them in a taxi," Nate protested. "What? Should I have checked the forecast before I sent them out on the road?"

"It's the sea," Flynn said flatly. "You don't take risks with the sea. You *always* assume that something is going to go wrong. That way you have a chance—"

"Oh shut up," Nate snapped, and kissed him.

In surprise Flynn rocked back on his heels as far as he could go with Nate hanging on to fistfuls of his sweater. That wasn't the usual reaction he got when he yelled at people. Of course, it was Nate. The man was weird. He had cold lips too, although his tongue was hot as he shoved it into Flynn's mouth.

The flare of anger was satisfying, something to do with all that jittery, leftover energy. But it folded as lust punched it solidly in the gut. Heat flushed the cold out of his marrow and pulled tightly in his balls. Flynn reached up and buried his hand in Nate's damply curled hair and cupped around the bones of his skull with his palm. He kissed him back, with a sharp new confidence in the press of lips, tongue, and spit.

This time it was Nate kissing *him,* and there was no audience to convince—not unless the hanging rubber suits joined the gossip circle.

So fuck it. Like it was the first bad idea he'd followed through on?

Flynn caught Nate's lower lip between his teeth and tugged at it. He let the soft curve slip free and pulled back from the kiss. "I hope you don't want the cake back," he said. "I ate it."

The reminder made Nate's ears flush again. If he ever decided to try poker as a career, that tell would ruin him.

"I thought I told you to shut up," Nate said. "I'd try that."

He shoved Flynn down on the bench and crawled into his lap. His ass pressed down against Flynn's dick, and the pressure made his balls ache with pleasure. He groaned raggedly, and Nate smirked down at him.

"That noise you can make," he allowed.

Flynn snorted. He shoved Nate's jacket down off his shoulders and bit wet, openmouthed kisses against his neck. His teeth branded red rosettes into Nate's pale skin. Probably a shit move, but seeing possession bruised down that elegant throat gave the lust in Flynn's gut an extra punch.

It made Nate hot too. He knelt on the bench and ground himself against Flynn. There were just a couple of layers of fabric between their hard dicks. Fuck.

Flynn braced his feet on the tiles, muscles pulled tightly up into his thighs, and slid his hands down to grip Nate's ass. He dragged him closer and tried to remember the last time he'd been that close to coming in his pants. Probably the last time he'd had a stealth fuck in a locker room.

He didn't have long to think about it. Nate slashed a hard, demanding kiss over Flynn's mouth and fumbled impatiently with his jeans. Flynn lifted his hips off the bench and helped shove the denim down toward his thighs. Nate's fingers were cold as they skimmed down the flat of Flynn's stomach and even colder as they wrapped around his dick.

"Sonofabitch," Flynn groaned into Nate's mouth and felt the smug as it curved the lips pressed against his.

Pleasure throbbed down his shaft and twisted into his groin as the liquid pressure of it swelled. Nate squeezed and tugged at his dick with clever fingers, more roughly than Flynn handled himself and with an impatience that made Flynn's mouth go dry. The scrape of old wool against tender skin was less appealing.

He leaned back awkwardly and dragged the sweater off, one arm at a time. Nate shifted his weight and raised himself up on his knees. He let go of Flynn's dick as he unzipped his trousers. His erection pressed up toward his stomach, the head of it dabbing precome stains onto his T-shirt.

"Didn't say you could go anywhere." Flynn growled as he grabbed a handful of shirt.

A laugh snorted inelegantly down Nate's nose as Flynn dragged him back down. He slid a hand between their bodies and traced the hard lines of Flynn's ribs and tight stomach. His breath tickled Flynn's lips as he muttered, "Never taking my fucking shirt off around you."

"You're beautiful," Flynn said. It was the truth, and it made him cringe. "If you keep your mouth shut."

"Yeah?" Nate's eyes flicked up and looked sharp with amusement. The corner of his mouth tilted in a wicked smirk. "Never had any complaints about what I did with my mouth before."

It was self-preservation to grab the back of Nate's head and pull him into a kiss. If Flynn didn't stop thinking about all the other things he could do with that mouth, it was going to be over quickly.

Nate went along with being shut up and kissed back enthusiastically. He returned his hand to Flynn's dick and squeezed it against his own. Each thrust of his hips rubbed their dicks together and trapped them between their bodies. The scruff of hair that trailed down Flynn's stomach prickled against tender skin and matted with a mixture of come and sweat. He could feel the twinned pulse of blood through both of their erections and the way Nate's dick slid to the right with each thrust.

Flynn reluctantly dragged his mouth away from Nate's and tracked kisses along his jaw. He felt weirdly smug at the faint prickle of stubble against the sharp line of bone. It felt more intimate than it should have—a chink in Nate's considered presentation of himself. He tasted of salt and the sharp alcohol base of cologne. A hint of smoke.

Nate spit a curse out in ragged pieces and pressed his face into Flynn's shoulder. His breath was hot against skin that had gone from cold to sweaty, and he chewed with blunt teeth at the taut flesh over Flynn's collarbone.

The liquid pressure in Flynn's balls felt like it was about to spill, and its surface tension strained to hold with each thrust. He ran a hand down Nate's back to the bare slice of skin between his shirt and the waistband of his trousers and then farther, so his hand cupped the bare cheek of Nate's ass as the muscles flexed and relaxed with each thrust.

Nate came first, with something inaudible panted into Flynn's throat. His come was slick and wet against Flynn's cock and sticky against their stomachs and between Nate's fingers. The thought of it was enough to crack whatever control Flynn had been hanging on to. He pulled Nate in tightly, squeezed their bodies together until it ached, and let the pulse of his orgasm wring him out.

They sprawled against each other for a second. Then Nate crawled off Flynn and lay back along the bench. He left his legs stretched over Flynn's thighs and combed his fingers through his sweat-tangled hair. There was come on his shirt and slowly drying on his dick.

"You have any idea why you did that?" Flynn asked.

Nate propped himself up on his elbow and rolled his shoulders in an awkward shrug. "Long term? No," he said.

"Short term?"

There was a pause. "I guess I just really wanted to."

CHAPTER NINE

"You know, I think my cousin's gay. He says he's not, but he's really into fashion. Maybe I could set you up?"

BREAKFAST IN bed for the happy-couple-to-be was on the house. Breakfast for Nate was a slice of toasted pumpernickel-and-olive bread and a furtive escape before his mother asked any questions.

Nate sat in his office and frowned blankly at the stunning view through the huge, spotless window. That morning's escape was counter to the whole bad-boy-friend scheme, of course. It was hard to be scandalized by something you didn't know about. Nate just needed a chance to process what had happened. A locker room hookup wasn't exactly part of the plan.

Sweat, salt, and the rough grasp of Flynn's hands on him. The hard length of Flynn's dick grinding against his, and the wet slick of come mixed on his stomach—the memory was sharp enough that Nate could practically taste Flynn on his tongue, and interest cramped hot deep in his balls.

Okay. It had been unexpected but not exactly unwelcome.

Nate shifted in the chair and dragged his mind out of the locker-room gutter. He had work to do, and that, at least, was something he actually understood.

Katie and Bradley's wedding—other than the near drowning—was set to go off like clockwork. The prewedding photo shoot had been rescheduled to give Bradley time to recover, and the tailor was pushed back until that evening. Nothing else was going to go wrong, not until the last minute, when it would screw up his blood pressure as usual.

That just left the twenty-five other weddings they had booked, a dozen new clients to touch base with, and some new suppliers to explore. He had plenty to keep his mind off salt-chapped lips and that lean, offensively ripped body.

He picked up the phone.

"Hello?" a pleasant alto voice answered on the other end of the line. In the background a faintly electronic voice rattled through "The Wheels on the Bus." "This is Fi Calders of Harpy Endings, how can I help you?"

The name made Nate wince. Some couples liked cute, but still…. Still, Ms. Calder's branding was her business.

"This is Nate Moffatt. I'm calling from the Granshire Hotel," he said. "You sent me your reel—"

"Oh, Mr. Moffatt, of course." He heard a door open and close. "Did you want to book me? I'm quite busy at the minute, but if you have dates, I could see if it would be possible to fit you in?"

"One of our clients really liked your reel," he said. "However, there's a few details we'd need to agree on before we even talk contracts."

"Like what?" Her voice went up quizzically.

Nate sympathized. He'd felt much the same going through the details with the bride and her representatives.

"You'll have to sign a nondisclosure agreement." He leaned back in his chair and put his feet up on the desk. "You'll also need to agree to have your image used for broadcast."

She snorted out a laugh. "Seriously?"

"Yes," Nate said. "I'm afraid that's nonnegotiable for the bride. There are a few other musicians she's interested in, but if you—"

The door opened, and Max came in sideways, his tongue stuck out the corner of his mouth as he balanced two overfull coffee cups in his hands.

"Shit," he muttered as coffee slopped out and scalded his fingers.

"Pardon?" Fi asked uncertainly.

"Sorry. Just my other phone," Nate fibbed smoothly. He raised his eyebrows curiously at Max but pointed to the couch by the window. It wasn't often he saw him awake that early in the morning, and when he was, it was usually to beg for coffee, not provide it. While Max made himself comfortable and scuffed a coffee stain into the carpet, Nate focused on the call. "If you're interested, we'll need to set up an audition with the couple."

She hemmed. She hawed. She agreed to a date. Nate hung up and flicked through screens to his email inbox. He tapped away with his thumbs as he swung his legs off the desk and stood up and sent an email to the production company to add the date to their schedule.

It was Teddy's idea. Nate was not sure it had anything to do with business benefits as much as Teddy's love of trashy reality TV. He owned the Granshire, though, so it was his call.

Nate hit Send, flopped down on the couch, and slung his legs over the arm. "Coffee?"

"With vanilla and hazelnut." Max handed him the cup. "Busy morning?"

"Productive," Nate said. "Of course for you, movement before noon is a busy morning."

Max slouched back and draped his arm along the leather cushions. His T-shirt dragged tightly over his shoulders as he toasted Nate mockingly.

"Shows what you know. I haven't been to bed yet." He paused, pursed his lips, and corrected himself. "Well, I've been to bed. I just haven't been to sleep."

Nate would usually have snorted something disparaging, but he still had dents in his knees from the bench the night before. He wasn't sure if he was smug that, for once, his sex life was more interesting than Max's, or if he wished he'd thought of the bed himself.

"So now when you want to boast about who you pulled, I get coffee?" Nate took a drink. "I can live with that."

"Yeah, well, I am a class act." Max scratched the side of his nose. "So what about you? Anything interesting happen last night?"

"What?" Nate choked down a mouthful of coffee. He reached up to scratch the back of his neck. "No. When does that happen? I just went home. Why?"

Max tilted his head to the side and narrowed his eyes curiously. "Yeah? You didn't, I don't know, nearly lose a guest at sea?"

Right. Of course Max wanted to know about that. Nate dropped his hand, wrapped it around the coffee mug with its mate, and tried to pretend he hadn't just flapped about like an idiot.

"I didn't actually lose him. I knew where he was. It was just... at sea. Something went wrong with the boat on the way back over. Not ideal but—" Max stared at him. "What?"

Wrinkles creased the skin around Max's eyes as he squinted. "Is that concealer on your collar, Nate?"

Technically it was thickly applied tinted moisturizer. Nate tucked his chin in as he looked down to find the smudge. Even though he knew it would only make it worse, he licked his thumb and rubbed the smear of midtan Maybelline.

"It was a long night," Nate said. "And nobody wants to deal with an event organizer who looks like, well, you."

Usually Max would have absorbed the insult with a snort and tossed it back. Not this time. He reached out and smeared his hand over Nate's neck, and his fingers came away covered with foundation that had been hiding the bloom of mouth-shaped bruises on Nate's skin.

"Hickeys?" Max snorted and wiped his hands on his jeans. "For God's sake, Nate, I know you had a crush on Dishy Delaney when we were fifteen. You don't have to act like you still are."

That had been their nickname for Flynn, Nate remembered. He tried not to flush at the cringe of his teenage self, but wasn't sure he succeeded.

"Trust me," he said. "At fifteen I wouldn't have gotten up to what I did last night."

Wanted to, probably. Definitely, if he were being honest. Just never went through with it. He'd always been the wallflower to Max's slutty social butterfly.

"Ugh," Max said. His lip curled in disgust. "I can't believe you're doing this after how long we've been friends. You know how I feel about Flynn Delaney."

"I don't think the guy code covers twenty-year-old crushes," Nate snorted. "Besides, you're one to talk. It didn't stop you back then."

Both of them had snuck into the club that night and spent an hour stuck to the wall as they goaded each other into approaching someone. Then Flynn stalked in, all black leather jacket and swagger, and Max found the balls to make a move. All Nate found was that he didn't like vodka and coke.

"Yeah, and what did it get me?" Max asked. There were two flags of angry color to his face, and again Nate wondered why Max held on to his grudge so tightly. "Dragged back home on the ferry and outed to my dad because Flynn Delaney is a prat. He was a prat then. He's a vicious old bastard now. Everyone on the island knows what he's like, Nate. He didn't even come back to see his dad when he was dying. Didn't even go to the funeral."

That pinched a gut-level discomfort in Nate's stomach. Most of the rumors about Flynn were rootless and gleefully off base. Gangland connections. Abandoned wives and children. Witness protection. But him not attending his dad's funeral was just a fact. It was the sort of thing that didn't go unmentioned on Ceremony. No one's funeral went unattended, even if the mourners were just there for the gossip and a sausage roll.

"Some people don't get on with their family."

"Yeah," Max said. "Assholes and psychopaths. Come on. It wasn't like Mike Delaney was a monster."

"I'm not going to be at my father's funeral."

"You don't know him," Max said dismissively. "Not like you'd miss my dad's."

Nate bit his tongue. He didn't know why he was defending Flynn. People weren't supposed to approve of him. That was the point.

"I thought you were going to back off and let me get on with it."

Max looked sour and took another drink of his coffee. "I thought you'd go on one date with the cheap bugger and come to your senses," he said. "You can do better."

"Like who?" Nate asked. His voice sounded a bit sharper than he intended. "I'm a middle-aged gay man who's living with his mother and works ridiculous hours in a very harp-heavy profession. And I live on Ceremony. Maybe Flynn's not perfect, but I like him. So unless you have another option…."

Max stared at him for a second with his lips squeezed together in a tight line.

"What about me?" he asked abruptly.

Nate sat back and waited him out. His coffee was going cold, and it wouldn't take long.

"I mean, in theory," Max said. His expression was a mixture of stubbornness and panic that made him look like a hangover had just hit. "Why not?"

"Well, for a start, because the last time you saw me naked, you said 'is that it'?'"

"I had been watching a lot of porn." Max muttered the excuse awkwardly. "And it was cold, so you were not... looking your best."

Nate snorted. "You're my best mate, Max, but I'd smother you in your sleep if we were dating. To be honest, when we shared a flat, there were a few nights I came in and stood over you with a pillow."

"Very funny," Max said sulkily. He slouched down and absently picked at the rim of his cup. "Flynn, though?"

"I like him," Nate said. "Maybe he's a prat, but he makes me feel good."

Max mimed sticking a finger down his throat and gagging. Then he sighed and leaned over to hook his arm around Nate's neck and bump their heads together.

"You really want to do this?" he asked. "Him?"

"Yeah," Nate said. "He makes me happy."

It was a ridiculous thing to say after two dates, even if they had been real dates. Despite that, it sounded so convincing that Nate almost believed it himself. He wasn't usually that good a liar. Maybe that's why Max bought it.

"Fine," Max grumbled and sat back. "It's your funeral, which the dickhead probably won't attend."

"Well, at least I get a funeral," Nate said. "Last week I just got eaten by cats."

Max rolled his eyes, finished his coffee, and slouched back onto the couch. He grabbed a cushion and stuffed it under his head. "I'll enjoy saying I told you so when it all goes wrong."

A niggle of annoyance caught in the back of Nate's throat. Okay. So he knew it was going to go wrong, but he had insider knowledge. Max was just making assumptions. If he really liked Flynn, he could make it work.

He couldn't get into it with Max right then, so he swallowed hard and redirected the annoyance into something more immediate.

"What are you doing?"

Max folded his arm over his eyes. "I need some shut-eye."

"You have a bed."

Max lifted his elbow enough to give Nate an arch look. "And you said you aren't interested." He wagged the eyebrow that Nate could see. "Now you want to know about my bed."

"Get off my couch." Nate whacked Max's leg.

It didn't do any good.

"There's someone in my bed," Max said. "And Dad's looking for me. Just give me an hour to nap, Nate. You can judge my life choices while you still have the high ground."

Nate picked up the spare cushion and mimed smothering his friend with it. In the end he just whacked him with it and took his coffee back to the desk. He had five other wedding-music auditions to arrange, along with one "dramatically offbeat" musician, and then back to Katie and Bradley.

He checked the time and mentally sliced the rest of the day into manageable segments. It was doable—if a certain someone didn't spend any more time distracting him.

On cue, Max started to snore.

"IT'S JUST so weird," Katie said. She sat cross-legged on the loveseat, wearing bright pink yoga pants and a bra. The view didn't do a lot for Nate, but he couldn't help but see she had abs too. He tried to sit up straighter. Maybe he should revisit exercise. Katie didn't notice. She slapped her hands on her knees to underline what she was saying. "We just met your boyfriend last week, and then he saves my fiancé's life. It was, like, some weird fate."

The fiancé in question gave her a fond, slightly skeptical look. "I wasn't on the *Titanic*, love," he said. "I could probably have swum to shore if I needed to."

Despite everything, Nate was still an island boy at heart, and he knew better. Even in the height of summer, that was a stretch of treacherous water, with unpredictable riptides and no easy shore to wash up on. At the dog-end of the season, at night, and in a storm? Bradley was an athlete, but fitness wasn't enough. But the story of how the island had lost a rugby player out there one August—drunk, stupid, and on a dare—wasn't wedding appropriate.

"I'm just glad everyone got a happy ending," he said.

Katie sniggered. Bradley looked up from a book of specialty cocktails. "Huh?"

She primmed her lips and said innocently, "Nothing, love."

"I've arranged for the tailor to come this evening around six," Nate said. It had been a while since he had reason to make innuendos, and he was out of practice at subtlety. "He can make any alterations needed for your suit, Bradley. So everything will be ready for the big day."

"Yeah," Bradley said. He drew the word out in a way that, in Nate's experience, never ended well for him. "I've been thinking about that."

Oh, that was even worse than the drawn-out *yeah*. Even Katie looked worried—possibly reminded of her doubts about his willingness to be there.

"What about, babe?" she asked. "I mean, you haven't changed your mind about the kilt?"

"Naw," Bradley said. "Ma says it'd look stupid. Thing is, Nate, I hate ties, man. Can I just not wear one?"

Katie blinked a few times, a bit too quickly. She looked like she was trying very hard not to be horrified.

"I can say to Harvey to bring a few options," Nate said. He made a note on his phone with quick swipes of his thumb. "We can see what a collarless shirt would look like with the suit... or possibly tiepins. You and Katie can decide then."

They chatted briefly about the other plans for the wedding. Nate was about to excuse himself when there was a polite tap on the door.

"Come in," Katie said.

The rest of the wedding party was expected to arrive that day and the next. So Nate expected to see one of Katie's bridesmaids or Bradley's lanky teammate or his best man. Instead Teddy Saint John strolled into the room.

"I just wanted to drop by and wish you both the best," he said effusively. Bradley got a firm handshake with a kiss on the cheek, and Katie got a squeezed hand. "I'm so sorry about what happened last night."

Katie blushed a delighted pink. "Oh, never mind that. Bradley's fine, and it wouldn't have happened if he got here on time anyhow. Although I wanted to ask Nate to pass on a message." She shifted her attention to Nate, her eyes wide under her dark, manicured brows. "We would love it if Flynn could make it to the wedding. He's so lovely, and if it weren't for him, we might not even be getting married."

Before Nate could say anything, Teddy patted Katie's hand. "I'm afraid Mr. Delaney's a very busy man," he said. "So many dogs to rescue from the high tide."

Katie's expression didn't exactly change, but her smile was more steely than sweet.

"But I'd like him there."

"We all would," Teddy said. "But there's—"

Behind her back Bradley pulled a "better him than me" face at Nate. He might be underestimating Teddy. In Nate's experience, the bride expected to get what she wanted for maybe twenty-four hours. Teddy Saint John had expected to get what he wanted for nearly seventy years.

"I'll ask him, of course," Nate interrupted. "Hopefully he'll be able to make it."

Sweetness flowed back over Katie's face, and she promised to find a spare invitation and to cover the extra meal. Teddy looked grumpy about it, but graciously changed the subject.

"If you don't mind," he said smoothly, "I'm just going to steal Nate away for a bit. Have a wonderful day, and tell your father I'm up for a rematch anytime."

They exchanged a few more pleasantries, and Teddy led the way out of the suite. Nate followed on his heels, head down as he quickly checked his phone. He'd received a few emails while he was talking to Katie, but nothing alarming or immediate.

"Is something wrong?" he asked when the doors were closed behind them. They walked down the hall toward the stairs. Shadows sliced through the long rays of sunlight that glowed through the huge lead-ed-glass windows. "Did the production company call about the cake? Because I told them they need to bring in another chef if they don't want a tantrum. It's not Star's—"

"No. That's fine," Teddy said. "It's actually... well, I don't want Flynn Delaney at an event in my hotel."

The statement hung starkly in the air. Nate stopped and gawked at Teddy's back, lost for what to say. He hadn't expected the disapproval of Flynn to go beyond his private life. It certainly wasn't something he expected from Teddy, who'd sat through a disastrous parade of Max's flavors of the month.

By the time he got over the surprise, Teddy was halfway down the stairs, and he had a death grip on the handrail. His ankle must hurt. He snapped it coming off a horse last year, but he refused to take the service lift.

Nate bit his tongue and kept pace with Teddy down the stairs and out onto the long, narrow balcony that clung to the front of the hotel. Seagulls took off from the wall as Nate closed the glass doors behind him.

"Katie wants to invite Flynn," he said. "It is her wedding, but I doubt he'll want to come."

"Even to see you?" Teddy asked dryly. He turned around and gave Nate an arch look, his eyebrow

raised. Max had been trying to master that look for
years, with no success. "His, what are we calling it,
boyfriend?"

Nate took a second to swallow his first response.
The tone pissed him off, but he wanted to have misun-
derstood it, misheard it.

"I've been calling him my date so far." Nate
crossed his arms. "I don't want to scare him off by
jumping the gun."

The tone was sharper than it had been in Nate's
head. From the flush of irritated color in Teddy's
face—two stripes of red across his cheekbones, as
though he'd been slapped—it was even more edged
by the time it got to his ears.

"He's not welcome here," Teddy said flatly. "Not
even as your guest."

Nate took a deep breath of salt-fresh air. "I guess
I'll have to do my drinking in town, then," he said.

"You're always welcome. Always," Teddy said
firmly. "Just not with him. He's bad news. He's trouble. Always has been. Even Mike Delaney saw that."

"Maybe fathers aren't always the best judges of
their sons."

Apparently Teddy wasn't the only one who could
get inappropriately personal. The tension hummed
between them like a plucked string, the thrum of it
hard in Nate's chest. He wanted to apologize. It wasn't
worth fighting with Teddy, who was his friend as well
as his boss, over his dislike of a man who wasn't even
Nate's boyfriend—or his date. But the words just
couldn't quite squeeze past his clenched jaw.

"Well, I always thought you were a sensible boy,"
Teddy said. "But then I'm not your father. So it's not

my business if you aren't. The Granshire is, though, and I don't want Delaney associated with it. Now I'm sure you have work to do, Mr. Moffatt."

Teddy left and closed the glass doors precisely behind him. Nate watched him disappear down the corridor and then slouched back against the wall. It had been a polite, if curt, exchange of words, but the aftermath felt like a fight. Nate's heart was going too fast, he was sweaty, and his head hurt.

He wanted to punch something, and his knuckles ached as though he already had. He wanted a smoke. He wanted to tell Teddy he was wrong about Flynn. Even though, for all Nate knew, he might not be. So he leaned back against the pitted stone wall. He guessed that was what it was like dating the most unpopular man on the island. Not as much fun as you might think.

Fuck.

CHAPTER TEN

"Well...you know what his mother was like. The apple doesn't fall far from the tree."

SEASIDE COMMUNITIES were not, traditionally, fond of seagulls. They were unmannerly, covetous avian mobs, always ready to crap on a car or steal a handful of chips. So Flynn supposed there was something particularly contrary about feeding one, even if it was a sad specimen.

He sat on the narrow metal balcony that wrapped around the top of the lighthouse, and his legs dangled carelessly over the drop as he tossed digestive biscuits out over the sea. The lame seagull that he'd been seeing around the cliffs for the last few weeks snatched them out of the air.

In between tosses it flapped back to perch precariously on the balcony, its white feathers fluffed, and it shrieked at him and showed the bright pink inside of its beak until Flynn tossed it another biscuit.

"End of the packet, bird," he said as he shook the last biscuit out into his hand. A flick of his wrist sent it frisbeeing into the air. The gull toppled off the balcony after the treat. It dropped like a fluffy stone for a second, and then the wind lifted its wings and it caught the biscuit just as it started to fall.

It made its usual tail-over-beak landing on the metal and screeched at him. One of its feet was clubbed awkwardly. Scar tissue stuck the webbing together. Could have been a lucky sea lion. Could have been a fishing line.

"You don't give up do you," Flynn said to it. The corner of his mouth twitched. "I should call you Nate."

The gull tilted its head sharply to the side and trained one beady yellow eye on him. Flynn pulled himself up as something under his kneecap grated, and he shooed it away. It didn't come back.

Maybe it was smarter than Flynn. It kept its life simple.

He went back into his bedroom. The duvet was creased where he'd crashed on it the night before, and his skin still smelled of sex and stylish posh boy. He resisted the brief temptation to grab a pillow and see if the scent had stuck to it.

It wasn't that he regretted it. Beautiful men didn't crawl onto Flynn's dick often enough for him to think it was a bad idea. It was the aftermath that nagged at him. He had dismissed the possibility that a quick fuck could ever happen. But it had, and his brain worried at his other assumptions, like whether or not it could be something more. Did he even want it to be? Nate was handsome and cat confident in his physicality, but Flynn couldn't imagine him in his life. What would it be like? Converse sneakers in his kitchen and ashtrays in the bedroom, footballers on speed dial and Max over for lunch?

No, he corrected himself, the Granshire lot would probably have brunch instead.

The two of them stuck on the island—drinking in the same bars, eating in the same restaurant, seeing the same people—until they got old.

He stretched and felt something under his shoulder catch and then pop. Older.

The coffee was on in the kitchen, and the extra-strong brew fermented on the element. Flynn poured himself a cup and added milk. The first gulp scalded his tongue and made him grimace. He leaned back against the counter and took another drink.

He needed to stop second-guessing Nate. It didn't matter what his actions suggested. His words had made it perfectly clear that he wasn't interested in a relationship. The only boyfriend he wanted was a bad one.

Maybe Flynn wasn't as bad as people on Ceremony wanted to believe, but all his relationships ended badly. So he couldn't be that good at them. And if Nate wanted to crawl on his dick again…. Well, thinking that Flynn was an asshole had never stopped any of his lovers from fucking him.

Or eventually fucking him over.

USUALLY FLYNN just propped up the bar at the Hairy Dog, but since it was a date, he grabbed a table. It gave the gawkers a good three hundred sixty degree view. Flynn's plan to embrace his inner shit-relationship material—he'd even scrawled out a list of some of the things his exes had complained about, from "unavailable" to "always thinks job makes him better than me"—was under threat because Nate was turning out to be a worse date than he was.

For the last ten minutes, he'd been on his phone. He set it down twice and then picked it back up again the minute it beeped.

"Is it really that hard for you to stay single?" Flynn asked.

Nate didn't bother to move his attention from the screen as he grunted absently. After a second his brain caught up with his ears, and he looked around. His expression teetered between apologetic and peevish. Apology won. He flicked the phone to silent and turned it over.

"Sorry." He leaned back in his chair and picked up his pint. The long sprawl of his body briefly distracted Flynn. The way he sucked the head off the beer, fingers wet with froth, didn't help Flynn keep his mind out of the gutter. Nate wiped his thumb over his mouth and added, "Although to be fair, I never actually said that."

"No?"

"I could get dumped in a nunnery," Nate said blithely. He set his glass down and held up his hand to tick points off with his fingers. "I work too hard, it freaks blokes out that I spend so much time thinking about weddings, I'm aggressively unhealthy, and I'm emotionally unfaithful with my phone. In the end everyone's happier if I'm single. This"—he toggled his finger back and forth between himself and Flynn—"is just making that point to my friends and family so they stop trying to set me up with whatever random gay man they know."

The prickly irritation in Nate's voice was charming in an odd, possibly "just when Nate was doing it" way. Flynn took a drink of his pint and raised his eyebrows.

"You talk a good game, but I heard you were quite the shagger."

"Max is quite the shagger," Nate corrected him. He tapped his finger against his chest twice. "I'm a serial monogamist."

"The difference?"

There was a pause, and Nate glanced down into his pint. His face twisted into a rueful expression, one side of his mouth hitched up in a self-mocking smile. It didn't quite hide the regret. "Max never tries to turn a one-night stand into a relationship."

Flynn winced. He'd planned to play the asshole, not to actually be an asshole. Maybe it wasn't an open wound or even a scar, but he'd obviously ground his thumb into what was at least a bruise on Nate's emotions. It definitely didn't help his resolution to not get tangled up when a flash of vulnerability made him want to comfort Nate.

Luckily he'd always been shit at that.

"Well, you know what they say," he said. "It's better to have loved and lost, than—"

Nate interrupted him. "It really isn't."

No. He was probably right. Flynn took a drink and tasted the sour tang of jealousy along with discomfort and hops when he swallowed. He ignored it. No more overthinking—about Nate or himself.

"I need to go to the loo." Nate broke the silence. He slid off his seat and stood up. "Get me another beer if Gennie brings the food over?"

Flynn let himself admire the long stretch of Nate's body as he stood and as he walked away. Even for a drink in the pub, Nate was wearing a silk T-shirt and jeans you could tell had a designer label stitched to them somewhere. With what they did for Nate's ass, Flynn thought he might actually have to rethink whether paying that much for denim was a waste of money.

He took a swig of his beer. One of the barflies holding up the bar, a ginger in a shiny tracksuit, staggered over to the jukebox and punched his money in. The freshest hits of the 90s blasted out and Britney Spears told someone to hit her one more time.

"Jesus," Flynn muttered.

While ginger scuffled with his friends at the bar— apparently they didn't have anything else to do on a Tuesday night—Gennie came out with two plates of food. She stalked over and shoved them onto the table.

"Here." She pulled two napkin-wrapped sets of cutlery out of her pocket and smacked them down. Her mouth stretched in an empty, glossy red smile. She had lipstick on her teeth. Her voice dropped so it was disguised under the tinny chorus from the juke-box. "I hope you choke."

That made Flynn blink in surprise. Gennie had never had a problem with him before. He paid for his drinks and kept to himself. What else he did with himself she didn't care about. Until then, apparently. "What?"

Gennie sniffed. "Ally Moffatt got my boy through school, got him an apprenticeship, still asks about him when I see her down the street. She's a good lady, she is, and I don't like seeing you taking advantage of her son."

"He's a grown man," Flynn said.

"And he's got enough on his plate right now with his mum being sick," Gennie said. "He doesn't need you cozening up to him to get some contract with the Saint Johns. It's not on, Flynn."

She sniffed at him, turned on her heel, and stalked off. A few of the regulars at the bar nodded their heads in approval at her. And there was Park on the end of the bar, his face florid with whiskey and smug with whatever gossip he was spreading.

"Can I get a couple of beers with that?" he called after Gennie. "Thanks."

Apparently, however she felt about him, it didn't extend to his money. She pulled two pints and put them onto the bar—just in time for Nate to come out of the toilet, wiping his hands fastidiously on a paper towel. Flynn raised a hand to catch his attention and then pointed to the waiting beers.

Nate handed a tenner to Gennie, traded a minute of small talk, and then brought the beers over.

"Apparently I can do better," Nate said, looking bemused. He handed a beer to Flynn, sat down, and frowned at his plate and the pile of lettuce topped with a crumble of cheese and chopped almonds. "What the hell?"

"You said whatever sounded good," Flynn said. He unrolled the napkin to free his knife and fork. He'd gotten the chili and chips—Gennie's specialty. A bubbling crust of cheese was slowly dissolving into the spicy stew. It coated over the macaroni shapes mixed in it and soaked into the chips. "Salad *sounded* like a good idea. Besides, it was cheap."

"You're meant to be the bad boyfriend, remember?" Nate said absently as he ground a generous coating of salt onto the plate. The lettuce wilted like a slug under the onslaught of sodium. He gave Flynn's chips a longing look. "You should be encouraging me to eat onion rings and fried chicken."

Flynn pointedly turned the plate around so Nate would have to stretch across the food to steal any chips. He speared one and used it to gesture with.

"Fuck that," he said. "Apparently I'm using you for your connections, so I need to keep you alive and well for as long as possible."

"I'm slightly offended that the assumption isn't that you're using me for my ass." Nate prissily rolled a tomato out of his salad and positioned it on the edge of the plate. Apparently its fate was to watch the rest of the salad be consumed. The tines of the fork clicked against stoneware as Nate messed with the greens and glanced up at Flynn from under the flop of his bangs. "About what happened on Friday. It was—"

"It was fun," Flynn said, because better to burst that bubble himself. "And it was adrenaline. That pretty much covers it, doesn't it?"

He ate the chip. It was still half-frozen in the middle. He grimaced and glanced sourly toward Gennie, who was behind the bar, industriously occupied with cleaning pint glasses. When he glanced back at Nate, he caught the tail end of a fleeting expression as it slid off his mobile face. It might have been disagreement, or even regret, but Flynn wasn't overthinking things any more.

"Yes, I guess it does," Nate said. "Although it wasn't just adrenaline."

"No?"

"The rubber suit and musk of excessive manliness might have had an impact too," Nate said. He rolled his eyes at whatever look Flynn gave him, and a rueful smile curved his lips. "I know, I know. I like sailors. I'm a cliché. Don't rub it in."

The tomato had apparently suffered enough. Nate stabbed it and popped it into his mouth. Maybe it was the airy way he dismissed their attraction—even though Flynn had done it first—or that he'd lumped Flynn in under the catchall of "sailors." Either way it bugged Flynn enough that he had to wash it down with a gulp of beer.

"If it helps, I wasn't always a lifeguard," he said. "I used to be in the army."

It was a fairly prosaic statement, but it was only the second time Flynn had told someone on the island that bit of information. The first had been his dad, and the old man wasn't impressed. No one else on Ceremony cared enough to ask. They'd rather make up their own stories, and Flynn didn't care what they thought he'd done.

Apparently he *did* care what Nate thought—that or watching Nate choke on a tomato from surprise would be bizarrely satisfying.

"Fuck." Nate coughed and blinked tears out of his eyes. He took a gulp of beer and narrowed his eyes at Flynn suspiciously. "Are you screwing with me?"

Flynn dipped a chip in the cheese. "Nope." He was the one who brought it up, but it was a whim he regretted. He braced himself for questions he didn't like having to answer even in his own head—like why he left the army, if he missed it, if—

"Do you still have the outfit?"

That wasn't one of the questions he expected. Flynn took a bite off a chip and gave Nate a curious look. "The uniform? No, I never saw the point of hauling it around with me."

"Shame." Nate took two deep gulps of his beer and set the glass down. He raised his eyebrows at Flynn. Unlike his hair they were dark and gray-free. "Do you wanna make out?"

It was Flynn's turn to choke as the chip went down the wrong way. "What?"

Nate smirked over the table. "Serves you right."

"So you were kidding?"

"No. I meant it," Nate said. He set the pint glass down and stood up. His jacket was slung over the back of the chair, and he picked it up to shrug it on. "It still serves you right. So, do you want to take advantage of me or not?"

The chili wasn't the most tempting thing on the menu anymore. Flynn drained his beer and stood up. He leaned over and curled his hand around Nate's neck as he leaned in.

"In that case, you can pay for dinner," he growled against warm skin. His lips grazed the skin. The taste of alcohol and cologne were sharp against his tongue, and he felt the muscles move as Nate gulped. "And I can take advantage twice."

CHAPTER ELEVEN

"Everyone knows that his problem is he's in love with that friend of his. He just needs to get over him."

GENNIE *TCHED* her tongue at Nate when he paid, asked after Ally, and threatened to call around. He wouldn't tell his mother that. From experience, most people seemed to feel that promising to visit was the same as actually turning up. Under normal circumstances a quick chat about his mother would have put a boot firmly on the throat of Nate's libido.

But.... Flynn Delaney had been a soldier. That was two of Nate's more persistent teenage fantasies—and the soldier one actually lasted well into his twenties. He had a thing for men in uniform, bundled into a gruff, "faded jeans wearing" package. Nate put his change in his pocket and walked out of the propped-open door into a drizzling rain.

Besides, it wasn't like any of it was real. It came with a pre-established expiration date, so he didn't need to worry about… well, any of the things that usually preoccupied him during real dates.

His friends *didn't* like Flynn, but it didn't matter because they'd be broken up in a month. If Flynn didn't answer a text, it wasn't because Nate had been too fucking much or not fucking enough. It was because it wasn't a real relationship. If Nate screwed up the balance between stylish sophisticated lover and neurotic control freak who was always early, it didn't matter, because Flynn wasn't deciding whether or not to go for date three.

Best of all Nate didn't have to worry that he was wasting his diminishing days as a datable prospect on a guy who might or might not be a long-term prospect. He wasn't a prospect at all.

He paused midstep to admire the sight of Flynn leaning against the battered door of his jeep, arms crossed and eyes hooded like six foot one of very bad news. His mouth went dry. Okay. So last night he tried to do a push-up. But other than that, the arrangement with Flynn was a very tension-free affair.

"You're a cheap date," Nate said as he reminded his feet to keep moving. "I got change."

Flynn smirked. The drizzle had dampened his dark hair, and as Nate got closer, he could see it glistening in the stubble on Flynn's jaw. "I think you'll find that's just the booking fee."

He hooked his fingers in the waistband of Nate's trousers and pulled him two steps closer—near enough to kiss. The hair on the back of Nate's neck prickled with nervous goose bumps. It was one thing to buss a date in the Tax Shelter, where the worst that would happen would be a disapproving cluck from a rich old lady and the island-gossip version of a vague post about your behavior—a snide comment to your mother. It was a bit riskier outside the Hairy Dog, where the drink was stronger and the drinkers were resentful.

That didn't stop Nate from leaning into the kiss. He slid his hands around to grab Flynn's ass—the muscle was taut and flexed under his fingers—and chewed his lower lip appreciatively. Flynn buried his free hand in Nate's hair, twisted his fingers in the curls, and shoved his tongue into Nate's mouth.

The rough thrust of slick muscle between his lips pulsed a hot suggestion down Nate's spine and made his ass twitch. He groaned. The sound was trapped in his throat as he pressed himself against the hard, lean planes of Flynn's body. His mind was only too happy to call up, in high definition, the image of what lay under Flynn's T-shirt and leather—swarthy skin, a treasure trail of rough, clipped hair, and muscles that looked like someone had twisted them out of metal wire.

It was a body that made push-ups seem worthwhile, at least until you were in the middle of a set. Of one.

A car drove past and interrupted them, the headlights on full beam. The driver hit the horn, a cheerful rattle of "bra-bra-brap" that was more *fancy seeing you here* than *gonna circle the block asshole*. It still made Nate draw back. He licked his lips, and his tongue lingered where stubble had chafed the tender skin.

"You taste like chili," he said.

Flynn's hand was still buried in his hair. He used the handle to tilt Nate's head back and pull his throat into a tight line.

"Bad boys don't use breath mints," Flynn growled, the usual rasp of his voice exaggerated.

"I think they should." Nate reached up and cupped Flynn's face in his hand and felt the stubble against his palm. He brushed his thumb over the stern line of Flynn's mouth. "We should probably move off the street."

Flynn nipped his thumb with a quick, rough bite. There was a chip in his front tooth. Nate could feel the sharp edge of it against the meat of his pad. It prickled over his skin, and his imagination was all too eager to imagine that scrape against other parts of his body.

Frankly Nate wasn't too sure he'd enjoy that, but at the moment, his dick insisted he definitely would.

It was distracting enough that he almost missed Flynn's question.

"Your place?"

God, no. Nate might need his mother to find out about him dating on the dark side, but not the same way she found out he was gay. There was only so much humiliation a man could take, and his mother interrupting him and a boyfriend *once* with a cup of tea and a plate of condoms instead of biscuits had put Nate at that limit.

The lighthouse felt… too intimate. Nate might know what Flynn's come tasted like on his fingers, but he didn't know his bedroom. Besides, the lighthouse was the center of Nate's promise to leave Flynn alone once the fakery was over. It felt off-limits.

After a second of racking his brain, Nate realized the choice was obvious. If he was reliving his teenage years with all the sex he'd hoped for back then? He might as well commit.

"I got an idea." He couldn't quite keep the smirk off the corners of his mouth. "The Castle."

Flynn rolled his eyes. "You're kidding."

Usually Nate would have been kidding. Or, on the off chance that he wasn't, he would have pretended he was. He shrugged and let the smirk slide over his stubble-scraped lips.

"Come on," he said. "Not like you ever got to take anyone up there either."

Flynn snorted and wiped his hand over his face. "Ask around. I think you'll find I disappointed plenty of the island girls up there when I was a teenager."

For a second Nate wondered how he hadn't heard about that. Then he remembered that when Flynn had been pretending to be into girls, he'd been pretending that his bike was KITT. It was an odd moment. Nate had no idea how Max did it with his parade of guys who hadn't even been alive when *Knight Rider* was a thing and not just reboot fodder.

In his head he could hear Max's drawled answer. *We don't do much talking.* Maybe that was unfair, but after decades of friendship, his imaginary Max was pretty accurate. Nate supposed it wasn't his business, any more than what he was doing with Flynn was Max's.

"How about going with someone you're not going to disappoint?" Nate asked Flynn. He glanced up at the sky and wrinkled his nose against the rain. "At least we'll be dry."

After a heartbeat, Flynn growled in frustration and dragged him back in for a rough, quick clash of mouths.

"Why do I let you talk me into stuff I know is a bad idea?" Flynn grumbled between their wet lips.

"Oh, I know this one," Nate said. He gave Flynn's cheek a teasing pat. "It's because you want in my pants."

He pulled back, ignoring Flynn's growl, and circled around the bumper of the car to get in the passenger side. His damp trousers dragged on the pleather as he slid in and pulled his seat belt out. A glance out the driver's side window showed Flynn shaking his head before he climbed into the jeep.

"If Father Bly drags his arthritic old ass up the hill to roust us," he grumbled as he put the car in gear, "you get to give him mouth-to-mouth when he has a heart attack."

Nate laughed. Back when they'd been in school, the Father had been a lot less arthritic and a lot more of a firebrand. His blood-and-thunder sermons about the dangers of premarital sex, delivered car-side to horny teenagers, were legendary.

"Did he really do that?"

"Caught me twice." Flynn turned the engine over and put the jeep in gear. The heavy growl of it cut across the chatter from the pub like a snarl. "Not sure who was more relieved, me, my girlfriend, or Bly, since I'd just been to confession the week before. Pretty sure he thought fifteen Hail Marys had made me straight."

"How long did that last?"

The corner of Flynn's mouth that Nate could see curled up in a slow, lecherous smirk. "Not long."

Nate shrugged as they pulled away from the curb. His balls ached under silk and expensive denim, and his phone buzzed quietly in his pocket. He didn't know what he wanted to touch more.

All right. He could, and it was his balls. The phone was still distracting.

"At least it gave you something to talk about on Sundays," he said.

The low rub of Flynn's voice, like rough silk on his skin, made Nate shiver. He relaxed back into the hard seat and watched the dark, damp countryside race by through the window. His nerves fizzed under his skin, and his heart stuttered along too fast. He reached over the hand brake and rubbed Flynn's thigh. The way the heavy muscle tightened under his fingers and the low noise from Flynn's throat made his stomach clench with anticipation.

Sometimes being with Flynn felt like falling in love, without all the pressure of having to actually do it.

Either that or he was having a heart attack.

ASK A blow-in where The Castle was and most of them would eventually point out the Granshire. It had turrets and a grand ballroom. There was even a ghost, if you believed the stories.

None of which The Castle had. It didn't even have a roof. A banker had bought the land to build a summer home, but halfway through construction he'd lost either interest or means. It had most of the external walls and the weather-rotted remains of a fully fitted kitchen, but inside it was all wet plasterboard and half-tiled floors. For a five-year-old, it was a playground, and the fancy black toilet they'd left stored in the middle of the living room made a brilliant throne. For a fifteen-year-old, the huge, curved drive, half pitted tarmac and half gravel, was the perfect place for a bit of privacy—whether they wanted it for sex or to sell drugs and bottles of harsh, unlabeled liquor.

Or it used to be. Tonight it was empty, the stretch of unfinished tarmac free of muddy tire tracks. Maybe it was the time of year or the weather. Maybe kids were buying their drugs online and having them sent through the mail these days.

Nate didn't really care. He was folded across the hand brake, and the bar dug into his hip as he kissed Flynn. It was hot and rough and kind of funny as Flynn swore around Nate's tongue at the steering wheel for getting in the way, and Nate got tangled in the loose seat belt.

"Any chance we can give up on this and go find a bed?" Flynn grumbled. He ran a hand over Nate's shoulder and down to his hip. "Something with better springs at least." Despite his complaints he hooked his fingers in the waistband of Nate's trousers and tugged him closer.

With Flynn's spit on his neck and breath in his mouth, Nate's earlier hesitation over going back to the lighthouse seemed ridiculous. It wasn't like leaving Flynn alone would be absolute. It was a small island.

On the other hand....

"You really want to stop?" Nate reached down and palmed the taut ridge of Flynn's dick through his jeans. The zipper was rough against his fingers as he squeezed hard enough to startle a *fuck* out of Flynn as he lifted his hips into Nate's touch. His thighs hit the steering wheel, and he ground another curse out through clenched teeth.

"I can't believe you talked me into this." He reached down the side of the door and jerked the lever to jolt the seat back. His legs stretched out, and the planes of his body shifted under Nate.

Nate licked the stern curve of Flynn's mouth. "It didn't take much." He trailed his mouth over Flynn's jaw and down the line of his throat. A hickey wouldn't show up under the stubble that tickled his lips, but Nate chewed one into his skin anyhow. See how he liked it.

From the groan that Nate could feel as well as hear, he liked it quite a lot. So it was a surprise when Flynn pushed him back. He sprawled onto his side of the car, his arm braced against the window. Before he had a chance to catch his breath enough to complain, Flynn crawled after him.

His tanned, scuff-knuckled hands caught Nate's knees and repositioned his legs with one hooked up over Flynn's shoulder. The discomfort at not being in control, not setting the order of events, made Nate squirm. So did the impatient jerk of Flynn's hands at his trousers as he unbuttoned the fly and tugged them down. The night air was cold against his balls for a second and made them twitch up to his body. And then Flynn's mouth was there.

"Son of a bitch," Nate groaned. He let his head fall back against the window with a soft crack. He could feel the wet slick of Flynn's mouth around his dick and the hard pressure of his tongue pressed against the shaft and then flicking the head. He could feel the tight pressure as his dick thickened and ached under Flynn's ready tongue. "That feels... fuck... good."

He reached down and wove his fingers through Flynn's dark curls as Flynn worked his tongue around Nate's dick.

Pleasure twisted around and through Nate's shaft and balls, pulled at the nerves with satin fingers, and tugged at his spine impatiently. Nate braced his sneaker against Flynn's back and felt his sweaty ass sticking to the pleather seat. It was unbelievably hot, yet still ridiculous.

Or maybe the word he was looking for was fun— "sticky, sweaty, completely inappropriate for men of their age" fun.

Nate chewed on the inside of his mouth. The nip of his teeth on tender skin was a leash for the release he wanted… but not just yet. He flexed his fingers against Flynn's head and felt the salt stiffness at the roots of his hair.

Parked up in the hills, no one around for miles unless the Father was cursing his way up the road, it was quiet. It made the wet sucking noises of Flynn's mouth around him sound louder and more lewd.

Flynn tugged Nate's trousers down further and slid a hand between his legs. He kneaded the heavy weight of Nate's balls, and the rough squeeze of his fingers was payback for earlier. It dragged a whine out of Nate, and the noise was so ridiculously vulnerable that it made him flinch and made his balls throb with tight pleasure.

"Flynn, fuck," Nate rasped out. His ass clenched, a feathery tickle of warning flickered down at the base of his dick, and his control gave up the ghost. "I'm going to come."

Some guys didn't like it. Flynn apparently didn't care. He made a smug sound around Nate's dick, and the sound vibrated all the way down to the root as he swallowed the length. The slick squeeze of it, of Flynn's

tongue pushed hard against the underside, just wrung
the come out of Nate. He clutched the back of the seat,
dug his fingers in so deeply he had to leave nail marks,
and bucked up into Flynn's mouth as he orgasmed.

Flynn swallowed and let Nate's dick slide wet
and slippery out of his mouth. He crawled up Nate
and kissed him hard. His tongue pushed the salt and
warm-penny taste of Nate's own come into his mouth.

"You know what?" Flynn asked. He cupped Nate's face in his hand and dragged his thumb along his
lower lip.

"What?"

Flynn's eyes looked pale in the moonlight, and
something wicked sparked in them as he smirked.
"Your turn."

"Really?" Nate teased. "Because I paid for dinner, and—"

The abrupt angry clatter that interrupted made
them both jump back to their side of the car. Nate fumbled at his dick as he tried to stuff it back in his trousers. He didn't have the instinctive Catholic guilt that
creased Flynn's face, but no one wanted to be yelled
at by an angry priest with their genitalia drying in the
wind. It wasn't as though he could even run—his leg
had gone dead from the knee down.

Except the windows were empty, with no scowling face peering through the raindrops. Nate finished
zipping up anyhow. Just in case.

"What the hell?" Flynn growled. He shifted uncomfortably and reached down between his legs to tug
at his jeans.

"He died on the way up, and his ghost is pissed?"
Nate suggested.

It took a second burst of rattling before they realized what it was. Phone. Nate sniggered—well, he'd gotten his—as Flynn scrabbled for his cell phone on the dashboard. Once he had it, a glance at the screen made him curse.

"Hell, I need to take this," he muttered.

"Really?" Nate asked.

"It's Rescue. I don't get to blow them off."

Nate raised his eyebrows. "Does that mean I don't get to blow you?"

For a moment Flynn looked conflicted. He let out a breath that was almost a groan and answered the phone.

"Delaney," he said. There was a pause as he listened. To Nate the voice on the other end was an almost unintelligible chatter. He caught a few words—*emergency* and *fucking idiots*, but not the gist. After a second, Flynn broke in again. "I'm off duty tonight. I've had a beer. What about—"

Whatever the buzz on the other end of the line said made Flynn's jaw clench and his mouth twist in annoyance.

"Fine. I'll go, but I'm not happy." Flynn hung up and tossed the phone at Nate. "There's a kid fell down a sinkhole at the old Deacon farm. I need to go provide backup. You're going to have to come along. Just stay in the car."

Nate glanced pointedly down at Flynn's crotch. His erection was a stubborn bulge against the fly of his jeans. "You going to pole vault them to safety?"

Flynn threw the jeep in reverse and hit the accelerator. Gravel sprayed out from under his wheels as he backed up at speed down the drive. He hooked one arm over the back of Nate's seat as he twisted around, and steered the car with the other.

"I'm going to do my job," Flynn growled. He spun the car as they reached the end of the drive and hit the accelerator. "Then I'm going to do you."

That shut Nate up, and his skin prickled at the images the gruff promise conjured up. Even though he was starting to doubt he'd be able to sell the "bad boyfriend" thing to anyone but Teddy and Max. Even his mother would doubt the gossip if it got out that Flynn went around rescuing small children on weekends.

As he wriggled his numb toes, he supposed that he should call the whole fake-dating thing off. The idea stood there for a second with its chilly feet on the forecourt of his brain. After an uncomfortable second, he dismissed it.

Nobody liked a quitter. He might just need to… rejig the running order of it all. No reason to call it a day yet, not without giving it a chance to work. That was only fair.

Besides, he didn't want to call it off. Not yet.

CHAPTER TWELVE

"I can't tell you where I heard this, but I have it on good authority that he had a wife and child in Bristol. Ran off on them. Huge court case now. Don't be surprised to see a 'For Sale' sign slapped on that lighthouse soon."

THE LATEST owner of the old Deacon place was a tall, thin man with receding brown hair and a chicken. The bedraggled hen was squeezed under his arm, its eyes bright and beady with resentment.

Behind him, in the house, Flynn could see a woman silhouetted against the window as she peered out and then jerked the curtains closed. The sense of "something off" got stronger in the back of Flynn's brain.

When children were in danger, sometimes only one of the parents could function enough to interact.

The other parent was usually *there*, though, even if not exactly present. Maybe she was the child's stepmother or she was minding other children inside. Or it could be something worse. That didn't happen often— and less on Ceremony than on the mainland—but the times it had stuck with him.

"I don't know how he got out," the man said. He hugged the chicken like a security blanket. "We locked the door. We always do."

Flynn glanced at Mac, who was already there when Flynn screeched up in a spray of mud and puddle water. It didn't help. Mac hadn't been at it long enough and was too intent on doing a good job to pick up on the "off."

"I'm sure it couldn't be helped," Mac said, carefully on script. He hitched his bag up his shoulder. "Can you take us to him, Mr. Harris? Do you remember where it happened?"

"Sure. Of course," Harris said. "Just let me put Hennibal back in her pen. She got out along with him."

He turned and loped away through the rain to the small teal-blue barn. They watched as he shoved the hen inside, blocked her escape with his foot, and finally slammed the door in her beak.

That that wasn't quite right had sunk in even for Mac. He gave Flynn a nervous sidelong look and muttered out of the corner of his mouth.

"The boy was in the barn? Should we call someone—"

"Wait," Flynn said. "Do our jobs first. Then we can report on whatever we find."

"You sure?" Mac questioned, his eyebrows furrowed together over his eyes. Rain ran down his nose, found a way between the spots, and dripped from the end. "This is—"

Whatever Mac thought it was would have to wait. Mr. Harris slid back over to them. His Hunter boots were clogged with so much muck and silt he looked like he was on stilts.

"Okay. I'm ready to go."

"Do you need to tell your partner where you're going?" Flynn asked.

His answer was a blank stare. "No, she's fine."

He turned his flashlight on, and a pencil beam of light poked the darkness as he headed into the scrub. Mac patted his belt and looked panicked when he didn't find what he needed.

"Go on. I'll grab mine."

He jogged back to the jeep. Nate waited next to it with a map held over his head as a makeshift shelter. His cigarette cast shadows and glow over his face, and the sight of him, clothes wrinkled and hair rumpled, even the damn cigarette, made Flynn's balls ache. Somewhere Father Bly probably felt smug without knowing why.

"Is everything okay?" Nate asked.

Flynn reached over and took the cigarette from between Nate's fingers. He dropped it to the grass and ground it out under his boot. Nate rolled his eyes at him but didn't complain.

"Don't know yet." Flynn popped the boot, grabbed his flashlight, and flicked it on. It was always recharged after use, but better to find out the batteries had gone bad there than out in the weeds. The glare of 1000 lumens made Nate wince and bring the map down as a soggy shield for his eyes. "Stay in the jeep."

If it turned out for the worst, he didn't want to confuse things. Nate didn't pick up on that, though, so Flynn got a dry look over the edge of the map.

"Because I look like the sort of man who goes yomping in the dark," he said. Then his expression softened. "I hope the child's okay, and umm... be careful."

Flynn slammed the back of the jeep shut. "Worried?"

He caught the wry tilt of Nate's mouth for a second as he swung the beam of the flashlight away from him.

"Don't want to have to find another bad boy," Nate said.

Flynn snorted and jogged away, and the light bounced along the path ahead of him in time with his steps. He swept it briefly over the cottage, but the heavy curtains were still tightly pulled.

He hopped the fence. His feet landed in mud on the other side, and it sucked at the bottom of his boots as he moved. The beam of the flashlight had already caught up with Mac's heels as he tromped through long, scrubby grass.

Flynn stretched his legs and caught up. Instinct twitched his fingers to hand the light off to Mac, but the kid was the lead rescue. Flynn was just there for moral support and advice.

"This isn't like him," Harris said over his shoulder. He tripped over a tussock of grass. His long legs gave him a comical air, but he caught himself. "We've had him since he was born practically, and he's never any trouble. The dog is the one you can't trust. She found a dead... thing... the other day and dragged it back."

Flynn grimaced at the unsubtle self-edit. So that would have been a lamb, then. He would decide whether to pass that news on to the local farmers later. A sheep-worrying dog would cause problems and wouldn't last long.

"He maybe just wanted the adventure. You know what kids are like, they love breaking the rules."

"And eating," Harris said. "That's probably why he snuck out, looking for food."

Mac gave Flynn a desperate, sidelong look. The whites showed around his eyes as he mutely mouthed "What the fuck?" Flynn shrugged and kept walking. He could just hear the edge of a bawl on the wind, attenuated by distance and the dark to a thread of sound.

"What's your boy's name, Mr. Harris?" he asked.

Harris's stride faltered long enough for him to glance over his shoulder. The flashlight gave enough light to pick out the baffled expression on his face.

"Oh, umm… Bilbo," he said. "Ah, sorry. I misheard you there. We're almost there. I hope he's all right."

Bilbo Harris.

By the time they reached the slipping edge of the sinkhole and Flynn pointed the light down to the bottom, he was kind of expecting what he saw. The light reflected back from barred, horizontal pupils.

"Bilbo's a goat, isn't he, Mr. Harris," Flynn said while Mac gawped in disbelief.

Harris gave him that dubious look again, like he was wondering what Flynn was going on about. He crouched near the edge of the hole and made encouraging noises down at the trapped animal.

"He's a prizewinning angora goat," he said proudly. "Or he will be when he grows up."

The goat, who was small and dog-sized with a cream-and-tan coat, bawled up plaintively. It was lying on its side on the slope of the hole, its hooves braced against the rest of the drop. Mac turned his back on the hole and stepped away. He had his hand clapped over his mouth, either to hold in a laugh or a burst of swear words.

"When he grows up," Flynn said. He rubbed his thumb between his eyebrows in an attempt to squash the headache he could feel brewing. "Because right now he's just a kid, right?"

Harris looked like he was questioning Flynn's intelligence. "Yes. He's four months old. His breed don't reach maturity until…." He trailed off as his brain caught up with his mouth and he realized what had happened. He pursed his mouth around a dismayed "oh" and lifted the wavering beam of his flashlight to Flynn's face. "I did… wonder… why you came so quickly. I mean, for a goat."

Yeah, well, Flynn would have come even quicker if he hadn't been dragged out on a wild *goat* chase. He dragged his hand down over his face.

"I'm *so* sorry," Harris said. His apology had a desperate "not sure how much trouble he was in" note to it. He glanced from Flynn to Mac's back and then at Flynn again. "I didn't… when I said 'kid,' I didn't realize they'd think I meant a *child.*"

Mac turned around and glared at him. His face was flushed red—redder around the spots—and he jabbed an angry finger in Harris's direction.

"Do you know what the penalty is for wasting Rescue's time?" he asked sourly.

Flynn was tempted to wait and see if either of them knew the answer, because he didn't. Instead, since he still had better things to do that night, he interrupted. "Mac, why don't you call in to Dispatch and let them know about the crossed wires." He slung his kit off his shoulder and crouched down to unhook the looped rope. "I'll get Mr. Harris's goat."

No one laughed at the joke.

"Oh, come on," Mac protested. "We're not frigging Animal Rescue."

About 50 percent of the time, they were—mostly dogs and the occasional wayward sheep. Bilbo was the first goat. But Mac was still into trying to impress girls with his exploits—or boys. Flynn had never asked. It had definitely been a better story for him when there was a helpless child involved.

But there wasn't, and Mac needed to suck that up.

"Just call Dispatch," Flynn said, "before they have the cops out here."

"I don't see why I should have to—" Mac spluttered indignantly.

Flynn stood up. He rolled his head to the side and made his neck pop. Maybe he wasn't as bad as most people in town thought, but he could still be pretty awful—enough to make Mac swallow and take a step back. Flynn was his dad's son, after all, and the old man had always been ready with his fists.

Too ready sometimes, but that was chipped teeth under the bridge.

"Because I told you to?"

For a second he thought Mac was going to call his bluff—not that he couldn't take the kid in a fight. It would be one way to vent his frustrations, but he didn't particularly want to. In the end the threat of it was enough. Mac backed down resentfully.

"Fine," he muttered sourly. "Let's rescue the bloody goat."

Flynn relaxed his face into a smirk. "You can still tell people you rescued a kid," he pointed out as he shook the twists out of his rope. "They'll jump to the same conclusions."

If Mac didn't seem to take much comfort in that, it wasn't Flynn's fault.

A HOUR and one more complicated rescue than he'd anticipated later, Flynn limped back down toward the farm. He was carrying the goat this time, after Harris let it slip out of his arms fifteen minutes before and the squirmy little devil threw itself back down the hole. It had taken its name a bit too much to heart.

"Sorry," Harris said again from behind him. At that point it wasn't entirely clear what part of the night he was apologizing for.

The goat squirmed and kicked at Flynn with hard, sharp little hooves. It *blatted* its displeasure with the whole situation through a mud-covered muzzle. Flynn hoisted it up under his arm. "We got him out in the end," Flynn said.

Mac picked mud out of his ear and grunted sourly. His mood hadn't improved. But at least it had stopped raining. As they got down toward the fence, the security light over the back door clicked on and flooded the space with light. The back door opened, and Nate stepped out. He was grinning, or maybe it was more of a smirk, but he did come bearing cups.

"I thought I told you to stay inside," Flynn grumbled as Nate met them at the gate.

"Rebecca asked me if I wanted some coffee. Speaking of which…." Nate held out a cup to Flynn. "Milk, all the sugar."

Flynn handed Bilbo to Harris—who muttered a final apology and stumbled off to the barn—and replaced the goat with the hot mug. It wasn't that cold a night. It was damp and the air was mild, but the mud and the rain had sucked the heat out of Flynn. His fingers were chilled enough that the heat against his skin actually hurt. "Thanks."

Nate gave Flynn a quick up-and-down look, from muddy boots to muddy hair, and then glanced at Harris's squirming burden. "I guess you found out for yourself that Bilbo's a goat, then?"

"Fuck off," Mac spat. He squared up to Nate. Mac was slightly shorter and a lot more solid. "You think this is fucking funny?"

Instead of backing down or apologizing, Nate tilted his head and gave a fox-like smile that hid more than it revealed. "I do," he said.

Flynn grabbed Mac's shoulder before he could throw the punch that jerked his elbow up. He could sympathize with the urge, but he kind of liked the face under the smirk.

"Don't be an idiot." He felt no obligation to be clear who he was talking about. "Mac. Go pack up your car and go home. I'll see you tomorrow to rip strips off Dispatch. Okay?"

He kept hold of Mac's shoulder and pressed his fingers hard against his collarbone until Mac deflated and nodded his agreement. A shove sent Mac on his way with an angry glance tossed back over his shoulder as he stamped over to his Fiesta.

"You didn't have to do that," Flynn said.

"What?" Nate asked.

Escalate the situation. Play right into Mac's stereotypes of the Granshire lot. Poke the younger man right in his pride, all the time hiding behind that smirk like it didn't matter.

"Be a dick." Flynn figured that covered all of the above.

The polished composure slid off Nate's face and left the hint of a scowl. "I've found that backing down never actually makes people leave you alone," he said.

"I won't always be here to save your ass."

Nate gave him a wry look. "I can take care of myself."

"Really? When was the last time you were in a fight?" Flynn asked skeptically as he drained the last of the coffee and pushed his legs into moving again. The brief pause had been long enough for the strained muscle in his thigh to tighten. Shit. He limped across the garden to leave the cup on the back window.

"Not since I learned how to take a punch and call 9-9-9," Nate said. He tentatively touched the small of Flynn's back and tucked his hand under the jacket so Flynn could feel the heat of his fingers through his T-shirt. "You okay?"

Flynn couldn't deny it felt good—the nudge of a shoulder against his, the offer of support if he needed it, hell, even the concern that wasn't based on whether or not he'd be able to do his job tomorrow. It felt warm, and he caught himself wanting to lean into it.

Except it wasn't *his*. It was just basic humanity and an interest in being able to finish playing the bad boy for the climax of Nate's self-destructive little passion play. That was fine. It wasn't as though Flynn hadn't signed up for the role with a clear idea of what Nate wanted.

If he started to pretend otherwise, he'd fuck up both their lives.

"I'm fine." Flynn stepped away from Nate, his back chilly where Nate's fingers had rested, and took the last hitching strides to the jeep. "But I think the date's over for tonight. I'll drop you off back in town."

Lying to himself or not, he couldn't help but be disappointed that Nate didn't argue.

CHAPTER THIRTEEN

"Darling, I signed you up for that speed-dating event that the Deacon set up in the church hall. Just go and see. You might be surprised."

APPARENTLY, SINCE Nate hadn't gotten fucked the night before, the universe had decided to fuck him today instead.

It was raining in the wedding chapel. Water ran down the twisted wire that connected the chandelier to the ceiling and dripped from the multitude of tiny crystals. It oozed up between the planks of the wooden floor with every step and drenched the gold-and-white chair backs and pulled the carefully tied bows down in draggled knots. The flower arrangements had shed drifts of petals, and the delicate fronds of green fern were sodden and drooping. There were water stains on the old stone walls that, from experience, would take hours to dry. And everything smelled... damp.

"Fuck."

It wasn't the most eloquent response, but Nate felt that it summed up his feelings. He picked his way across the floor, tried to avoid the welling puddles, and poked at a broken vase and wet knot of daisies with his toe.

"What happened?"

Max followed him across the floor and stepped in all the puddles. He shoved his hands in his pockets and shrugged.

"Pipe burst."

"Fuck."

Nate scrubbed both hands through his hair and clenched his fingers at the nape of his neck. His brain tripped over itself as he tried to cope with all the different ways it was a disaster.

"Insurance will cover it," Max offered.

"By the weekend?" Nate asked. "Katie and Bradley's wedding is on Saturday morning."

Max glanced around and pulled a rueful face. "Yeah. Can't see that happening. You know... I *did* call you last night."

The way he dropped the comment made it obvious that Max knew he was on shaky ground. It didn't quite commit to being an accusation, but it was close enough to divert Nate's attention from the wreck of the venue.

"Not the time," he said flatly.

Max snorted and scratched his ear. "Don't know what you're talking about."

The muscles in the sides of Nate's jaw hurt because he clenched them so hard. He took a deep breath of air that smelled like damp stone and wet fabric. "Just drop it, Max," he said. "Does Teddy know?"

"Of course," Max said. "I called him after I called you. Told him you'd been having trouble with your phone."

"You don't have to lie for me. I didn't do anything wrong."

Max shrugged and reached up to hook his arm over Nate's shoulder. The solid weight of him threatened to make Nate stagger, but he braced his feet.

"I don't have to do anything," Max said. "But my dad hates Flynn even more than I do… and that's saying something."

"I know that," Nate said. "What I don't get is why. Flynn *didn't* fuck his teenage son, and *did* drag him home in one piece. Might not have been Teddy's finest hour as a dad, but what the hell does he think Flynn actually did wrong?"

There was a pause and then Max shrugged. "I don't know," he admitted and looked away. "Maybe he knows something we don't. What are you going to do about this?"

Subject changed, he waved a hand at the drenched mess that had been a wedding chapel until the night before. There were crumpled balls of wet kitchen roll in the corners of the room.

"Can you put it off?" Max asked.

Nate gave him an exasperated look. "Yes, Max. I'm going to just tell Katie that her wedding, the day she's been planning for a year, if not decades, has been rained out. Could she, her entire family, her groom, and his so-enthusiastic mother just come back next week? It's her *wedding day*, not a manicure."

"Trying to help." Max stuck his hands in his pockets and looked around. "I could clear out the bar for a night."

Nate rubbed his eye and pressed down with the heel of his hand until he could see stars. He could imagine the reaction. The whole thing was meant to be classy. "Classy as shit" was how Katie had described it. A stone wedding chapel where the lord of the manor—even if technically not their manor—had been married for three of his four weddings? That was the sort of classy she was after—the *Tatler* classy.

Hollyoaks actress and footballer getting married in a bar, however nice, sold to a different class of magazine.

"Max?"

"Yeah?"

"Stop helping."

"Whatever," Max said. He slapped Nate on the back. The impact was enough to make Nate stagger forward into a puddle. It soaked through his sneakers and wet the sole of his foot. "Let me know if you need anything. I mean, you could ask your current elderly friend—"

"He's only five years older than—"

Max talked over Nate's attempt to interrupt. "—to help. But what does he know about weddings, organizing, or anything that matters to your tightly wound soul?"

"Asshole," Nate muttered under his breath, but Max was already gone, so he didn't hear.

Right. Nate looked around, took in the devastation of the half-built wedding, and gave himself a minute to mentally throw up his hands. There was no way to rejuvenate an entire wedding basically from scratch—the wedding dress and food were the only things not in the room—repair the flood damage, or order up a batch of hand-calligraphed fancies to thank the guests.

That only took fifty-six seconds. He used the remaining four to curse out the fucking old plumbing that had sprung a leak. That felt good. But it was time to actually fix the mess.

He pulled his phone out of his pocket. Some part of his brain that apparently felt it wasn't an "all hands on board" situation noted that Flynn hadn't called yet. Still hadn't called yet. He ignored the invitation to fret over that and dialed Canon Paisley.

The phone rang twice, and the canon's secretary picked it up. It would have felt more official if Nate hadn't known that Friday and Saturdays were Mavis's turn to man the desk.

"Mrs. Jenkins," he said as he headed out of the room. "This is Nathan from the Granshire. That's right. Ally's son."

He stretched a long leg over the puddle at the door, his left foot squelched as it hit the ground, and he pulled the door shut behind him.

"Mum's doing well." He bit his tongue on the frustrated need to hurry her up. Alienating one of the canon's church ladies wouldn't do him any favors in the future. "She liked the cake you sent around."

She hadn't, but needs must.

He traded niceties about his mother's health and Mavis's ailments on his way through the hotel. The latest manager—a sharp-voweled Londoner who had replaced a sharp-natured Frenchman—waved him down in the reception area to check he had the news.

"Just a minute, Mrs. Jenkins," Nate said and tucked the phone flat across his shoulder. "Thanks, Fiona. I'm sorting it out now. Could you make sure the plumbers get out as soon as possible?"

She pulled an apologetic, perfectly made-up face. "Sorry, Nathan. I've made the calls, but I can't follow up. I have an interview in Cornwall on Monday. So I'm catching the afternoon ferry over today."

It hadn't been quite a year since Fiona had moved to the island. That wasn't a record—life on an insular, unfriendly hunk of pretty rock wasn't for everyone— but if she got that job, it would be close.

The search for a replacement would be fun. Teddy was a fan of nepotism. If he had the choice, he'd appoint one of his relatives or close friends. Unfortunately none of them had the skills for the job… but he couldn't worry about it right then.

"Can't be helped," he said. "I'll get Max to chase it up. Good luck in Cornwall."

She smiled and then tucked the corner of her mouth down regretfully. "I know I haven't been here long, but…."

Nate could guess what the rest of the sentence would have been. Ceremony wasn't an easy place for a blow-in. "It happens." He lifted the phone off his shoulder and pointed at it apologetically. "I have to go."

She waved him off, and he apologized to Mavis on his way out the door.

"Can you tell the canon that there's going to be a change in venue?" he said. "I can't just yet, but I'll let you know as soon as I can. I know, I know. It is asking a lot, but it honestly can't be helped. Yes. Yes, I know. You're an angel, Mrs. Jenkins."

He hung up and strode across the last stretch of concrete to his car. The sole of his sneaker squelched underfoot as he walked. He could have just called, but when you were asking for favors, it was better to do it in person. Made it harder to say no.

"WHAT THE hell? I *just* delivered your arrangements to the hotel," Mahdi said. He snipped through the stem of a bird-of-paradise and pointed the secateurs at Nate. "If some porter has nicked them to take to his mother, don't try and lay it on me."

The sun beat through the dusty glass of the greenhouse windows and heated the damp air until it was muggy. Flowers bloomed in perfectly lined-up rows of pots, where crimson roses graduated into pink carnations and then white daisies.

Those were only the basics. The special-order stuff Mahdi nurtured in the smaller hothouse behind his house. Madhouse Flowers supplied all of Granshire's floristry needs and additionally shipped rare roses and orchids across the British Isles.

Surprisingly enough, Mahdi could be charming when there was money on the table—less so when it was a favor.

Nate held up his hands in surrender. "Nothing like that," he said. "We had a leak at the hotel. The flowers are ruined. I need new ones… by Friday."

Mahdi raised a perfectly manicured eyebrow at him and snipped the secateurs. "Yes? Well, I want my boyfriend to move back to the mainland and stop shearing sheep for a living. Life is full of wanting and not having." He scooped the neatly trimmed flowers up off the table, turned his back on Nate, and poked four orange-petaled stems neatly into the bouquet already constructed in its vase. They nestled in among the furled ferns and baby's breath sprays.

"So you can't do it?" Nate asked.

Mahdi spun dramatically. "Can't? Can't?" he blustered. Then he deflated with a snort and a curled lip. "What am I? Six? I can't do it because I don't have four dozen ranunculus to hand, or—what was it—six feet of gold-plated wire to hold them together?"

"The wire could probably be salvaged."

He got the gardener's gloved finger for that.

"I fulfilled the contract," Mahdi said. "It's your problem now. I have other clients to tend to."

Nate crossed his arms and rocked back on his heels. The sole of his sneaker was finally dry. No more squelching. He raised an eyebrow.

"Better than the Granshire? Because I manage the event accounts, and we pay you a considerable sum for the various weddings, parties, balls, and golf tournaments we run. So I'd love to know who else around here could use that many flowers."

There was a pause as they stared at each other. Mahdi's eyes narrowed.

"Are you threatening me?"

"Yes."

"So, if I don't sort out this mess, you'll take your business elsewhere?"

"Exactly."

Mahdi scoffed at him. "Good luck with that. Before I moved here, I worked for the florist you used.

Remember? I know how much it cost to ship flowers in from the mainland."

That was a fair point. It had been expensive enough that the memory of the invoices still made Nate wince. Obviously he needed to change tack.

"It doesn't have to be the same flowers. You don't even have to stick with the color scheme." He hadn't particularly liked the yellow and orange anyhow. Hopefully he could sell Katie on that too. "Just get me flowers that look pretty—by tomorrow—and I'll pay you *and* owe you one."

Mahdi pursed his lips and glanced around as he totted up stock in his head. Finally he nodded slowly. "On one condition."

"Done."

The ready agreement made Mahdi smirk. He braced his hands on the table, leaned over it, and dropped his voice to a suggestive whisper.

"Is it true that Delaney was a whore you and Max used when you were in London?"

And just when Nate thought he had the most out-landish theories about what Flynn's past life was, the island gossip mill proved him wrong. He supposed he should be grateful. Without a lot of actual bad-boy-friend behavior to go by, people generated their own reasons for disapproval. Still. Bloody hell.

"No, he fucking wasn't," Nate said—snapped, even. Mahdi looked surprised and then smug. He probably read more into Nate's voice than was actu-ally there. "Whoever is coming up with these rumors should work for the *Daily Mail*. He wasn't a whore."

Mahdi pushed himself off the table and showed his still-gloved palms in a gesture of surrender.

"Hey, I'm just asking. I have nothing against sex workers," he said. "I used to strip when I was at college."

That threw Nate for a second. His extremely helpful imagination decided to toss its interpretation of a stripping Mahdi into his brain—all amber skin and sharp angles in a very small amount of skintight vinyl and glitter. Not that it was the first time he'd thought about it. Mahdi was a good-looking young man, and Nate wasn't dead, but it wasn't wildly helpful where the flushing was concerned. Particularly not when Flynn joined imaginary Mahdi on stage in low-slung jeans, a smirk, and a strut.

Nate knew he looked guilty... of something. He ignored it. "Neither do I. Flynn wasn't."

In Nate's imagination Flynn tossed a smug wink his way and dropped his hands to the already low-riding waistband of his jeans.

It was distracting enough that, when Mahdi threw up his hands and agreed to "put something together" it took Nate a second to pull his brain back out of the gutter.

Jesus Christ. Nate took a deep breath. It should have smelled like flowers, but he could swear he tasted Flynn's aftershave on the back of his tongue. Apparently he really was hitting his second adolescence.

"Great," he said. His second breath was appropriately floral, enough to tickle the back of his sinuses. He cleared his throat. "Let me know when you have some idea what flowers you'll be using. Please?"

"Sure," Mahdi said. "Don't hold your breath, though. Won't be until later."

Nate shrugged his surrender and turned to leave. He was halfway out the door when Mahdi called after him. "If he's not a sex worker," he asked. "What did he do time in prison for?"

"He didn't," Nate snapped over his shoulder. He slammed the door behind him. It made the whole structure rattle, or it felt like it did. Nate was pretty sure Mahdi tossed a curse word his way.

Of course, he couldn't swear that Flynn wasn't an ex-con. It wasn't like they'd had a chance to talk about his career last night when Nate's libido took the wheel. For all he knew, a jail term *was* why Flynn was back on the island.

Maybe he should ask more questions. As an obstacle to Nate's lighthouse-guesthouse plans, and occasionally a fondly revisited wank fantasy, Flynn had never needed that much biographical detail. But now that Flynn was his pretend boyfriend, Nate supposed he should show a bit more interest. After all, he was supposed to be the catch in the relationship.

His phone was already in his hand, two items on his to-do list marked as done, when it rang.

CHAPTER FOURTEEN

"Changed man, my ass. He was nothing but trouble when he was a kid, and since when does a leopard change its spots?"

"SONOVABITCH."

Flynn snatched his hand out of the engine block and shook it as though that would dislodge the sting of grated knuckles. All it did was spray drops of blood over him and the fresh white paint on the side of Mrs. Allen's Ford Focus.

He swore an unimaginative stream of *fucks* under his breath and grabbed for the oily cloth to wrap around his hand. Raw knuckles were run-of-the-mill for mechanics, but he'd already stripped the skin off both sets of fingers. His mind wasn't on the job.

Not because of the dull ache in his thigh, though. Not *just* because of the dull ache in his thigh. It was just a hobbling reminder that he was too damn old to have this bad a dose of blue balls.

After an early morning start in the garage, Flynn knew he stank of burned oil, sweat, and the eye-watering wintergreen sharpness of liniment. So why couldn't he get the lingering smell of smoke and sex out of the back of his throat?

It wasn't like he hadn't brushed his teeth after he sucked Nate's cock.

Okay. That didn't help. Flynn's tongue curled around the texture-memory of hard flesh and velvet skin, and the taste of salt and copper bloomed in the back of his brain. He screwed his eyes shut for a second and thought about wrenches, brake lines, and the sting of his knuckles. If it worked, he would know he was really getting too old.

Since it didn't, Flynn reached down and tugged the crotch of his jeans away from his aching balls. His knuckles had stopped bleeding, more or less, so he shoved the bloody cloth back in his pocket and got back to work. He needed to find out what Mr. Allen had "fixed" on his wife's car before he came to pick it up.

Just when he finally thought he was on the right track, Kenny yelled across the garage, "Hey, Flynn, something's going on outside."

Flynn didn't bother to pull his head out from under the bonnet. "Unless they're pushing a car, leave it outside."

He wiped his face on his shoulder and slotted a notched metal ruler into the engine. Yeah. The pulleys weren't square. The belt didn't look new, but Mr. Allen and eBay auto parts were old friends. He pulled the ruler out and absently shoved it into his back pocket.

Flynn reached around and scratched the nape of his neck. He twisted his mouth to the side as he considered the engine. The bolts on the tensioner needed to come off so he could realign the pulleys, but it looked like they were badly stripped.

Somewhere on the edge of his attention he could hear the rattle of the door and muffled conversation outside. That meant Kenny hadn't listened to him, but he mentally cut the kid ten minutes slack. It was what he'd get for a tea or cigarette break. They were about eight minutes in when Kenny yelled again.

"Oy, Flynn. You got Nate Moffat's number?"

Flynn felt his hackles go up. As much as he groused about the island rumor mill, he didn't really care about the gossip doing the rounds about him. That was because it was all lies. The thought of them chewing over his actual life made him bristle.

Even if his relationship with Nate wasn't real and wasn't his.

"Not sure how that's your business, Kenny," he rasped out as he straightened up. The minute he caught sight of Kenny's face, Flynn realized he'd gotten it wrong. Kenny's face was screwed up in worry, and he had blood on his hands. The tracks in Flynn's brain switched from island asshole to rescue. "What happened? You okay?"

"Me?" Kenny glanced down and seemed to catch sight of his bloody fingers for the first time. He scrubbed it off against his overalls. The addition of blood to grease and oil didn't make much difference to the dense black fabric. "Oh, no. It's not mine. Ms. Moffatt, she's had a tumble. I think she's hurt real bad.

There's blood all over, but she won't let us call an ambulance or anything."

"She can't remember Nate's number?" Flynn asked as he cut across the garage to grab the first-aid box from the wall.

"She told me not to worry him," Kenny said. He fidgeted with the ring in his eyebrow. "But I think maybe we should. This last year Ms. Moffatt's been real poorly."

That was Islander understatement. Half the church ladies on Ceremony had been planning Allison Moffatt's funeral the year before, from the music to the flowers. They liked a good funeral, since most of the weddings on the island were held up at the Granshire. But Flynn had heard she'd gotten better—maybe from spite, if she was anything like Nate.

Flynn tossed Kenny the phone with a brisk order to call him and ducked out the door onto the narrow street. His garage squatted at the dead end of the road. The sea wall beside it was an industrial holdover from when Ceremony's fishing industry supported more than tourism and chip shops. Halfway down the street, a small crowd had formed on the pavement, hunched nervously under the cloud of screeching gulls that filled the air.

"Call your doctor!" Dani Hale, who owned the glossy little boutique tucked into what had been the fishmonger, said. "You could have hurt yourself. I saw you go down. That was a nasty fall."

"I'm fine!" an irritated voice that Flynn assumed belonged to Nate's mum said. "I just need a minute, and I'll be grand."

"We could call you a taxi, Ms. Moffatt," the little girl who worked in the chippy said. "Get you home."

She was a year younger than Kenny and he was going to end up with a bad heart if he kept buying chips so he could talk to her. But they both said *Ms. Moffatt* the same way. Ms. Moffat had probably been their teacher.

Flynn tapped a man's shoulder and edged through.

"For goodness sake, Lisa, I'm fine," Allison snapped. "I'm quite capable. I didn't lose any gray matter to the cancer."

She had lost her leg, though, Flynn realized as he finally reached her. A crutch lay next to her, the metal shaft kinked where it had caught on the curb, and the leg of her trousers was pinned neatly closed below the knee—or it had been before it soaked through with blood. A halo of spilled chips surrounded her, which explained the seagulls.

"Hey, Ms. Moffatt," Flynn said. He crouched down next to her and felt the cobbles dig into his knees through his overalls. "You look a bit worse for wear."

Nate's eyes must have come from his mystery father. His mother had dishwater blue eyes and a sharp way of looking that made Flynn very aware of all the dirty things he'd done with her son. Not something he should be dwelling on right then.

"I slipped," Allison said. She shifted on the stones gingerly, and a grimace pinned her lips together. "People do. I don't see why it has to be such a production."

Her hands were shaking, and the two splashes of humiliated red in her cheeks looked like she'd been

WANTED · BAD BOYFRIEND

slapped. Not many people liked being weak, especially ferociously independent people like Allison Moffatt.

"Did you hit your head?" Flynn asked.

Allison reached up to touch the fuzz of short gray curls. Her fingers left grubby prints on the fine strands. "No." She shifted her weight and shakily tried to get her good leg folded under her. "Just my tailbone."

It would be best to keep her where she was until an ambulance got there. Chemo had more side effects than the cancer did, and it could leech the elasticity out of bone. If she hit the cobbles hard, she could have fractured her coccyx. That would mean a visit to the hospital, but there was no way Flynn would get Allison to stay put that long, and a second fall would do more damage.

"Okay," he said. "Tell you what—let's get you to your feet and out of the weather so I can have a look at that leg."

The expression on her face suggested she didn't like that idea, but she liked the thought of staying on the ground even less. She dipped her chin in reluctant agreement and held out her hands.

Flynn didn't haul her to her feet. He got his arms under her shoulders and helped her up. He knew she'd been sick, but the narrow span of her bird-delicate back under his hand drove it home.

The chip-shop girl—Katherine—darted in and grabbed the undamaged crutch. She passed it to Allison with a bashful "I hope you feel better, Ms."

"Thank you," Allison said stiffly. She dug her fingers into Flynn's arm in a mute but clear plea to get out from under everyone's attention. "I'm *fine*, really. No one needs to worry about me."

"I'll take care of her," Flynn said. "Just give her space."

The small crowd muttered and fussed with demands for updates and promises to come and check on Allison later. In the end, though, they were happy to give up the responsibility of dealing with the situation. That left them free to start judging.

"... don't know what Nathan was thinking," Dani tutted to one of her customers as she shooed them back inside. "She's obviously not capable of taking care of...."

"... not that she'd ever listen to anyone else," a man snorted. "Allison Moffatt's always done just what she wanted...."

"... goodness Mr. Delaney was here." That was Katherine, as she kicked the spilled chips into the gutter. "Her son's so lucky."

It was the first time anyone had ever said that about Flynn—on or off the island.

"DOES IT hurt?" Kenny asked. He hovered at the door to the office, his head craned to watch as Flynn cleaned off Allison's stump. "It looks sore."

The muscles in Allison's leg twitched under Flynn's fingers, and a dribble of fresh blood oozed out from under the gauze.

"Don't you have work to do, Kenny?" Flynn asked.

"Not really."

Flynn glanced back over his shoulder. "Find some."

Embarrassed color slapped Kenny's face, and he muttered "Sorry, Miss. Sorry, Boss," and ducked back into the garage. Without him propping the door open, it swung shut behind him.

"He didn't mean any harm," Allison said.

"Didn't mean he wasn't doing any."

Flynn carefully peeled the gauze off her skin. Scar tissue zippered across the stump just under Allison's knee. It was swollen and bloody where it had split against the ground, but it looked worse than it was.

"You're still going to have to see the doctor," Flynn told her. "Any injury to the amputation site can be—"

"I know." Allison paused for a second and tried again in a more moderate tone. "I do know. I'm usually very careful. The last thing I want is to end up back in the hospital. I just... I wanted everyone to stop looking at me."

Flynn grunted. "I get that."

He grabbed the can of antiseptic out of the first-aid box and applied it over the injury. The chill of the spray hitting the stump made Allison start. She hissed and shifted in the chair and made it rock on its dubious wheel.

"It's just so frustrating," she said bitterly. "I've got a clean bill of health. Better than that. Do you know what Dr. Mathers said? He said I was in better shape now than I've been in years. Yet every time I sneeze or stumble, everyone acts like I'm going to keel over dead from sudden onset... death."

"They care about you," Flynn said. He wrapped a dressing around the stump and taped it in place.

"I know," Allison said. Once he finished with the dressing, she pushed the leg of her trousers back down over her knee. "That's why I can't yell at them."

Flynn snorted out a laugh and tidied up the first-aid box. He balled up the used dressings for disposal, put the wrappers in the bin, and pushed himself to his feet to hang the box back on its hook.

"So you're the one that gave my son a hickey," Allison said mildly.

Flynn dropped the box. It hit the ground with a sharp crack and popped open. Two rolls of gauze disappeared under the sagging sofa, and safety pins scattered over the floor.

"Crap," Flynn muttered.

"I'll take that as a yes."

He scuffed the box into the corner for later and turned around. Allison was perched neatly in his office chair as though it belonged to her, hands clasped in her lap, and her expression somewhere between amused and challenging.

Flynn wasn't sure which was worse. It had been a long time since he had to do the whole "meet the parents" thing. He hadn't missed it. Not that it would matter if he made a bad impression this time.

"I think you should probably talk to your son about that," he said.

Allison raised her eyebrows slightly. "He's a grown man," she said. "It's his own business what he gets up to and with whom."

"So then, why ask?"

"I'm his mum," she said, and a slow, sweet smile lit up her face. "I get to stick my nose in."

"Even if it was with the island asshole?"

"Somebody thinks a lot of himself, don't they?" Allison said. "Trust me. When it comes to being the island asshole? You have plenty of competition.

Besides, I know what this place is like. It's fun to listen to gossip, but 85 percent of the time, it's nothing to do with reality. As long as someone is good to my son, I don't care what anyone else around here thinks of them. All I want is for him to be happy."

"I really am an asshole," Flynn pointed out.

"Not even what they think of themselves," Allison said. "Do you care about my son?"

"We've been on a couple of dates. That's all. It's just casual."

Allison rolled her eyes. "You've been going out for a month nearly. I'm not asking if the two of you are planning to adopt me some grandchildren. Just... do you care about him? Do you like him, I guess."

I like his ass.

I don't need to like him to fuck him.

I care about ending this conversation.

Flynn could come up with a lot of bad-boyfriend comments that would do the job and convince Allison her son was better off single. But he wasn't going to do that.

Compared to some, Flynn's dad wasn't so bad. He'd never beaten Flynn or chucked him out on his ear, and when he died, he left everything to Flynn. But the old man would never have had this conversation. He wanted Flynn to pretend he wasn't gay, to do what he liked as long as he kept it to himself. He could be happy, but somewhere else. Flynn had wanted more than that from his dad.

"Nate's all right."

Of course all the good intentions in the world wouldn't help him talk about feelings. He scrubbed a hand through his hair and struggled to think of something to say. Even if the relationship were real, it had just been a couple of dates. Hot dates, but he wasn't about to tell Allison Moffatt that he really liked the way her son tasted on his tongue.

"It's nothing serious," he said. "Neither of us want that. He's okay."

That wasn't any better—more words, not more content.

Allison looked amused. "Well," she said. "That's what I was going for when I brought him up. All right. Middle of the road. Unobjectionable."

Flynn sighed and gave up. "I like him," he admitted. Out loud. For the first time. "I don't think it's going anywhere, but I really like him."

It still sounded stupid to him, but Allison gave him a slow, wide smile and nodded.

"Good." She leaned forward and confided, "I think he likes you too."

She looked delighted with herself. Flynn didn't have the heart to disillusion her. "Maybe," he said. "We'll see."

"You'll see. I know my son." She steadied herself against the desk and reached down for her bag. "Just let me call a taxi—"

"Nate's on his way," Flynn said. "He can give you a lift."

"You called him?" Allison said. "I told them I didn't want to call him."

Flynn shrugged, leaned back against the door, and crossed his arms over his chest. "I told you already I'm an asshole. And he's your son. He's not going to mind coming to get you."

"He worries about me. He's worse than any of them out there, and he should be living his life, not fussing over me," Allison said. She dropped the phone into her bag and sat back in the chair. Then she sighed and admitted sheepishly, "Also, I'm on this low oxidant, raw food, anticancer diet that I've been trying to convince Nate he should try."

"Chips not on it?" Flynn asked.

She pulled a face. "It's good for you. Nothing nice is on it."

Flynn snorted. Apparently being surreptitiously unhealthy was a family trait.

CHAPTER FIFTEEN

"Look, you just need to get back on the horse. So what if he's married, he's hot."

THE DOOR to the boutique was propped open with a heavy black coat stand. A pale blue floral shift dress that Nate had seen on five mothers-of-the-bride so far that year hung on it and flapped listlessly in the breeze.

Dani popped out from behind it as Nate walked up. She must have been keeping an eye out for him through the window. A client stood abandoned in the middle of the shop, posed in front of a full-length mirror in an unzipped jumpsuit.

"Nate. Sweetheart," Dani gasped, her hands held out. "Thank goodness someone got in touch. I would have called, but I only have your work number."

That was on purpose. Dani had a good eye for fashion, but she was always at the bottom of any list of boutiques that Nate recommended. She'd caused at least three wedding-party fights that he knew about, and when they were sixteen, she spread a rumor that his hair was going gray because of all the spunk he got in it.

"I'll have to fix that," he lied smoothly. "What happened? Mum fell?"

"Yes. Right there." Dani pointed dramatically to a wet patch on the pavement. "She slipped on the cobbles. How often have I complained to the council about them, Nate? How many of my ladies have taken a fall coming down here?"

Nate made a noncommittal sound. Everyone knew the cobbles weren't a good idea, and everyone knew the council wasn't going to tear up a half mile of kitschy touristyness. Dani wanted to turn his mother's accident into another chance to talk about how her business was suffering.

"What happened?" He let her clutch his hands and pet the back of them. "The message just said Mum had hurt herself."

"Oh, it was awful," Dani said. She looked genuine for a second. "She must have fallen and hurt her... umm...."

Discomfort made her trail off. Instead of using the word, she gestured vaguely down at her knee and pursed her lips. It reminded Nate of his nana and the way she'd always marble-mouthed anything to do with reproduction.

"Her stump," Nate filled in flatly.

Dani wrinkled her nose like he'd said a bad word. "Well, yes. I wanted to do something to help, but she just wouldn't let us. She said she didn't want to go to the hospital, but there was blood everywhere. The girl in the chip shop had to come out and mop it up. You know I've never liked the sight of blood. Remember when I fainted in Home Ec after Mr. Davies cut his finger off?"

"Where's my mum, Dani?"

She blinked hard and blushed under the veil of her carefully applied makeup.

"Of course," she said. "I'm sorry, Nate. Flynn took her down to his garage to patch her up."

"Flynn."

She nodded and peered up at him. "Is that okay? He does all that rescue stuff, and he had a first-aid kit. I mean, I've got a first-aid kit, but it's a bag with plasters and a tube of hydrocortisone. And you know, you two are…." She paused and leaned in. "I wouldn't have thought he was your type, but I can see it."

Nate carefully freed his hands from hers. "I'm going to check on my mum, Dani."

"Give her my best," she said, wide-eyed and earnest.

He left her to get back to her client and jogged to the garage. The sign over the door hadn't changed in twenty years. It had been *Delaney and Son* when Flynn was gone for ten years. It was still *Delaney and Son* when the father had been dead for five.

The weathered wooden gate was painted bright blues. Strips of it had peeled off to reveal the faded green underneath.

Nate pushed the small door open and stepped into the chilly concrete box. A skinny kid with a pierced eyebrow and grease up to his elbows rolled out from under a Ford. He squinted up at Nate.

"Mr. Moffatt?"

"Is my mum still here?"

The kid propped himself up on one elbow and absently added a fresh black smear to his forehead with the other hand.

"Umm, yeah," he said and pointed to the office. "Ms. Moffatt's in there. I think she's okay now, though. Sorry. Maybe I shouldn't have called."

"No. I appreciate it," Nate said. "Mum thinks she's bulletproof."

A wide grin split the kid's face. "Yeah, Ms. Moffatt is pretty damn tough."

"No kidding," Nate said. He gave the kid a grateful nod and crossed the floor. The door opened before he got there, and Flynn waved him in. Despite everything else going on, Nate felt that hot tug of attraction as he took in Flynn's scruff, stubble, and shoulders. It was a hot, tight bubble low in his stomach, and it made him feel even shittier when he saw his mother.

Ally was sitting on a tattered office chair with one crutch balanced across her lap. The leg of her trousers was blotched with blood.

"Jesus, Mum," Nate said. He went to her and bent down to skim a kiss over her cheek. "I told you this would happen. You're doing too much. Why not use your chair?"

"Because I don't want to," Ally snapped. "And I didn't do too much. I went into town on the bus. You were doing that when you were eight. If an eight-year-old can do it, so can I."

"When I was eight, I wasn't recovering from cancer, and I had both legs."

"No sense, though."

Flynn cleared his throat. "I'll just go out," he said. "Get back to work."

He brushed against Nate on the way past, briefly gripped Nate's forearm, and leaned in to murmur in his ear. "It does look worse than it is."

Then he left and closed the door behind him.

Silence dragged out for a second as they both waited for Flynn to walk away. Nate took a deep breath and tried to hang on to his composure. There was no point in turning it into an argument. Ally was right. She was an adult. If she wanted to go shopping—

"I hope you're happy," Ally said. "You made the poor man uncomfortable in his own office."

Nate bit his tongue. He didn't know when Flynn had gone from "that Delaney boy" to "poor man" in his mum's lexicon, and right then it didn't matter.

"He'll survive," he said. "You should have called me. I could have been here sooner."

She flapped her hand dismissively. "You have work to do, Nate," she said. "Besides, I didn't need you. If everyone hadn't made such a fuss, I'd have just called a taxi and gone home. I can take care of myself, you know. I'm not an invalid."

The *anymore* hung in the air between them. The *yet* might just have been in Nate's head.

"What if you'd really hurt yourself?" he asked. "What if you *have* really hurt yourself? Flynn's not a doctor."

"It's a graze."

"What if it's not? What if—"

"Oh, stop it," Ally said sharply. "I know you're worried. Do you think I'm not? That doesn't mean that every sneeze, every spot, is me getting sick again.

I fell. I've got a cut on my leg, and my ass is killing me. That's all. God knows, it feels like enough."

Her voice cracked, and there went the anger. It popped like a bubble and left him with the stale taste of guilt and fear. What sort of terrible son argued with his mother—his still-recovering mother, after she'd had a nasty fall?

Nathan Moffatt, apparently.

"Sorry," he said. It sounded like he'd reached back through time and yanked that apology out of the mouth of his eight-year-old self. Small, grudging, and shamefaced, all at once. There was a wedding to relocate, a venue to find, and a couple to sell on the change, but that would have to wait. "Come on. Let's get you home."

"Don't you have anything better to do than fuss over me?" Ally asked. "I told you it was nothing. It was the shock more than anything else that threw me. I'll get a taxi. Kenny can help me out when it gets here."

"That's daft. I'm here now. Just let me drive you home."

"You don't need to, Nate."

"I want to."

"Sweetheart, I love you—"

"I know. I love you t—"

"But I'm sore, I'm tired, and I'm not crawling into your ridiculous car so you can rattle my bones all the way back to the house."

Nate had already taken a breath to disagree, but that was a hard point to counter. His car wasn't a smooth ride on old roads full of ruts and occasional stretches of cobbles.

"Fine," he said. "We'll call a taxi. I can swing back for my car and—"

"No."

"Mum, I can't leave you alone."

Ally pursed her lips and made a rude sound. "Please, Nate. I fell down in the middle of town. There's already a line of gossips forming at the front door with cake and theories on whether I'm dying or have taken up drink. I won't be alone."

"Hardly the same."

"Nathan."

He knew what it meant when she said his name that way—end of discussion. She used it when she forbade him to sleep over at the Granshire or take off with Max for one of the St. John family's four-week-long summer vacations. She refused to brook any discussion.

Of course, that was when he was a teenager. He was a grown man, and she couldn't even throw "while you're under my roof" at him anymore.

But it still worked.

SUMMER WAS on its last legs. The sun was bright enough, but there wasn't much warmth in it. Nate slouched in the alley behind the row of shops and tried to suck the day's heat from the brick wall through his shoulder blades.

His head was full of to-do lists—find a venue, call the nurse, chase up the canon, find better crutches online. The longer he dwelt on them the more things he added to the list. Yet somehow his brain still had enough processing power left to run through a dark little play called "imagine if your mum died."

It was brutal the first few times he saw it—the pessimistic underpinning to his relentless external confidence. But he'd gotten numb to the basics of grief, and his mind's eye had resorted to pulling "last season of *Lost*" tricks to elicit a reaction from him.

Imagine if Ally… dies in a car crash on the way home. Because you wouldn't give her a lift.

He lit a cigarette and inhaled. The smoke was hot as it trickled over his tongue and still warm as it reached his lungs.

"Most people have a stab at giving up when someone in their family gets cancer." Flynn motioned toward Nate's cigarette as he stepped out through the gate. He'd shrugged the top of his overalls off and knotted the arms around his chest. The old gray T-shirt underneath clung to his shoulders and arms. It was a V-neck, even if it hadn't started that way, and Nate could see the scruff of hair that dusted Flynn's chest.

"It's not like it was lung cancer," Nate said. Even before Flynn did a slow eyebrow lift at him, he knew that was a shitty thing to say. He exhaled and fogged the air between them with smoke. "I had quit. Years back. Then I started again."

This time he expected Flynn to pluck the cigarette out of his fingers, but he let him do it. Flynn stubbed it out against the wall, and a fresh smear of ash joined the gull shit, graffiti, and moss that already spackled the brick. He tossed the butt into a battered old bucket shoved against the wall, where a half-dead plant grew out of a pyramid of filters.

"Your mum going to be okay getting home alone?" Flynn asked.

Nate had wondered the same thing. It still put his back up to hear it from someone else.

"It's Bernard," he said. There wasn't that much call for taxis on the island—drunks had a bad habit of just driving themselves home—but he also drove the school bus, ran tours around the island for the Granshire, and organized a delivery service run by the council. "He'll help her inside, make sure she's comfortable. I've already called the nurse to check on her. What more do you expect me to do?"

Flynn braced his arm against the wall. The sleeve of his T-shirt crawled up his arm to show off the lines of ink that followed the curve of his bicep. Nate had dug his fingers into the tattoo that night in the boat house, but he hadn't paid attention to what it actually was.

"You could stop lying to her."

"No," Nate said. "I can't."

You couldn't live with someone without arguing with them—even if it was just about putting the toilet roll on the holder wrong way around—and arguing with a parent as an adult was… fraught. During one fight over his refusal to date her hairdresser's son, he'd thrown some old childhood grudge in Ally's face—something he'd said a dozen times as a bratty teen. It made her cry.

It might have made her cry back then too. He was a kid, though, and that had shielded him from knowing what a shit he was.

"Really?" Flynn asked. "Because she doesn't seem that bad."

"Yeah. She said the same thing about you." Nate ran his hand up Flynn's arm and peeled the gray sleeve back from the tattoo. The skin was warm under his fingers. It wasn't fresh. The ink was faded and smudged under the tanned skin, but it was still legible. A cracked skull made of smoke, wrapped in a Maltese cross made of barbed wire and a tattooist's needle. He rubbed his thumb over the image. "Maybe you should try and get in touch with the guy that did this. Because right now you aren't holding up your end of our bargain. I'm paying for a bad boy, remember, not Mr. Reliable."

If Nate had rubbed just a bit of the edge out of his voice, it could have passed for flirting. Except he hadn't, and so it couldn't.

Flynn's jaw clenched, and a muscle jerked under the gray stubble on his jaw. He braced his other arm against the wall to make a cage of hard bone and muscle and leaned in. There was more heat coming off him than there was in the sunlight.

"You saying that you have a problem with my performance?"

"I'm saying that right now you seem more like marriage material than a disaster zone," Nate said. He raised his eyebrows and tilted his head to the side. "If I didn't know any better, I'd think you wanted to date me."

That might have slipped into flirting.

Flynn snorted. "God forbid. I have enough problems keeping up the payments on this place without having to take on the upkeep of the Granshire's golden boy." He bent his arm and leaned in until his mouth was almost touching Nate's. "I'd rather just fuck you."

The roughness of his voice and the soap and fresh, clean sweat of his skin made Nate's balls ache.

"You had your chance."

A smirk flicked at the corner of Flynn's mouth. "Like you'd turn me down if I put on rubber?"

"You make it sound weird."

"It is weird."

Nate opened his mouth to retort, but Flynn kissed him to shut him up. His mouth was rough and impatient against Nate's—all stubble and eager tongue—and he moved one hand to grip the back of Nate's neck. He dug his fingers into the tight tendons and pried them loose, and the liquid release of tension was nearly as good as the clutch of want in the pit of Nate's stomach.

He tightened his grip on Flynn's bicep and pulled him closer. The heavy sprawl of Flynn's body pinned him against the wall, and the edges of the bricks were sharp against his shoulder blades.

Lust might not make Nate forget all his worries, but it did shove them to the back of the line for later.

A startled gasp put a stop to that.

"Shit," Flynn muttered. The word bumped against Nate's lips, and he raised his head.

Dani stood at the back of her shop with her arms full of broken plastic hangers and bags. Her eyes were huge, and her mouth hung. Old habits made Nate flush and try to shove Flynn off him. Flynn stayed where he was.

"You're gonna catch flies, Dani," Flynn said.

She snapped her jaw shut. It was probably Nate's imagination that filled in the click of teeth meeting.

"Sorry," she said after a second. "I just... well, I'd heard the gossip about you two, but I didn't believe it. I mean, after what happened between him and Teddy—"

"Nothing happened between him and Max...." Nate's brain caught up with his mouth. "Hold on. What?"

"You don't know?" Dani gasped. One hand patted at her throat as if she'd forgotten she had no pearls to clutch. Then her eyes flicked to Flynn, and her expression of wicked glee faded into something more wary. She pursed her lips. "Not that there's anything to know. Not really."

"No one said there was, Dani," Flynn said flatly.

Dani shrugged a silk-covered shoulder. "If you say so. You'd know." She dumped her armful of rubbish in the bin and turned to go back inside. But she paused on the threshold. "Oh, I do hope your mother is okay."

Her sniff represented all the judgment that would be coming Nate's way. Then she was gone, and the door slammed behind her.

Nate dropped his head back to bounce against the wall, and he groaned. "Fuck." Then he opened his eyes and squinted at Flynn. "You didn't, right?"

CHAPTER SIXTEEN

"He thought he was too good for the island when he left. Well, maybe we didn't want him back."

FLYNN DIDN'T do denials. If people wanted to believe the worst of him, let them. It was no skin off his nose. But for the first time in a long time, he was tempted to defend himself. He overcame the urge.

"What if I did?" he asked. "Why do you care? Banging your father figure? It's what a bad boyfriend would do, right?"

For a second Nate looked conflicted. The expression on his handsome, mobile face was caught between accusation and apology. Flynn felt anticipation catch in his chest as he waited to see what it would be. He didn't know why it would matter, but it felt like it would.

Instead Nate shrugged.

"You're right. It's none of my business." He pushed himself off the wall and ducked under Flynn's arm, but he touched Flynn's hip as he did so. It was a casual touch, careless even, but it sparked heat under Flynn's skin. "I should get back to work. I'll call later if I can."

He took two quick strides down the alley, stopped, and turned back.

"Thanks," he said. "For helping Mum. I appreciate it."

Flynn scratched the back of his neck. "It's my job."

"Still." Nate gave him a tight smile, but it softened after a moment, and the edges curled into something more genuine. "Funny thing is, I don't think she's ever warmed to any of my actual boyfriends this quickly."

Nate gave a quick nod, and then he left.

Fuck.

Flynn groaned to himself and scrubbed his hands over his face. It felt like he'd just lost a game he didn't even want to admit he'd been playing. What exactly had he expected from Nate? That he'd buck the habits of a lifetime, of the island, and just have some faith in Flynn?

Actually, Flynn realized, yeah. Once he put it into words, that was exactly what he wanted. He could have just denied he'd ever gone near Teddy St. John, or even told the truth, but instead he'd dug his heels in to see if maybe, just maybe, Nate wouldn't think the worst of him.

Even though Flynn had been pretty sure he would. Or maybe it was *because* of that. It was why he'd come back to the island—because it was the one place on earth that he wouldn't be tempted to get comfortable.

"Idiot." He swung his foot in a short frustrated arc that connected with the red-glazed pot by the gate. It hit the wall and cracked in half, and a dead lavender plant and three years' worth of cigarette butts spilled over the ground.

Because that helped.

THE GULL was back. It perched precariously on the kitchen window and squawked insistently through the glass. Flynn leaned over the sink and banged his knuckles on the glass. It shut up but didn't actually move. Its feathers fluffed out from its body as it peered at him judgmentally.

"You're a pain in the ass, bird." Flynn left the dishes to soak in the sink, wiped his soapy hands on his jeans, and grabbed a tin of sardines from the cupboard. He peeled the lid off, opened the back door, and tossed the brine and slippery pickled little fish out onto the grass. The gull swooped down on them and hopped from fish to fish to snap them up. "I should have called you Max instead."

The gull ignored him. Once it was fed, it didn't care what he did.

Flynn leaned against the door, crossed his arms, and watched it for a second. The fact that he'd bought the fish just for the gull meant that it might be a pet now.

He shifted his attention to the horizon. The sun hung low in the sky and stained the shredded clouds in shades of rose and gold. Beneath it a ribbon of golden light that looked as solid as a path stretched across the sea toward the cliff. A few birds hung in the air, silhouetted against the sky like a child's pencil check marks.

They never had much when he was growing up. Even with the garage, his dad had only ever just about made ends meet—too many favors for his mates, too much time down at the pub after Flynn's mother died. But no matter how bad things got, he always had the view. Even when he was coming home to hot dogs and rice for dinner, he could look out on a scene that people were willing to pay a fortune for.

As he watched, a slack fin popped up out of the water, and he could see the shadow of a pale, round body under the golden water—a sunfish, although occasionally the sight disturbed tourists.

The old-fashioned jangle of the doorbell echoed through the lighthouse and jarred Flynn out of his contemplation. He glanced at the gull, who'd finished its fish and was a fluffed-out ball perched on the cliff edge.

"Looks like your namesake is here," he said.

The gull ignored him. Flynn went back inside and closed the door behind him. Despite the lingering frustration over their earlier conversation—although he wasn't even sure who he was frustrated with. Himself? Nate?—he stood straighter and rubbed a hand over the rough on his jaw.

He could have shaved. Not that Nate had complained about his grooming so far.

The doorbell rang again. Flynn grunted irritably and stretched his stride out, despite the lingering ache that was still lodged in his thigh.

"Hold on. I'm coming. If you're in that much of a hurry to get on with this, you could have called…."

He knocked the latch off the door and pulled it open. The flutter in his stomach was replaced with a sinking feeling. "What do you want?"

Teddy St. John leaned both his hands on a walking stick and tilted his head back so he could look down his ship's prow of a nose. He looked older. Of course he did, Flynn supposed. It had been twenty years, but it still managed to be a surprise.

"Would you have been here if I had?" Teddy asked dryly.

A muscle twisted in the corner of Flynn's mouth.

"Probably not," he said. "What do you want?"

Teddy tightened his fingers on the polished silver head of his stick. "Nothing that I want to discuss on your doorstep, Mr. Delaney."

Flynn glanced around. To the left there was clear blue sky, and to the right there was a mile of uneven heather and heath.

"Who are you scared is going to overhear you this time?" he asked. "The rabbits?"

"I don't discuss business at the door like I'm a salesman," Teddy said. He tapped the cane on the curved stone step impatiently. "I know your mother taught you manners, even if your father never bothered."

There was a bad taste at the back of Flynn's mouth—like blood and bitterness. He cleared his throat.

"Keep your mouth off my mother, Mr. St. John," he said. It would serve Teddy right if Flynn just closed the door on him and his assumption that everyone cared about what he wanted. But there was an itch of curiosity in the back of his head. It had been twenty years since he'd spoken to Teddy face-to-face and not through an intermediary or a lawyer, and he wanted to know why the old bastard had broken that habit. Flynn stepped back with a shrug. "Come in, then. Have your say."

Teddy stepped over the threshold, and the light-house didn't fall down. He walked over to the sofa, each step accompanied by a tap from the cane, and sat down without waiting to be asked. He propped the cane against the arm and fastidiously smoothed his trousers down over his knees.

"I don't see any point in beating around the bush," he said as he finally looked at Flynn. "I do not approve of your relationship with Nathan Moffatt."

Well, Nate couldn't complain that Flynn wasn't pulling his bad-boy weight anymore. Flynn leaned against the banister of the stairs, the metal cold against his back, and crossed his arms.

"I don't recall asking you to," he said. "Mostly because it is none of your business."

Teddy gave him a glittering look of dislike. "He is my employee. As such, his well-being and his be-havior are my concern. Not to mention he's one of my son's closest friends and someone I've known since he was a boy."

"All of which gets you an invite to his birthday party," Flynn said. "Not a say in who he fucks."

He used the word deliberately, just to see Ted-dy's mouth priss up in annoyance. If he had pictures of what he did to Nate the other night, he might have been able to make Teddy swallow his dentures.

"I care about him," Teddy said. "I care about the smooth running of my business. That gives me a say."

Flynn raised his eyebrows curiously. "Did Nate sign off on that?"

There was a pause and the flicker of something that might have been guilt through Teddy's pale eyes, and then he reached into his jacket.

"Nevertheless." Teddy pulled an envelope out of his inside pocket and leaned forward to lay it on the table. He tapped it pointedly with one gnarled finger and then sat back.

"What's that?" Flynn didn't need to ask. He knew. The question was just tinder for the smoldering anger lodged behind his breastbone.

A humorless smile twitched the corners of Teddy's mouth. "Call it the next installment." He reached for his stick and braced it against the floor for balance as he stood up. His eyes flickered over the curved walls and huge windows for a second and then came back to Flynn. "You can keep this place if you want. Even visit sometimes. However, I expect you to be gone within the month."

Flynn expected to be angry, but the black flash of dry rage was a shock. It parched his mouth and wiped away all his good sense long enough to clench his fist and take an angry step forward. He stopped himself before he did anything stupid. His hands trembled with banked adrenaline as he sucked in a lungful of air.

"You arrogant son of a bitch—"

"Once you've been bought, Mr. Delaney," Teddy interrupted, "it's disingenuous to act surprised when someone suggests repeating the transaction."

Flynn huffed out a laugh that didn't have any mirth in it. He shook his head slowly. "You're a piece of work, Teddy."

A shrug of Teddy's elegantly tailored shoulders was the response. "Maybe." Teddy raised his stick and waved it in the direction of the incriminating envelope. "However, it's a generous offer, and I would consider it if I were you. We both know that Nathan could do better than you, and eventually he'll realize it too."

Something in Teddy's tone caught Flynn's attention. He narrowed his eyes. "Better than me? Like who?"

"Anyone."

"Or Max?"

Teddy gave him a cold, untroubled look and a slice of a smile.

"Why not?" he asked. "They've always been close, and I think of Nathan as another son."

That jab caught Flynn on a raw spot he didn't know he had—not that he intended to let Teddy see that. "Get out," Flynn said.

"What is it they say? Back at you." Teddy paused at the door and looked back. "Oh, and while I'm here, consider your invitation to this weekend's wedding rescinded. Nate might think he wants you there, but you aren't welcome on my property or at my events."

"Never thought I was."

Teddy let himself out. Until he heard the car start, Flynn stood with his fists clenched so tightly he could feel ache in his bones. It was a relief. If the old man had taken a fall on the steps, Flynn couldn't swear he'd have gone out to help him.

The envelope lay on the table, expensively cream against the boot-scuffed wood. It made Flynn feel exposed, as though it were a sex toy that needed hiding away in a cupboard before anyone came around. Not that anyone would.

He shook himself, craned his neck from one side to the other to loosen the cramped muscles, and walked over to pick it up. It was heavy and textured, self-evidently expensive enough that Flynn felt a twitch of guilt for the damp marks his fingertips left on it. The last envelope had been the same. Thicker, though. Back then Teddy used cash.

When he flipped it over, the flap was unsealed. Flynn folded it back and slid the contents out. On the shiny rectangle of paper, Teddy's careful calligraphy inked out the words *fifty thousand pounds*.

It was an offer that should focus the mind, but Flynn couldn't get over the distracting question, "What wedding invitation?" Apparently Nate didn't want him there either.

"HO-LEE CRAP," Jessie squawked. She turned the check over and stared at the back. Maybe she expected a "just kiddin'" stamp to appear. "Is this real?"

"Looks like it," Flynn said. He plucked the check out of her fingers and frowned at it. "That's exactly how much Teddy St. John wants me to leave the island."

"Not like everyone approves of me dating their daughters, but nobody's ever offered me that much to go away." Jessie perched on the arm of the sofa, bare feet braced against the cushion. Her hands dangled over her bare, scuffed-up knees. "Gives some credence to the rumors about him and Nate's mum, eh?"

"Not really."

Flynn folded the slip of paper and stuck it back in the heavy wedding-invitation envelope. He rubbed the rich weave of the paper absently with his thumb.

"So?" Jessie pursed her lips and raised sun-bleached eyebrows. "What are you going to do?"

That was the question, wasn't it? Flynn wasn't even sure where to put the envelope. It felt irresponsible to just put it in the kitchen drawer with the rest of his mail.

"I guess I have a month to think about it," he said.

"Really?"

"What would you do?"

Jessie snorted and shoved a hand through her hair. Her fingers caught in the thick, salt-coarsened mass. "I'd have that cash in my hot little hand already," she said. "I'd have booked Katy Perry to do my farewell gig. I'd have ordered a cruise liner to take me over to the mainland. Tell me how to alienate Teddy St. John so badly he'd pay to get me to leave, and I'll do it twice."

"It wouldn't piss you off that he thought he could buy you?"

She wrinkled her nose. "Maybe," she said. "But the money would soothe me."

Flynn snorted. He wasn't even sure why he'd decided that Jessie was the person to talk to about it, other than the fact that she'd turned up at the right time to drop off the books he'd asked her to get. Maybe he just needed someone to talk to. Thing was, she was twenty-six years old. Of course she thought taking the money was a good idea. God knew, in his twenties, Flynn thought the same thing.

"He'll think he's won."

"So?" Jessie spread her hands expressively. "I mean, come on. It would be different if you had a life here or if he were buying his way into your partner's bed. Then I could see why you'd hesitate, but all he wants you to do is move. I mean, why not? You always said you weren't here long-term."

Her peace said, Jessie leaned over and grabbed her coffee from the table. Steam rose between her steepled fingers as she lifted it to take a careful sip.

She had time. It wasn't as though Flynn had a good answer.

CHAPTER SEVENTEEN

"Good news! His wife doesn't care, as long as she can watch."

"CRAP."

Coffee slopped over the table, soaked under Nate's notebook, and puddled muddily in the shallow saucer. Nate snatched his book and held it out of the way in one hand as he scooted the chair back to avoid the spillover. The legs of the chair scraped on the polished wooden floor. He glanced around for something to mop up the mess with and found nothing.

The little coffee shop was tucked into a sea-view corner of the Granshire. It had excellent coffee, an eclectic aesthetic of surfboards and bleached wood, and apparently no napkins.

Nate grimaced as coffee dripped down his arm, and he glanced toward the counter to catch someone's attention. The girl behind the counter nodded, held up a finger for "just a second," and rattled through ringing up an order of two hot chocolates and a huge slice of cake.

By the time she got finished with that, grabbed a cloth, and ducked out from behind the long, confectionary-laden counter, most of the coffee had migrated to the floor.

Nate shook his notebook out—the pages were already stained and wrinkled along the edge—and rescued the rest of his things from the table. The shell of his well-chewed Bic was half full of coffee, but his phone had gotten away unscathed.

"I'll get this, sir," the barista chirped. "Don't worry about it."

"Sorry," Nate said as he stood up. He glanced at his pen, sighed, and tossed it toward the bin. It dropped into the metal case just as Katie walked in arm in arm with her maid of honor. It took a second for Nate to scrape her name up out of his mind, but he got there—Hannah Daley. Both of them were exfoliated and beaming. He'd told reception to give the bridal party a free pass to the spa when they arrived. Cynical, maybe, but he wanted them in the best mood possible. He raised a hand to acknowledge her and gave the barista an apologetic grimace. "I'll have to change tables. I have a meeting."

Her smile slipped a little bit—that meant one more table to clean up at the end of the workday—but she nodded agreeably.

"Of course, sir," she said. "I'll get you a refill now."

Nate left her to soak up the spill and went to greet Katie. He touched her arm and leaned in to kiss her cheek. Her skin was peachy soft and smelled of salt and lavender.

"You look lovely," he said.

"We had a wonderful time at the spa," she said as she gave him a hug. "Thank you so much for booking us in. It was just what I needed."

"That's good," Nate said.

Hannah gave him a curious look. "Is everything all right?" she asked. "You look a bit stressed."

"Well, he's making my wedding go perfectly," Katie laughed. She nudged her friend. "Imagine if this were all down to you."

Hannah raised a perfectly arched eyebrow. "Imagine if I'd said no."

Well, that was the perfect opportunity to break the news. Nate *had* been hoping for a bit more time to ease into the conversation, but he supposed it wouldn't make a difference in the end.

"Actually, that was what I wanted to talk to you about," he said as he put his hand in the small of her back. "Come and sit down."

Worry creased Katie's face. "Is it the dress?" she asked. She brought her hand up to cover her mouth. Her eyes were huge over the cage of her fingers. "Oh God. Did Bradley lose the rings?"

Next to her, Hannah sniffed and crossed her arms. "More likely that mother of his." The word *mother* came out as if it were a curse. "She probably shaved his head."

"Ah, no," Nate said. He pressed gently on Katie's back to get her moving. "Nothing like that. We did have a bit of a situation, but I think I have it resolved."

A huge sigh escaped Katie as she walked toward the window. "You *think*?" she said.

Nate led her to a table tucked next to the window. It had a sweeping view down to the rocky shore and the high tide that covered the sand. He pulled out a chair for her and then turned to do the same for Hannah.

"That's up to you," he said. "Just let me explain."

"Please," Katie said. She clutched Hannah's hand on the table tightly enough that her knuckles poked white and bony against moisturized skin. "I knew this was going to go wrong. Ever since Brad was delayed, I was just waiting for the other shoe to drop."

She looked on the verge of a panic attack, despite the reassuring noises Hannah made. Nate glanced at the barista, mouthed "tea" at her, and held up three fingers. While she went to make that, Nate turned his attention back to the table.

"We had a flood," he said. "In the wedding chapel."

"Oh gaaaawd," Katie moaned. "I'm not getting married."

"Yes, you are," Nate said. The assurance was echoed by Hannah, even if she sounded a bit less certain. "If I have *anything* to do about it, you are. We just have to compromise a little."

Katie sniffed and chewed nervously on her thumbnail. "On what?"

"The venue," Nate explained apologetically. "The chapel isn't functional right now."

She looked dismayed. "So we came all this way, and we can't even get married here?"

"The chapel, no," Nate said. "Here, yes."

All the photos had been loaded onto his phone. Nate pulled it out of his pocket and tapped the album open. He flipped through the pictures with his thumb.

"Technically it's even the Granshire," he said. "It was built as a folly for the wife of one of the previous owners. Usually we'd have closed it up by now, since it's only used during the summer months, but we had a late fair there this year, so I can have it ready for tomorrow without too much trouble."

If he were honest, the photo he passed over the table wasn't entirely representative of the current state of the folly. It had been taken at the height of summer, when it was set up for a wedding fair. In the image, morning sunlight streamed through elegantly draped swathes of pale silk and illuminated the weathered stone and a tray of silver-iced cupcakes. But right then there were tarps draped over the benches and puddles of water on the floor.

He could fix that, though.

"Oh," Katie said. She blinked in surprise. "It's beautiful."

"Honestly, it's one of our popular venues," Nate said. "We just don't like to book it for this time of the year because brides are usually booking a year before, and we don't know what the weather will be like. This year, though…."

He gestured at the window, where the sun was still bright as it dipped toward the horizon. The Met Office claimed the next day would be even better, and the old wives said that cows wandering in the middle of the fields meant the same thing. He might be clutching at straws a bit.

Katie and Hannah put their heads together as they pored over the pictures.

"I've spoken to the florist," Nate said. "He can change up your arrangements to make it look a little more… cultured wildflower and tie it into the setting. It is stunning up there for photos, between the folly and the cliffs. What do you think?"

The rapid-fire delivery of information left Katie on the back foot. She chewed her lip while her knee bounced under the table in a nervous jitter.

"I don't know."

Hannah nudged their shoulders together. "It looks lovely."

"I have to ask Brad."

"Brad won't care as long as you're happy." Hannah squeezed Katie's hand. "You're going to get married."

Tea arrived in three glass cups with a bowl of uneven brown sugar cubes. Nate left his black and unsweetened. It wasn't his preference, but sweet and milky tea was soothing, and he needed to stay awake.

"Talk to Brad," he said. "Just let me know what you decide. If you do go ahead, trust me, it will still be a fairy-tale day. I know this isn't ideal, but it was unavoidable."

Katie picked up her tea and sipped it. Her mouth twitched into a wry smile around the lip of the cup. "At least it explains what all the plumbers were doing here today."

"We thought there was a convention," Hannah chipped in.

"That would have been more convenient," Nate said dryly. He glanced at his watch and grimaced at the time it told. Then he drained his tea, though the

liquid was still hot enough to scorch his tongue, and
left the gritty dregs on the table. "I'm sorry to have to
do this, but I have to go and make some arrangements.
You have my number."

"And your phone," Katie said dryly. She nudged
it back over the table toward him. "Could you send me
some of the pictures?"

"Of course."

Nate lifted the phone and stood up. He wanted to
find a sofa and have a nap like Max, but that wouldn't
get anything done.

"Let me know what you decide," he said. "The
Granshire—I—really hope you'll let us fix this for you."

He took his leave and headed out through the
maze of tables. There was a new barista behind the
counter, assiduously polishing the coffee machine.
Nate paused at the till.

"Mr. Moffatt!" the boy said with a wide smile.
"How's Ms. Moffatt doing?"

It took a second, but then the bleached hair and
eyebrow piercing clicked. It was Kenny, the kid who
worked for Flynn. That threw Nate off his expected
conversation track for a second.

"I didn't know you worked here," he said.

"Oh, yeah. I pick up a few evening shifts."

"Umm... well, Mum's fine. She's been to the doctor and got patched up and told off for pushing herself too hard. Look, put the tea on a tab and send over
some cake?"

Kenny nodded and made a note on a pad. "Will
do. Tell your mum I hope she feels better soon."

Most of the time Nate didn't mind living on an island. He could have stayed in London, found another

roommate to take over from Max, and lobbied for the promotion at the charity he'd been working for. Instead he came back, full of praise for tight-knit communities. But sometimes it felt more claustrophobic than anything else. You couldn't do anything without the entire neighborhood commenting on it a few hours later.

"I will."

"YOU'RE LUCKY I found this," Max said as he dragged the roll of heavy silver-gray voile out of the back of his car. In the moonlight the fabric looked nearly black. "I thought we chucked it in the last clear out."

"No. Those were tablecloths," Nate said. He brushed a hand over the fabric and felt the rough coat of dust that had settled on it. That could be dealt with. "Thanks, Max."

Max shrugged easily. "Not doing anything else tonight." He hefted the roll onto his shoulder as though it didn't weigh anything and balanced it there. "You want this in the estate car?"

Nate nodded. He patted down his pockets until he found his key ring so he could beep the car open. When he pressed the button, the lights flashed three cars down the street. The parking spaces outside his house had been occupied when he got in. He'd had to park outside Mrs. Saunders' house. So he could probably expect an "anonymous" note under his wiper in the morning.

"You sure you don't mind staying with my mum tonight?" Nate asked.

They reached the car, and he pulled the trunk open. He'd already dropped the seats in the back to make room for boxes of cushions and a crate of card-board-padded glasses. Max shrugged the voile off his shoulder, shoved it in at the side, and angled it so the end stuck between the driver's and passenger's seats.

"Don't be an idiot," Max said. "You know I think the world of Ally. I'd swap any two of my stepmothers for her in a heartbeat. What was she doing down there anyhow?"

"Shopping, apparently." Nate slammed the trunk shut and turned. The curtains over Mrs. Saunders's windows twitched open, and she peeked through the gap. Nate caught her eye and nodded politely. She glared at him as though it were his fault she'd been caught peeping, and scrubbed at an imaginary smear on the window with the cuff of her cardigan.

"Or maybe checking out your new boyfriend?" Max asked. His voice was aggressively neutral, and he raised his eyebrows innocently when Nate frowned at him. "He works down there, doesn't he?"

"I don't think even Mum would take a fall just to get a chance to interrogate my boyfriend," Nate said. "Though I'm sure she made the most of the opportunity once she had it."

A grin creased Max's face, and he slung an arm up over Nate's shoulder. The weight of him made Nate stumble. "Good to know," Max said. He dug his fingers into Nate's hair and pushed his head to the side. "We can trade theories on what you see in the useless bastard."

"I think she likes him." Nate squirmed out of what had turned into a headlock. He absently smoothed his jacket down, the fastidious tug of his hands a muscle memory that went all the way back to the days when he'd had a blazer and a school tie.

Max pulled a sour face. "That's only because he was there in her hour of need."

"It's a fairly good reason to like someone."

"I'm sure I can show her the error of her ways," Max said. "I heard that he was a loan shark, and he did time inside for breaking some kid's legs."

"He was a soldier," Nate said. "And a mechanic."

Max gave him a dubious look out of the corner of his eye. "Who told you that?"

"Flynn."

"So he was a loan shark, and now he's a liar." Max shook his head ruefully. "Can you believe that?"

Not really. Nate didn't think it would work on Ally either, for the same reason she'd always liked Max. Ally enjoyed a good gossip as much as anyone else on Ceremony, but once she saw something good in someone, she wouldn't let go of it.

Not even her son's bad-news boyfriend.

"You know, it was a lifetime ago," Nate said. "Don't you think it's time to get over it?"

He didn't think Max would agree. For someone usually laid-back, Max liked his grudges. But he expected a joke, another jibe at Flynn's reputation or age. Instead Max clenched his jaw, muscles working visibly in his cheek, and gave him a hard, almost unfriendly look.

"No," he said. "I don't think so."

"Oh, come on—" Nate tried to protest.

"No." Max stopped on the road and jabbed a finger into Nate's shoulder. "You want to date this guy, that's up to you. Go ahead. Hook up with Mr.

Disposable. Chase your teenage crush. Whatever gets you through this midlife crisis you're having. I agreed not to get on your case about it, but I'm not changing my mind either. So lay off. You don't know him as well as you think."

The conviction in Max's voice rocked Nate back on his heels for a second as Max stalked away. It wasn't like he could argue. He didn't know Flynn that well. Sex didn't actually give you an insight into who someone really was—which explained a few of the weddings he'd organized.

"Hold on." He caught up with Max on the doorstep to the house. "You don't know him any better than I do. Twenty years ago was the last time you spoke to him too."

Max jabbed the code into the electronic keyboard, to the familiar *beep boop bip* of the small keys.

"Yeah, well, maybe I just see him clearer than you do," Max said. He pushed open the door and glanced over his shoulder at Nate as he stepped inside. "Since I don't have to make excuses to justify climbing on his dick."

Heat flushed Nate's face like a slap. He scrabbled for a reply, but Max's enthusiastic "Aunt Ally" rang out before he could come up with anything.

"Shows what you know," Nate muttered to himself as he stepped through the door and closed it behind him. "I already climbed it."

There was a flask and a Tupperware box full of sandwiches waiting for him in the living room. They were set on top of his *Game of Thrones* box set. It reminded Nate uncomfortably of going away on school trips as a kid, although he hoped the flask had coffee and not soup in it.

"This is ridiculous." Ally was midprotest as Nate came in. She had stretched up off the sofa to hug Max. Despite the doctor's assurance yesterday that she was fine and all she needed was rest and a round of antibiotics, she looked pale and tired. "I'm not eleven. I can take care of myself. How many times do I have to say I don't need a babysitter?"

Nate would have snapped. He knew that. It was just *easier* than anything more reasonable. The words were already there in his throat. All he needed was a second to open his mouth and let them out.

Max didn't give him the chance. He flopped down on the sofa, swung his feet onto the table, and slung his arm over the back of the cushions.

"Good, because I am here to complain and get sympathy, not fuss over you," Max said. He leaned over and grabbed the box of sandwiches. The lid popped, and he peeled it off and picked out a cheese sandwich. "You know Flynn Delaney tried to pick me up once, right?"

That was Max. He reminded Nate why he loved him one minute and demonstrated what an ass he was the next.

"If that put me off dating someone, I'd never go out of the house again."

Nate abandoned the sandwiches to Max. Food was the last thing he wanted right then. His stomach was too full of stress and acid to add anything else. He grabbed the flask off the table. There was always room for coffee.

"Whatever," Max snorted through a mouthful of sandwich. "Just don't let him near your credit cards."

That was a step too far for Ally, who pulled a disapproving face. "Maxwell, that's enough. Don't be unkind."

"I'm not," Max protested. "Just prudent. You know when he left last time, he took the contents of my dad's wallet with him?"

After his conversation with Dani, that plucked the strings of Nate's interest. He hesitated but squashed the urge to ask any questions. If Max knew anything about what really happened back then or whatever rumors tied "Flynn and Teddy" together, he'd have brought it up years before.

"I shouldn't be too late." He leaned over the back of the sofa, between Ally and Max, and kissed her cheek quickly. "If you need anything, if anything happens, call me."

Ally reached up and affectionately ruffled his hair. "Don't be such a worrier, Nate. I'm going to watch *Fortitude,* drink some hot chocolate, and try to convince Max that he doesn't have to live down to his father's expectations."

"Good luck with that," Max muttered.

"Nothing is going to happen." Ally ignored Max's interruption and patted her thigh. The truncated leg of her yoga pants was stretched over the fresh bandages the doctor had dressed her stump with. "I might have to wait a bit longer before I get my prosthetic sorted, is all. But once I get my new crutches tomorrow, I'll be good as new."

The blithe confidence in her voice made Nate sigh. When she was sick, she was sure she'd get better. That was reassuring. Now that she was better, it seemed like tempting fate.

"I'll try not to wake you up when I get back," he said. "Don't listen to anything Max says."

CHAPTER EIGHTEEN

"Remember all that fuss over Flynn and Max St. John, back when he first left? He came to blows with Teddy and everything. Well, there's no smoke without fire is there?"

AFTER YEARS on call, Flynn woke up when the phone rang, even if it only rang twice. He rolled over, sat on the edge of the bed, braced his hands on his knees, and waited for it to ring again. It didn't.

The bed hadn't had time to get cold yet. If Flynn rolled over and went back to sleep, it would still be warm. It was a tempting thought, but he got up. The floor was cold under his bare feet as he padded over to the chair where he'd tossed his jeans earlier.

His phone was in the back pocket, along with a handful of change that fell out and bounced over the floor. There was only one missed call. Flynn rubbed his hand over his face, stubble-rough against his palm, and wondered why the hell Nate was calling him at 2:00 a.m. He supposed there was one way to find out.

He hit the callback button and let it ring. While he waited, he turned to look out the stretch of glass. It was dark outside, and the moon hung bright and low in the sky. It was a night you could never have in a city, where there was always some invasive glow. As though it had just been waiting for its cue, the image of Teddy's check popped into Flynn's head.

If he took the cash, he lost the view. On the other hand, greed nudged him. If he took the cash, he could find a new one.

Before he could get lost in the maze of options the money would open up for him, Nate picked up the call.

Flynn didn't give him a chance to say anything. "What do you want?"

The sigh on the other end of the line sounded… cold. "I changed my mind."

"That's up to you." Flynn tucked his phone against his ear and climbed into his jeans. He hitched the denim up over his hips and buttoned them and then grabbed his T-shirt to give it a sniff—petrol, sweat, and a hint of bitter smoke that reminded him of Nate. It didn't take long for Nate to crack. The sigh was loud in Flynn's ear as he gave up.

"My car broke down."

"That's because your car is a Fisher-Price toy."

"I need a lift."

Flynn swapped the phone from one ear to the other as he pulled his T-shirt on. A twitch of vanity made him shove his hand through his hair to brute-force un-tangle it.

"You can't ask Max?"

"Not really. Look, I shouldn't have called. I know that's not—"

"Shut up, you idiot." Flynn put the phone on speaker and sat down to get his boots on. He stamped his feet into them, but didn't bother to tie the laces. "Where are you?"

"The folly."

"What the hell are you—" Flynn stood up and started down the stairs. "Never mind. You can tell me when I get there."

"Thanks. It's fucking freezing here."

Flynn snorted and hung up. He shoved the phone into his jeans and grabbed his jacket from the door. The keys were already in the pocket, a weight drag-ging it down at one side. He was halfway down the worn steps when something occurred to him.

He backtracked into the lighthouse. Teddy's en-velope was still on the table. He hadn't been able to think of a safer place for it, so he picked it up and folded it in half.

Flynn was probably going to tell Teddy to shove his money, but he wasn't 100 percent certain. No one else needed to know about the offer until he decided—especially not Nate.

He put the envelope in the kitchen drawer. It was where all the mail lived, so technically he wasn't hid-ing it, even if he had stuck it under everything else.

Once the drawer was shut, he went back out to the jeep. The engine coughed as he started it, and the noise was shockingly loud against the night's stillness.

Unless you counted the gulls and the occasional fox, Flynn didn't have a neighbor for miles, but he still felt the urge to apologize to the countryside.

To get it out of his system, he yawned hard, his eyes squinted shut and his jaw popping, and threw the jeep into gear. It was usually an hour to the folly, but there'd be no one on the road. He could probably make it in thirty.

IN THE end it took forty minutes, thanks to a sheep he had to get out and physically shoo back into a field. Flynn pulled in at the foot of the hill. Last time he'd been there, decades before, for some half-assed play the school put on, the parking lot had been a crooked patch of rutted dirt halfheartedly covered with gravel.

They'd paved it since, although the cheap layer of concrete had already cracked and pocked in places. At the far edge, next to the staggered stone steps, a shiny black Ford Estate was parked with its hood popped to expose the engine.

Flynn didn't even need to look to make his diagnosis. The minute he opened the car door, he could smell the acrid stink of burned oil and hot metal. He sighed and dragged his hand down his face in old frustration.

"How hard is it to check the goddamn oil?" he muttered as he started the climb up to the folly.

The steps were roughly cut slabs of granite wedged into the side of the hill at uneven intervals. Flynn remembered nearly breaking his neck on them as a kid when he lost his footing on a damp patch of moss and bounced down to the bottom. They'd been cleaned up since then, the moss bleached clean and the sloping slabs propped up with pebbles and concrete until they were more or less level.

It wasn't much of a climb, but it was enough to jostle the ache in Flynn's thigh to life. The cold probably didn't help either. He stopped halfway up and stretched his leg. It didn't help, so he grimaced and dug his knuckles into the tender knot of muscle. That hurt enough to make him curse under his breath, but after a second, the muscle gave under the pressure. Flynn pushed himself back up straight and resumed the climb.

If he took a spill on the steps, he thought dourly, he'd probably break a fucking hip.

His ego flinched. He wasn't *that* old, and it wasn't that he was out of breath or wheezing. When hikers got lost out on the island, he hiked up cliffs and came back down carrying sodden, frostbitten idiots in shorts over his shoulder.

He just wasn't twenty anymore, when a pint and a bad night's sleep were enough to bounce back from a dislocated shoulder.

But it did make him think again about Teddy's offer. His thigh ached. What would it be like in ten years' time? Twenty? Going up and down the stairs at the lighthouse? The thought made him wonder whether Jessie might be right. Maybe cutting off his nose to spite his face wasn't the best thing to do with a fifty-grand check on the table.

He stamped firmly on that notion. Whatever he was going to do, he wouldn't make up his mind that night.

The last two steps brought him to the arched, empty doorway into the folly. It was an old ruined chapel, and had been an old ruined chapel since some St. John with a whim and too much money in his pocket ordered it built. The bare stone ribs of the roof curved overhead in the suggestion of a vaulted ceiling, and the far wall consisted solely of an empty Gothic arched window that romantically framed the moon.

It was also all decked out like a fairy orgy was about to take place. Drapes of silver silk hung from the walls, silver bowls glittered on the narrow altar in front of the moon window, and narrow wrought-iron benches had been lined up in the nave.

For a moment the idea that it could be some rom-com inspired setup flickered through Flynn's mind—complete with Nate in a suit and down on one knee and their loved ones gathered around as he popped the question. The thought of it made Flynn cringe. Well, maybe 75 percent of him cringed. The other 25 percent was apparently an idiot.

It was a stupid idea, anyhow. For one thing, Flynn didn't have any loved ones on the island, and for another, he caught sight of Nate. He was slouched against the folly's one complete wall. In the moonlight his graying hair blended with the old stone and he looked more like a jilted bridegroom than a hopeful one.

His shirtsleeves were rolled back to expose his wiry forearms, there was grease on his hands and his jaw, and he had an uncorked bottle of wine between his knees and a cigarette between his lips. When he saw Flynn, he sighed and took a swig of the wine.

"Come on, then," he said. He tilted his head back against the wall, and he looked at Flynn through the drifting smoke. "Let me have it."

Flynn thought about it.

"Maybe once you're warmed up." He walked over and held his hand out. Nate eyed it for a moment and then sighed and took it. Flynn hauled him to his feet and caught him when he staggered. "How much of that wine did you drink?"

Nate snorted and lifted the bottle so Flynn could see it was still half-full. "Not enough," he said dryly. "My ass is numb, not drunk."

Flynn plucked the cigarette out of his mouth and took a drag. It had been over a year since he'd stolen even a postpub lungful of someone else's cigarette, over a decade since he'd had his own pack in his pocket, but it felt like he'd never quit.

"I thought it was a bad habit," Nate said.

"It is." Flynn took another drag and then lifted the cigarette from his lips to look at the smoldering tip. He twisted his mouth in a humorless smile, and the smoke escaped the corners. "It's been one of those days."

"Tell me about it," Nate said as he pushed himself off Flynn's shoulder. He rolled his head from one side to the other, and his vertebra sounded like cracked knuckles as he took the cigarette back. It was halfway to his lips when a yawn interrupted the habit. He wiped watering eyes on his hand and smeared grease over his eyebrows. "Sorry. Not your problem. I shouldn't have woken you up. I just didn't know who else to call."

That curled something smug and petty on the back of Flynn's tongue. "Not even Max?"

Instead of taking that last hit on the cigarette, Nate stubbed it out against the wall. It left a ashy black smudge that he scrubbed away with the heel of his hand.

"I asked him to sleep over at mine, keep an eye on Mum." Nate flicked the butt away into the dark.

"I don't want to wake them up—not after Mum fell today."

The smug turned to ashes in Flynn's mouth. He shouldn't have asked, and he wanted a cigarette even more.

"But you didn't mind waking me up?"

That got him a tired shadow of Nate's usual "charming as a fox" grin. "I'd already drunk the coffee and broken the wine open by that point," he said. "Like I said, sorry. I am really glad to see you."

The idiot 25 percent of Flynn wanted to make something more of that. The rest of him just wondered how the hell his clotheshorse posh boy looked even hotter scruffy, grouchy, and covered with oil.

Because he was a fool, probably. He should remember the wedding invitation he hadn't gotten before he got all soppy.

"Come on." He slapped Nate's shoulder and gave him a shove toward the steps. "I'll take you home."

CHAPTER NINETEEN

"Well, at your age, it's not the sex, is it? It's the companionship you want."

FLYNN STOPPED the jeep, and Nate woke up with the realization that he was probably drooling a bit and that they weren't parked outside his house. He wiped his hand over his cheek as discreetly as possible—dammit, he'd definitely been drooling, that was a great impression—and peered up at the pale tower of the lighthouse.

"So, your place?" he said.

Flynn shrugged and got out. "If you don't want to disturb your mum, rolling in at this hour isn't a good idea," he said. "You can crash here if you want."

He headed for the front door. Apparently if Nate *didn't* want to crash there, he was going to sleep in the car. It didn't sound appealing, and besides... it had been a shitty day. It could do with a happy ending.

"Mr. Delaney," Nate drawled as he hopped out of the car. His voice carried on the still air. It was nice to get a chance to flirt without worrying a neighbor would give him evils through the blinds. "Are you planning to take advantage of me?"

"I'm just offering the sofa," Flynn said without looking around as he opened the heavy front door. There was an edge to his voice that Nate couldn't pin down. Maybe he was more pissed about a midnight disturbance than he acted earlier. "You're safe with me."

"That's a relief," Nate said. He gave Flynn's ass a glance. The old jeans should have sagged too much to be flattering, but the soft denim hinted at the firm curves Nate already knew were there. "Wish I could say the same."

Flynn finally glanced around at him. The light was on inside, and it illuminated the hard, lean lines of Flynn's cheek and jaw. It also caught the skeptical expression he turned on Nate.

"What?" Nate asked.

"You think you could take advantage of me?"

Nate tilted his head to the side to look Flynn up and down and quirked his mouth to the side thoughtfully. "Maybe with a running start?"

"Don't be cute," Flynn said as he gave Nate an unceremonious shove through the door into the lighthouse. "What do you want from me, Nate? From this."

The whole bad-boyfriend thing was meant for the public eye. What they'd been doing in private wasn't exactly covered in the original agreement. So a fair enough question, but one that Nate shied from answering. It felt like any answer he gave would end up with them agreeing it hadn't gone according to plan and they should wrap it up.

Nate didn't want that—not yet. He supposed it was time to admit it, though. As bad boyfriends went, Flynn didn't exactly make the grade.

"I want to see your bedroom." He lifted a hand and sketched a cross over his heart. "I promise not to talk about Airbnb profit margins."

The twitch at the corner of Flynn's mouth could have been amusement or old frustration at a well-trod topic. He narrowed gray eyes at Nate. "Tell me you won't be thinking about it," he challenged dryly.

"I might," Nate said, raising his eyebrows. "Unless you can distract me."

It was the sort of corny, over-the-top line that Max would try out—come-ons that worked when you were rich, cocky, and dating twenty-year-olds. Usually it would have made Nate feel like an idiot to be nearly forty and still using the same pickup lines he'd cribbed off Max as a teenager, but the dry tilt of Flynn's eyebrow offset that. Sure it was ridiculous, but they both acknowledged that, and they were in on the joke, not the butt of it.

"And after?" Flynn asked. He closed the door and leaned back against it with his hands tucked into his pockets. "Nothing has changed there, right? Once we call this quits, you shred your earning projections and never darken my doorstep again?"

"Sure." Nate shrugged. "It's not going to be an amicable breakup, remember. No one will expect us to stay friends."

A smirk twisted up the corner of Flynn's mouth, and a dimple carved into his cheek under the salt-and-pepper stubble. "Yeah, because everyone is going to be glad to see the back of me."

That was the plan. It was a bit late for Nate to suddenly have the sinking feeling that it was a *bad* plan. He couldn't even put his finger on why—because he was lying to his family or just because he should be focused on doing his job after today's—yesterday's—disaster.

Or was it something else? Nate wasn't stupid. He knew he was lying to himself. The truth would definitely have gotten in the way of Flynn grabbing his shirt and dragging him into a hard, insistent kiss.

Later. Nate gripped the back of Flynn's neck and traced the long tendons of his throat with his thumb, from the bristle of stubble to the soft plane of bare skin. His tongue tangled with Flynn's, trading breath and heat between their eager mouths. He could deal with the truth later.

He shoved his hands under Flynn's jacket and pushed the leather down over his arms. His T-shirt had short sleeves and exposed his lean, tanned arms. The flick of ink that peeked out from under the sleeve drew Nate's fingers.

"Your hands are freezing," Flynn mumbled around Nate's tongue as he shook the jacket off the rest of the way. It landed on the doorstep in a tangle of leather and he left it there. He caught Nate's waist, hooked his thumbs over his hip bones, and walked him backward toward the stairs.

Nate tilted his head out of the kiss and braced his palms against the hard muscle and bone of Flynn's shoulders so he couldn't chase Nate's mouth. "You could stop complaining," he said, "and warm me up."

"You could stop talking."

Nate grinned. "Give me something else to do, then."

That made Flynn laugh. He turned his head to the side and pressed a kiss against the underside of Nate's wrist. The contact of wet lips and heat sent a shudder through Nate that started in his fingertips and ended in his balls. He caught his breath.

"This time," Flynn said. "You go first."

He took another step forward, and Nate mirrored him. His heel caught on the first step of the stairs and made it rattle. Nate stepped back onto it and was briefly the taller of the two, but it didn't last long. Flynn joined him on the step, crowded his body up next to Nate's, and pressed against him from shoulder to hip.

A grin flicked up the corner of Flynn's mouth. He slid his hands back to grab Nate's ass and pulled him in ever closer, until their cocks rubbed together through their clothes. The jolt of pleasure that hit Nate was sharp enough to almost be pain. He bit his lip hard and hung on to Flynn for balance, his knees suddenly loose under his weight.

"Shit," he muttered into Flynn's shoulder.

Flynn laughed and pressed his mouth against Nate's ear. It tickled as he murmured, "Now that seems hot enough," and then traced his wet tongue around the shell—which didn't help Nate get his legs underneath him. He shuddered, clenched his fists, and pressed his knuckles against the long strap muscles in Flynn's back.

"Don't get me wrong. I really want to do this," he said. "But your stairs aren't made for fucking, Flynn."

Flynn snorted and gave Nate's ass a rough squeeze. "You saying my stairs aren't good enough for you, Granshire boy?"

"I'm saying the hickey was bad enough. I don't need a waffle pattern on my ass too."

"I liked the hickey." Flynn scraped his teeth down Nate's jaw—half kiss and half bite. "I might like the waffle pattern too."

"I wanted a bad boyfriend," Nate reminded him. "Not a weird one."

Flynn's laugh vibrated through them both. It was a rough rasp that dragged an answering chuckle out of Nate. He grabbed a handful of Flynn's T-shirt and pulled the thin material up and over his head. It ruffled Flynn's hair and then caught around his arms. He had to let go of Nate's backside to take it off the rest of the way himself.

Like the jacket, he left it where it dropped.

They stripped their way up to the bedroom. Nate toed off his sneakers on one step and lost his shirt and a couple of buttons to Flynn's impatient fingers on the next. Another step and Nate fumbled the button fly of Flynn's jeans open. His knuckles brushed against Flynn's stomach as he did so and made Flynn flinch and suck his breath in through his teeth.

"Your hands are still like blocks of ice, Nate," he grumbled.

"And I told you, warm me up, then." Nate grinned and slid his hand down into the gaping waistband and palmed the rise of Flynn's cock. It was heavy and eager in his fingers—soft skin over hard flesh and the hot pulse of blood. He rubbed his thumb over the come-slick head, and Flynn's hips jerked toward him. The groan that escaped him had nothing to do with the chill. "Better?"

It must have been.

Flynn bit out a strained curse between his teeth and dragged Nate up the last few steps. The lights were off, and the moon was the only source of illumination, but in a room that was 90 percent glass, that was enough. The walls curved in almost invisible lines, confusing the eye about where the room ended and the velvet-black, star-studded night began, and a massive rumpled bed dominated the room.

"Wow," Nate said as he paused to admire the view. "This is…."

"I can hear you writing the ad in your head." Flynn wrapped an arm around Nate's waist and pulled him back against his chest.

That wasn't entirely true. Nate had written the ad years before. He was just editing it on the fly in his head. It probably wasn't the time, but his brain had briefly skipped tracks.

Flynn slid his hand down until he cupped Nate's cock through his trousers. The quick squeeze, hard fingers, and the chill scrape of the zipper against sensitive flesh brought his mind back to what they were doing.

"Only a bit," he promised. His breath hitched, and caught in the back of his throat when Flynn squeezed again. His voice was ragged as he added, "Stunning vistas. What stunning vistas."

"Smartass."

Flynn pressed a kiss against Nate's neck. The sharp pressure of his teeth gave way to the wet softness of his lips, and he scooped him up. The sudden gesture made Nate yelp and grab for Flynn's shoulder as his feet left the floor.

"What the hell are you doing?" he asked, half laughing.

Flynn grinned, skimmed a kiss over the tilted corner of Nate's mouth, and tossed him onto the bed. "Distracting you."

It worked. Nate spluttered out a laugh as he sprawled back on the soft mattress. The memory foam gave under his elbow as he watched Flynn wrench off his boots and shove his sagging jeans down to his ankles. Moonlight glazed the heavy planes of practical muscle as he straightened up, and silvered the threads of gray in his hair and on his body.

Nate felt his mouth go dry. He knew what Flynn's body was like—the breadth of his chest, the dense, dark arrow of hair down to his balls, and the heavy, curved shaft of his erect cock. But it was like that story about the blind men and the elephant. He'd missed the heavy, dark-haired thighs and the knotted bloom of scar tissue that slashed across one leg like a twisted garter.

Flynn was hot in fits and starts of partial nudity, but he was beautiful taken as a whole.

The bastard didn't look forty.

Stretched out on the bed, his cock pressing against the fly of his trousers and his stomach sucked in so hard he could feel it behind his ribs, Nate wished he'd pushed through the pain to that second push-up. It wasn't that he was fat—he spent too much time running up and down stairs and hauling trestle tables for that—but he didn't look like *Flynn*. He didn't even look like the "before" version of Flynn they'd have in a sports magazine.

"You could grate cheese on your abs," he muttered. It sounded a bit more sour than he meant it to. He covered the moment by unfastening his trousers and lifting his hips off the bed to push them down.

Flynn crawled onto the bed and straddled Nate's thighs. He yanked the trousers down to Nate's knees and left him to kick them the rest of the way off himself. Then he leaned forward and braced his arms against the mattress so he could look at him.

"So, exactly how long do you think you can suck your stomach in like that?" he asked.

It should have been mortifying. Instead Nate creased up with laughter. It snorted ungraciously out of him on the breath he'd been holding. The grin on Flynn's face didn't help. It was slow and wickedly amused at Nate's embarrassment. Finally he covered his face with his hands, shoved his fingers into his hair, and admitted between snorted giggles, "I think I was hoping you'd just flip me over. Then I could let go."

Flynn lowered his body down on top of Nate. The weight of muscle and bone pinned him to the bed and twisted eager heat in his balls.

"That doesn't sound like me." Flynn caught Nate's wrists in his hands and pulled them away from his face. He pinned them down to the bed behind Nate's head and then took a second to cock his head to the side and admire the view. "I've rarely been a 'just flip 'em over' kind of guy. I like to take my time."

Flynn leaned down and kissed Nate as though he were trying to prove it. His kiss was slow, wet, and thorough, and Nate made a strangled noise in the back of his throat and squirmed under Flynn's weight. He wanted to touch Flynn, to trace the ink-etched cross on his bicep and map the scattered nicks and scrapes that a lifetime had left on him.

Mostly he just *wanted*. He'd thought he was happy enough on his own, with Netflix and his own hand, but he missed this. Not getting fucked—not *just* getting fucked—but the intimacy of being naked with someone, of being so close you were breathing their air.

Nate hooked a leg over Flynn's hip and rubbed a bare foot down his thigh. His toes caught on a thick seam of scar tissue, the mirror of the slash Nate had noticed on the front. That hadn't been a flesh wound.

"... used to be in the army," he remembered Flynn saying. He wondered if that was why the past tense.

"What happened?" he asked.

"Car accident," Flynn said. He bit kisses along Nate's jaw and down his throat and muttered the words into his shoulder. Lust prickled under Nate's skin, like pins and needles of pleasure. "It was in Somalia. A coach sideswiped a minivan, overturned it on the side of the road. I got a kid out, but then the vehicle shifted, and I got trapped. They had to cut me free. Army invalided me out before I left the hospital."

There was no emotion in Flynn's voice, but it obviously wasn't something he talked about often. None of the gossips had ever even hinted at that bit of backstory. It was an old scar, though, and well-healed.

"That's not why you came back."

"No."

Flynn didn't elaborate. He let go of Nate's wrists and trailed his fingers along the inside of Nate's forearms down to the crease of his elbows as his mouth found a path to Nate's nipple. He swiped his tongue over the flat bud and then sucked it into his mouth. His teeth scraped over the nerve-rich flesh, and Nate made a mangled sound that would have been a curse if he could have put the vowels together.

He reached down, ran his hands over Flynn's back, and traced the hard swoop of Flynn's shoulder blades and down across the taut drum of his ribs. The strips of dense muscle twitched and clenched as his touch set off a chain reaction that made Flynn's dick jump where it was pinned between their bodies.

"What about you?" Flynn asked. He pressed a last, wet kiss to Nate's chest and sat back. His weight settled across Nate's thighs as he idly stroked his dick. The head was wet and shining as he pulled the foreskin back and the thin skin wrinkled under his fingers. "What's with the Converse?"

Nate snorted again. "Seriously?" he asked.

"I'm curious." Flynn leaned back and reached toward the bedside table. He dragged a drawer open and pulled out a condom and a tube of lube.

"It's just my thing," Nate said as he got up on his knees on the bed. He plucked the condom out of Flynn's fingers and tore the packet open. "I was running late for school one day, and Max had hidden all my shoes. I grabbed a pair of his sneakers and ran in."

He rolled the condom slowly down Flynn's dick as he talked. His head was bent as he watched his fingers work around the hard shaft, and his tangled hair hung in his eyes. Maybe bare skin felt better, but he always liked the way condoms looked on a man's erection, the latex slick and shiny with lube, how *tight* it looked under the thin skin. He reached the base and slid his hand back to cup the heavy swing of Flynn's balls. They twitched in his hand, and Flynn groaned. His thighs clenched, and his muscles knotted like cords under the skin.

"That was the first day that no one asked why I was gray at nineteen," Nate said. "So I made it my thing."

Flynn pulled him into his lap. Their dicks pressed together, slick and hard between their stomachs, and Nate's belly clenched eagerly as Flynn reached around to press a slippery finger into his ass. Another finger joined the first and worked more lube inside him. Nate gripped Flynn's shoulders and groaned as he pushed back against the fingers inside him.

"You know," Flynn said raggedly as he pressed deeper into Nate. It stretched Nate almost uncomfortably wide and made him mouth eager pleas for more against Flynn's throat. "I think you're old enough that no one's going to wonder why you're gray anymore."

"You're a bast—" The curse turned into a whine of protest as Flynn pulled his fingers out. Nate squirmed so their cocks rubbed together. The press of hard flesh, sweat, and precome twisted pleasure through his balls until he ached with it. "Jesus, Flynn, just fuck me."

Flynn snorted. "You're a brat."

"Well, if you want to, you can spank me later. Right now?" Nate pulled away from Flynn and sprawled back onto the bed. He grinned at Flynn, cocked a knee up, and braced his foot against the tangled sheets. "Fuck me, bad boy."

That got him a disdainful look, but it didn't keep Flynn from joining him in the jumble of sheets. Nate mouthed encouragement as Flynn gripped his thighs and pushed his knees toward his chest. He reached back and steadied his hands against the headboard, his cock slick and wet against his stomach and his balls tight with frustration.

"I suppose you should get your money's worth," Flynn rasped. Something about the way he said it jabbed at Nate, like a pin through the heady throb of hunger and want that filled him. He *would* have said something. He was definitely going to explain that it wasn't... that. But before he could, he felt the blunt pressure of Flynn's cock pressed against his ass. He groaned and sank his teeth into his lower lip, but the pinch of pain wasn't a particularly effective distraction from the flare of heat that settled like a weight between his hips as Flynn slowly pushed into him.

Later.

Nate kept promising that, but... later.

It burned as his ass stretched around Flynn's cock and a dull ache jostled his hip bones. In any other situation, it would have been painful, but right then it was co-opted by his dick for pleasure. His body felt feverish with lust, heat prickled at his balls and nipples, and he was so full of Flynn's cock that there was no room for anything like breath or words or thinking.

Flynn was finally all the way inside him, his balls pressed against the taut curve of Nate's ass, and he paused for a second. His jaw was set and tension corded the muscles on his shoulders and forearms. He shifted his weight, leaned forward, and somehow managed to fit his cock even deeper into Nate. The shock of pleasure shot black and prickling down Nate's spine, and he groaned out a ragged *fuck* through clenched teeth.

"Was this part of your plan?" Flynn asked. He let go of Nate's thighs, braced his hands on either side of Nate's shoulders, and clenched his fingers in the sheets. "When you came here that first night?"

"No," Nate said. He hesitated. It wasn't that he was going to lie. He just needed a second to remember what the truth was when he was on fire with Flynn. "Maybe part of a few fantasies, but not the plan."

Flynn laughed a breathless huff on Nate's not-quite humor. "For a hotshot wedding planner," he said, "things don't often go according to plan for you, do they?"

He had a point. Nate wrapped a hand around Flynn's neck and pulled him down. He mouthed his answer against Flynn's lips. "Maybe, but I'm kind of okay with that."

At least he was for the moment.

Flynn kissed him. It was slow and salty and sweet, and he started to rock his hips against Nate. It was careful at first, and his cock slid just a bit at a time, but the pace quickened with each thrust. Nate wrapped his legs around Flynn's hips, dug his heels into the bunched muscles on Flynn's thighs, and moaned encouragement as he arched his hips up to meet each thrust.

Each thrust shoved Nate down hard against the mattress, pinned him under the weight of Flynn's body, and sent a jolt of pleasure up his spine. His cock was trapped between their bodies, ground against Flynn's taut stomach with each thrust. There was a hot knot of pleasure in his gut that twisted tighter and tighter and yanked ragged jolts of pleasure down his nerves each time Flynn's cock bumped up against his prostate.

He caught Flynn by the shoulders and dragged him down into a kiss. He pressed his mouth against Flynn's for a moment and then slid down his jaw to his shoulder and bit kisses along the bony jut of Flynn's collarbone. While Flynn growled at him, Nate claimed the span of skin with his tongue and teeth and slid his hands down the laboring length of his back. The long muscles stretched and flexed under his hands as Flynn fucked him.

"God, Flynn," Nate groaned against Flynn's throat. "I wish...."

He didn't need to wish for anything. There was no looming obstacle he had to shrug his shoulders at and give up. It was his for the taking if he wanted it. If Flynn wanted it.

That was kind of terrifying.

Before he could think on it anymore, Flynn claimed his mouth in a searing kiss as his cock hammered his prostate. The sensation of it slammed down Nate's spine on sharp black wings and yanked loose the knot of pleasure between his thighs. Ecstasy flashed through him and drained him dry. He came in a wet spill across both of their stomachs and his ass clenched around Flynn's dick as he did so—an involuntary cramp of muscle that made Flynn groan into his mouth.

"Fuck," Flynn ground out through clenched teeth. He thrust hard into Nate's body—as though he needed to be even deeper—and came. The twitch and pulse of his release filled Nate's ass as Flynn's body collapsed on top of him. He panted unsteadily against Nate's neck while the sweaty weight of him pinned Nate to the mattress.

After a second, Flynn rolled off Nate and onto his back. His cock lay wet against his thigh, the filled condom slick and shiny, and Nate's come was smeared and wet on his stomach. He ran his hand through his hair. Sweat glued the dark tangle flat to his scalp.

"So? Am I worth the money?" he asked as he stared up at the ceiling.

"Don't be an asshole."

Flynn grimaced and rolled onto his side. He slung an arm over Nate's chest, tucked his hand around to cradle the nape of Nate's neck, and pressed a kiss against the bony angle of his shoulder.

"Yeah," he said. "That wasn't about you. Sorry."

Nate reached up and tangled his fingers in Flynn's hair. It felt almost naughty, as though that were closer to breaking the terms of their agreement than the sex had been. "If it helps, I've got no complaints. Maybe a few pointers...."

Flynn snorted. "Go to sleep, Nate," he said.

CHAPTER TWENTY

"He's never denied any of it."

IT HAD been… a while since Flynn had woken up
to company. The breakup with Kier hadn't exactly been
out of the blue. It had been brewing for a dry spell, and
when you lived on an island, a one-night stand was actually a fair amount of commitment. Not that he'd been
celibate, but he stuck to hookups in back rooms and back
seats, and at some point, he settled into the idea that he
preferred it, that he liked his space and his privacy.

Yet there he was, and there Nate was, and all Flynn felt was lazy contentment and a bit of surprise that
Nate hadn't snuck out with the dawn.

Or maybe he meant to and just got caught by the
view.

Flynn propped himself up on his elbow, stifled a
yawn against the back of his hand, and looked down

to where Nate was sitting cross-legged on the end of the bed. The teasing comment on Flynn's tongue went dry, and he wondered who the hell had told Nate that he wasn't a beautiful man.

His back was long and narrow and his arms were slim and elegant in a way that Flynn had assumed was down to the expensive suits and silk T-shirts. The tilt of his folded legs drew his long, lean thighs tight from knee to hip, and the marks of Flynn's fingers were still visible as pale prints on his skin. Maybe Nate didn't have much muscle, but there was no spare flesh on him. He just looked like a runner instead of a weight lifter— soft like he enjoyed his body, but not like he was weak.

"You know you're gorgeous, right?" Flynn asked. His voice sounded harsher than just morning dry mouth could justify.

Nate snorted without looking around and shifted his shoulders as though he could shed the weight of the compliment. "I clean up okay." He glanced over his shoulder, his messy piebald curls fell over his face, and he bit his lip as he gave Flynn a once-over. "You look like a Greek statue."

The easy, open appreciation on Nate's face made Flynn's balls tighten and his cock twitch. Apparently his body thought he could be up for another round if he put the effort in. That was wishful thinking. The swell of warmth and… affection in his chest was delusional.

"The ones with small dicks?" he jibed.

Nate laughed and turned to crawl up the bed. He reached between Flynn's thighs, his hand cupped his ever more lively cock, and squeezed thoughtfully. Interest yanked back to Flynn's spine with a hot cramp of hunger, and he had to hold back a groan.

"Like I said." Nate leaned in and brushed a closed-mouth kiss over Flynn's bitten lips. "I've no complaints." Fuck morning breath. Flynn caught Nate's arm and pulled him back down for a proper kiss—slow and leisurely, tongues tangled, and hands free to explore. Flynn's ended up on Nate's ass again. It didn't feel that narrow from his angle.

After a long, distracting minute, Nate broke the kiss. He tilted his head back and looked regretful. "I really need to go," he said.

Flynn rolled them both over and pinned a laughing Nate to the bed. He cupped Nate's face in his hands and grazed his thumbs over his cheekbones.

"Just tell your mum you're here." He caught Nate's lower lip between his teeth and tugged at it gently. "Let her think I'm leading you astray."

Nate draped his arms over Flynn's shoulders and snorted. "I'm pretty sure she knows I've had sex—considering she walked in on me the first time."

He said it as though it were funny, with maybe 20 percent leftover embarrassment. If Flynn's old man had walked in on that, one of the two wouldn't have walked back out again. The jab of odd, old jealousy deflated a bit of the lazy, sweaty balloon of early morning lust.

"But," Nate added, "I do have to get to work, and I probably shouldn't go in smelling like sex and burned oil."

Yeah, there was that.

Nate's shove wasn't particularly effective, but Flynn sighed and rolled off him. Nate sat up and stretched like a cat, with his shoulders rolled back and his stomach caved in under his ribs. As he dropped his hands back to his sides, he gave Flynn an uncertain look. "Do you mind if I use your shower?" he asked.

Flynn sighed and folded his arms behind his head. "Help yourself." He unlaced one finger long enough to point. "Behind the wall."

He sprawled out on the bed and listened to Nate turn the water on, swear, and turn it back off again. While Nate fought with the water pressure—it was okay, but the boiler on the ground floor wasn't meant to run water up for twenty minutes—Flynn stared down his stretched-out body.

Most of the time, he didn't really *look* at himself. It was his body. It was just there, as long as it did what he needed it to do. He knew his thighs were sprinkled with dark hair, that his stomach was flat, and that he was lucky his scarred leg worked. But he didn't dwell on it.

The old white seam on his leg looked raw and new, as though it were the first time he'd seen it. It looked ugly and function impairing, but it wasn't that bad—little muscle damage, no tendons, just a split bone and torn flesh. It was nearly as good as new. He was starting to feel like he was too.

"I never meant to stay here," he said. His voice carried over the splash and gurgle of Nate's shower. "That wasn't the plan."

"Mine neither," Nate yelled back. "I figured you'd be joining me in here."

Not what he meant. Flynn glanced down at his cock, which lay at half-mast against his stomach, and decided it wasn't in his interest to argue. He rolled off the bed, and his bones still sounded like gravel as he headed around the curved glass-brick wall to the shower.

Nate stood in the sunken wet room, hair plastered to his head and soapy water glistening on his bare skin. One of his hands was curled around his cock at the start of a lazy wank, and he grinned at Flynn through the dripping water.

"Just in time," he said.

Flynn stepped down onto the slick tiles. The water hit his skin and made him flinch. Nate apparently liked tepid showers and had turned the temperature way down. He tilted his head back to let the water soak his hair and wash the sleep out of his eyes. Nate pulled him into the shower and pressed up against his back. He ran wet hands down Flynn's body, over his ribs, and down to his thighs. His fingers stalled at the twist of scar tissue.

Nate traced the scar from the thickest point at the front of Flynn's thigh, where he could barely feel the pressure, to the thread-thin surgical scar on his inner thigh. "So what was the plan?"

It was Flynn who brought up the question, but when he was on the spot, he didn't want to talk about it. The hand on his cock was a good distraction from that reluctance, though—slow, steady strokes from base to tip, a bit too gentle.

"Fix this place up, sell it, leave," Flynn said. He reached down and wrapped his hand around Nate's. He pumped it faster along his cock and squeezed just hard enough to make pleasure throb down into his balls and back into his ass. "Go back to work. There's always a garage, always rescue work."

Nate groaned and pressed an open-mouth kiss against Flynn's shoulder. He sucked the water off his skin and bit down on a mouthful of flesh. His cock was slotted between Flynn's thighs. It was hard and wet as Nate ground against him.

"You're still here. You could have sold to Teddy anytime."

Flynn reached back with his free hand and caught Nate's thigh to pull him closer. Each thrust rubbed velvety hardness over the tender ridge of skin between his thighs. Arousal was a hot clench of weight, and his balls were tight and twitching.

"I guess, just once, I didn't want the old bastard to get what he wanted. This time he didn't get to win."

An unsteady laugh escaped Nate, and he ground against Flynn's ass in time with the steady pump of their interlaced fingers.

"That's cutting off your nose to spite your face," he said. "Trust me, living your life to spite Teddy doesn't get you far. Ask Max."

Flynn let his lip curl. "I'd rather not."

He felt Nate's body shift behind him. The hitch of muscles and slip of flesh translated into a shrug in Flynn's head. Maybe he was going to say something else, but whatever it was got lost in his harshened breathing and the desperate squirm of his hips against Flynn's ass.

Flynn tightened his grip over Nate's fingers and turned the slow pump into an impatient yank. He twisted on the downstroke and choked back a groan of aching pleasure and a mouthful of tepid water. It drew the orgasm out of him, and he arched his back into it.

He had to grab the wall for support and brace his fingers against the slick glass as his muscles went slack and loose with his release. Nate swore against the nape of his neck and thrust roughly against him. He came with a shudder and a drawn-out rasp of

Flynn's name. The stickiness clung to Flynn's thighs and washed away with the shower.

"For this," Nate said as he panted like a winded horse. "I could be a morning person."

Flynn snorted and reached back to ruffle his fingers through Nate's hair. "This and coffee."

THE COFFEE was black, thick, and store brand. It was also strong, which was all Nate seemed to care about. Flynn leaned against the sink, his cup cradled in his hands, and watched Nate distractedly juggle between drinking the coffee and checking his phone.

Despite the borrowed T-shirt and scruff-dried hair—it had taken him a while to believe Flynn didn't have a hair dryer—Nate looked like he should be in the pages of a magazine. Maybe not fashion, but some high-end "home and gardens" thing at least.

"If I chucked that thing over the cliff, you'd probably go with it," Flynn said dryly.

Nate didn't look away from the screen, but he set his cup down long enough to give Flynn the finger.

"After yesterday I'm playing catch-up. It's the wedding rehearsal dinner tonight, and I've got to convince the mothers about the change in venue and get in touch with the photographer." He looked up at last and grimaced apologetically. "It's not always this bad."

"Katie and Bradley's rehearsal dinner," Flynn said. "So his dip in the sea hasn't cooled the groom's enthusiasm?"

Nate shook his head. He turned his screen off and dropped the phone into his pocket. "No. Once I made sure he didn't have to wear a tie, he was all for it. Now I just have to make sure nothing else goes wrong between today and tomorrow night." He paused and glanced over at the back door and the pale blue sky bright as crayon through the window. "And somehow make sure it doesn't rain."

"It's not meant to."

"That means nothing." Nate tipped his head back and drained the dregs of coffee. He put the mug in the sink and looked at Flynn uncertainly for a second. "So, I was thinking—"

His phone went off before he could finish the sentence. Nate grabbed it from his pocket and frowned at whatever the screen said. He gestured "just a second" to Flynn as he took the call.

"Hi, Max, I—No, I'm not dead. I just—yes, I'm still here. Why tell Teddy that? I'm not even going to be late." The stuttered rhythm of the call marked the habitual interruptions of people who knew each other too well to need to hear out the whole sentence. It paused for a second, and Nate absently rubbed his fingertips against the back of his ear as he listened. Whatever he heard made him pull a face, but he didn't argue. "I do appreciate it. Max, don't spoil it."

Nate took the phone away from his ear.

"You called Max?" Flynn asked.

"I didn't want Mum to worry," Nate said. His mouth twitched into a stiff smile. "And I, umm… needed a lift into work."

Flynn hid the bitter twist of his mouth in his mug. The car was outside. He ran his own business, so if he wanted to be late, he could.

"He's nearly here," Nate said. There was a pause that condensed twenty years of old resentments and older secrets into an awkward shuffle of avoided eye contact. It was Nate who broke it. "Look, this whole bad-boyfriend plan… maybe we should talk about it?"

"Tonight?"

Nate laughed. "Rehearsal dinner, remember?" he said. "Then the wedding. Maybe in a couple of days?"

Flynn finished his coffee and put it down. The odd, candy-floss fluffiness that had stuffed his chest since he woke up finally started to melt. It left a sour stickiness behind.

"Katie and Bradley," he said. "Give them my best. They were a cute couple."

Nate nodded. "I will."

Flynn was relieved when the brash blare of the car horn outside interrupted them. Nate glanced around and twitched like he'd forgotten Max was on the way.

"I better go." He stepped forward and leaned in for a quick, dry kiss. "Soon as this wedding is in the bag, we can talk."

Flynn clenched his jaw against the urge to kiss him back, to bruise his lips and mark his neck so that when he went outside, Max would know exactly why they'd kept him waiting. Instead he slouched where he stood and listened to the front door slam and the rev of the engine idling outside.

It didn't take long—Max obviously wasn't interested in wasting any time—and Flynn was left alone with Teddy's check and his own thoughts. They weren't the best company.

When he'd left Ceremony twenty years earlier, he swore he'd never come back. When he came back, he swore he wasn't going to stay. His leg was good enough for rescue work. He could probably pass the physical to get reinstated in the service. If he wanted.

Even if he didn't, fifty thousand was a lot of money to do exactly what he always said he would—leave. What did he have here after all? A view, a bad reputation, and a fake boyfriend who was happy enough to fuck him but didn't want to rock his comfortable boat.

He tossed the dregs of his coffee into the sink and flicked the tap on to wash it away. The sour taste in the back of his throat had spoiled the cup. In a couple of days, Flynn was going to get ditched, Nate would go back to his nice, unruffled life, and Teddy St. John would get the stand-in son he always wanted.

Money in his pocket or not, that didn't seem entirely fair to Flynn.

CHAPTER TWENTY-ONE

"You should get a dog. Dogs are great for meeting people."

THE PHOTOGRAPHER, Dale Lau, was a stocky, genial man who drove off the ferry in a car packed with camera gear and an old surfboard strapped to the roof. He grinned at Nate from behind a pair of polarized sunglasses and said he was going to get some surfing in while he was there. He leaned out the arched window of the folly to check the waves below. His T-shirt crawled up his back to flash a glimpse of tanned skin and the sun-blurred lines of a black tribal tattoo.

"Do you surf?" he asked Nate over his shoulder. Then, as though the answer were obvious, "Where's the best spot on the island?"

"I tried it once. Not really my thing," Nate said. He added casually, "If you want, I could ask my boyfriend for recommendations. He's with the Coastguard."

"Huh, maybe."

Nate left Dale to admire the scenery and turned around to adjust the hang of the sheer curtains while he thought about what he'd just said. It was the first time he'd really called Flynn that and meant it. He might have said he wanted a bad boyfriend, but even when he poked at Max about it, he stuck to "dating." It didn't sound quite right.

It could be that he was too old for *boyfriends*. He might need to upgrade to *partner*. Or the not-so-casual way he'd slotted *Coastguard* in there, as though he were a teenager with a boyfriend in a band.

Of course, Nate popped his own bubble firmly, it could be because he hadn't actually had any sort of conversation with Flynn about it. One night of sex didn't automatically upgrade to a relationship. Hell, it didn't usually upgrade to another night of sex. Otherwise Nate's occasional Facebook stalking of his exes would be all-nighters, not an hour to pass the time until someone died during an *Emmerdale* two-parter. And Max would be a bigamist.

"Anyhow, we'll be shooting up here around this time of day?" Dale said as he dragged himself away from the window.

"The wedding starts at 11:00 a.m.," Nate said. He checked his watch. "So right about now we'd be walking the bridge to the altar."

Dale nodded and pushed his sunglasses onto the top of his head. One eye was a slit in a puffy nest of yellow and green bruising, with blood-blisters scattered over the lower eyelid. Nate stared for a dismayed moment as "defaced photographer" was added to the list of things that had gone wrong. Before he had to think of how to ask, Dale caught him staring.

"Oh this?" He poked gingerly at the puffy underside of his eye. "Christening in Oxford got a bit rowdy. Don't worry. I shoot with my other eye." He held his hands up to demonstrate, his fingers crooked around an imaginary camera in front of his face.

"Just keep the sunglasses on as much as you can," Nate said. "Even if you won't be in the pictures, the bride doesn't need to see that."

Dale obediently popped the shades back down onto his nose. They headed down the steps to the car, through the dapples of sun and shade cast on the stone by the branches overhead. Nate made it halfway down, and gave three sidelong looks at what he could see of the bruising. "Okay, so who punched you?"

"Grandma."

He waited expectantly, as though he expected Nate to call him a liar. But after so many years of organizing the annual Ceremony Harvest Festival, that sounded about right. Nate had seen a seventy-year-old widow batter her rival's husband about the head and shoulders with the parish magazine because of a squashed cupcake. He wouldn't put anything past an irate grandmother at a ruined christening.

"Well, it could have been worse."

"How?"

"It could have been the baby."

The broken-down Granshire car was still parked in the corner, waiting for someone to collect it. Nate folded himself into Dale's Mini instead. The inside of the car smelled like salt and sugary sweets, and the floor under Nate's feet was covered with discarded wrappers.

"Sorry for the mess," Dale said. "I keep meaning to clean it up. Never do. So you want me at the rehearsal dinner tonight?"

Nate nodded and pulled his phone out of his pocket. He filled Dale in on the wedding party and their quirks on the way back to the Granshire. The groom would have shirtsleeves rolled up the minute he got a chance after the ceremony, the maid of honor was quite short, he was to include the groom's mother in every picture the bride's parents were in....

"To a long and happy marriage." William McCreary raised his glass, and the gathered guests followed suit. Bright candlelight glowed through dozens of red wine filled flutes as they all took a dutiful sip. Then a grin cracked William's broad pink face—a few too many hours on the golf course with Teddy—and he added an unscripted epilogue to the toast. "I figure about twenty years will get us our money's worth."

He got a laugh. It made him beam and open his mouth again. Before he could go on, his wife caught his sleeve and tugged at it.

"Sit down, Billy," she ordered. "You're embarrassing Katie."

"Yeah, Bill," Bradley said. He grinned at his future father-in-law. Then he winked and downed his wine. "Save something for the wedding."

Katie rolled her eyes, and Nate leaned over the table to pour her a fresh glass of wine.

"Thanks," she said. "I don't suppose you can organize my dad's speech?"

"I'm sorry," Nate said. "I convinced the best man it wasn't a roast. My persuasive powers are tapped out."

Katie laughed and took a sturdy gulp of her wine. She'd been up to see the folly in the afternoon and was cautiously won over by the "fairy-tale grotto" appeal of it. It was still a big change from what she'd originally planned, and she wasn't entirely confident she could risk being happy about it yet.

"I still think we should postpone the wedding," Sheila said darkly from her seat at her son's elbow. "So many things have gone wrong. It's like a sign."

While Bradley hushed his mother, Katie took a deep breath and another sip of wine.

"I know. God, I just hope nobody blows off a cliff tomorrow," Katie said through tight, bright pink lips. "That would really dampen everyone's spirits."

Sheila narrowed her eyes and pressed her lips together in a tight, unhappy line, and the main course came out in the middle of it all as Granshire servers in fitted black delivered orders of coffee-grilled steak, pecan-crusted chicken, and risotto. There were other vegetarian options, but apparently Sheila actually wanted risotto.

Max slid her plate onto the table in front of her with a most charming smile.

"A special dish for a special lady," he said. "I hope you enjoy."

It didn't work on Sheila, any more than it had worked on Max's own mother. She poked at the risotto with her fork, regarded the mixture of rice and pomegranate with pursed lips, and put it back on the plate. "It's a bit wet," she said. "But that's fine."

While Max argued that he could definitely get her a much better risotto, Nate turned back to Katie. She pulled a face and vengefully sawed a chunk off her pecan chicken.

"It'll be fine," Nate mouthed to her.

Katie rolled her eyes, but relaxed her fingers on the knife. She lifted the piece of chicken off her plate and then put it back down as her eyes shifted to focus over Nate's shoulder.

"Oh!" she said. A pleased smile folded her mouth, and she raised her free hand in a wave. "I thought you said he couldn't make it?"

Nate twisted around in his seat. He knew who he was going to see, but he wasn't sure why. Flynn was slouched against the door of the hall in old jeans and a black leather jacket, his hands shoved into the pockets.

"Umm… I didn't think he could," Nate said. He scooted the chair back from the table. "Maybe something came up. Excuse me for a minute."

He got up and headed across the floor. Flynn watched him weave through the tables and then pushed himself off the doorframe so he could meet him halfway.

"Flynn? What are you doing here?" Nate asked.

"Just here to wish the happy couple the best," Flynn said. His mouth tilted up at the corner in a hard smile, and he reached out to tug Nate's jacket straight. "Support my boyfriend."

Nate couldn't resist the lure of that drawled word. Despite everything he'd said to… basically everyone… it felt good to have someone call him that. To have *Flynn* call him that. Of course, he didn't know if Flynn meant it or if he was just playing his part.

"This isn't the place—"

Flynn twisted his hand in Nate's lapel and tugged him in close enough that Nate could feel the heat of his body. He quietly asked, "Why not? The audience not big enough?"

Instead of giving Nate a chance to answer, he yanked him even closer and kissed him. It was hard and impatient, almost angry, with roughly mashed lips and the sharp-sour taste of whiskey on Flynn's breath. A murmur rippled through the background noise of the hall as people reacted with a mixture of disapproving mutters, gasps, and the scrape of chair legs as they turned to gawk.

It should have pissed Nate off—it *did*—but it still made hunger twist in his balls. His breath was sticky in his throat.

Flynn leaned back. He licked his lips and looked almost regretful for a second. But it passed quickly, and he smirked instead. He straightened Nate's jacket for him with a tug and brushed his shoulders off.

"There you go," he said. "Now everyone knows who you've been doing."

Nate quickly glanced around. It wasn't like everyone was staring at them, but Nate cringed with self-consciousness at those who were. It felt like they were all waiting for him to do something so they could either clap or boo.

"What the hell?" he said as he tried to ignore them. "Flynn, this is my job. It's not the place—"

Flynn shrugged. "Afraid Teddy won't approve?"

"Yes," Nate said. "He's my *employer*. He pays me."

"Yeah, well." Flynn leaned over one of the tables, winked, and grabbed a bottle of wine. He smirked and raised it to his mouth. "Teddy pays everyone. Welcome to Ceremony, where the St. Johns own our asses."

He took a swig of wine. Nate grabbed his arm and dragged him back the way he'd come. He shoved him out through the lobby doors, nearly knocking over a tipsy bridesmaid on her way in. Flynn scuffed his feet over the tiled floor and took another swig of wine straight from the bottle.

"What are you doing?" Nate demanded.

Flynn shrugged. "You wanted a bad boy. What? Wasn't I bad enough?"

Nate shoved his shoulder. It rocked Flynn back on his heels and flashed a brief expression of surprise over his face.

"Don't feed me that bullshit," Nate said. "I don't know what the hell this is, but it's not about me."

Flynn wiped wine off his lips with the back of his hand and contradicted him. "Don't undersell yourself. It's a little about you."

"You know what?" Nate said, raising his eyebrows. "You're not a bad boy. You're just an asshole. I'm not doing this. Come back when you're sober, or don't. It's up to you."

Behind Nate, someone wolf-whistled. He jerked around and found Max standing in front of the doors with a shit-eating smirk on his face as he slow-clapped the argument.

"About time, Flynn," he said. "Just when I was starting to think you'd buck the trend and not fuck up."

"Max, not now—" Nate tried to say. Neither of them were listening to him.

"Maybe I should have asked you for advice," Flynn said with a sneer. "You know all about fucking up, don't you? Almost forty years old, still waiting bar in your daddy's hotel."

Dull color flagged across Max's tanned cheekbones as though he'd been smacked. His smirk slipped into more of a grimace.

"Fuck you." He shoved past Nate's attempt to block him and squared up to Flynn. "You think you're so much better than me? Only person on this island that had the time of day for you was Nate. Now he's fucked you, and you've disappointed him like everyone else in your pathetic—"

Flynn 's knuckles caught Max on his outthrust jaw and knocked him backward. Nate had to jump out of the way of Max's suddenly limp body as he hit the tiles with a bone-rattling thud.

"Why don't you shut up," Flynn suggested flatly. He shook his hand out while a dazed Max rolled onto his side and nursed his jaw. Blood dropped onto the floor in fat splodges. He looked reluctantly back at Nate. "I didn't mean to—"

"Get out," Nate said.

Everyone in the lobby looked around and craned their necks to see what was going on. Out of the corner of his eye, Nate saw the receptionist pick up the phone and speak into it urgently. Nate dropped to one knee next to Max. He peeled Max's hand off his jaw long enough to check the damage. Blood covered Max's chin, and his lip was already puffed up and purple. Nate grimaced and dragged a handkerchief out of his pocket to mop up the mess.

"Nate. You don't get it," Flynn said.

"I know you aren't going to convince me this was even a little bit about me."

Max looked up and smirked bloodily over the handkerchief. "You heard him. He wants you to fuck off, just like everyone else." He turned his head and spat blood on the marble. "So go before I decide to press charges."

"You can shut up," Nate said. He shoved the handkerchief back up over Max's bloody mouth to muffle him. "Just go, Flynn."

There was definite regret on Flynn's face that time. He pushed his hair back from his face and opened his mouth, but nothing came out, and he closed it again. With a last apologetic shrug, he turned to leave just as the elevator doors slid open and Teddy limped urgently into the lobby. The two men stopped and stared at each other.

Nate groaned under his breath. That was all he needed.

"Here." He placed the handkerchief in Max's hand. "Don't choke."

He braced his hand on the cold tiles, ignored Max's mumble-mouthed complaints, and pushed himself to his feet.

"Teddy… Mr. St. John." He took two steps forward and stopped abruptly, pinned by Teddy's cold, gimlet glare. It made his mouth go dry and the back of his neck itch as though he were still a kid called on the carpet because he was caught stealing apples from the cider press. "I know this looks bad. It's just a misunderstanding—"

"Don't bother," Flynn interrupted. "I don't need you to apologize for me, Nate."

Teddy curled his lip in a sneer. "Perhaps he's apologizing for himself, Delaney. I don't appreciate employees' private lives bleeding over into my business—especially not when their private lives involve such poor decision-making."

A flick of anger cut through Nate's embarrassed discomfort. That his sort-of lover disrupted an event at the hotel was his problem. It was unprofessional, even if he hadn't encouraged it. But the fact that he *had* a sort-of lover was no one's business but his and Flynn's.

"My private life didn't turn this into a problem. Max's mouth did," he said. From the floor Max protested halfheartedly. Nobody paid any attention. "Flynn's leaving now, and there's no reason for him to come back. So unless you want to suspend me, I'm going back to work."

He waited. For a second, under Teddy's cold glare, he thought he'd pushed too far and was actually about to be asked to leave. Part of him almost hoped for it. He could go home, get sloppy drunk, and cry on his mother's shoulder. He wouldn't even try to pretend he didn't want to.

Instead Teddy pursed his lips and inclined his chin in a brief, stiff-necked nod. "Fine," he said. His eyebrow twitched up toward his forehead, and he added ominously, "But we will revisit this when the Ferguson wedding has wrapped up. You acted against my specific orders in bringing Delaney here."

Flynn snorted. "Nate? He didn't even tell me I was invited, Teddy. I came off my own bat, and I'm leaving the same way."

"Before you're dragged out," Teddy said.

"Yeah, well, I wouldn't want to damage business—not until the check has cleared." Flynn glanced at Nate and lifted one shoulder in a shrug. It might have been an apology. It probably wasn't. "You were right. This was never going to work."

Nate lifted his chin. He didn't want to do this in the lobby of the hotel, under Teddy's withering glare, but it didn't look as if he'd get another chance.

"I told you already," he said. "This isn't anything to do with me. So don't try and give me the blame. Have a good life, Flynn."

He didn't wait to see if Flynn had anything to say. He went back to Max, who stuck out a bloody hand for help getting up. Enough time had passed for the idea of consequences to have caught up with Max. Just like always.

"Nate, I'm sorry," he said. His lip split afresh as he talked, and he absently licked the dribble of blood away. "I never meant—"

"Just shut up," Nate told him. He turned Max around and shoved him in the direction of the toilets. "Not happy with you right now either."

"I got punched," Max said indignantly.

"You deserved it."

Max grimaced and rubbed his jaw. "Maybe," he admitted. "Sorry. C'mon, though, it's best he fucks up now rather than later, right? Before you get attached."

"Yes. Before."

Despite his resolution, Nate looked over his shoulder to see what Flynn was doing, but Flynn had already gone.

THE REST of the rehearsal dinner went without a hitch. That wasn't going to stop Sheila, though, since apparently a gay man getting his ass groped in the middle of dinner was a bad omen—like a single magpie or Halley's Comet. Thankfully she'd missed Flynn laying Max out. That was probably up there with a black cat crossing your path.

"It's obvious the world is trying to tell you something," Sheila said loudly. In an attempt to placate her, one of the servers had been overgenerous with drink refills. Four vodkas had turned Sheila's conversational tone up to shrill and narrowed her focus until she forgot the rest of the table was there. "All I'm saying is maybe you should listen. I've said, right from the beginning, that this wedding was all about her. It was her idea to come here instead of getting married in our church. It was her idea to hire that flighty 'wedding planner' boy instead of listening to me."

Nate tuned her out because he'd already heard that bit twice. He gave Katie an apologetic look. "I'm so sorry, Katie. I don't know what Flynn was thinking—"

"Well, I know what I'm thinking," Katie said. She took a prim drink of her wine and left the last of her lipstick on the glass. The plates had been cleared away, and only crumbs and sauce stains were left on the heavy tablecloths. "Flynn saved Bradley's life. He can kiss his boyfriend at my rehearsal dinner if he wants. All Jim's done is agree to be the best man, and he passed out facedown in the crème brûlée."

Explaining that Flynn wasn't his boyfriend—never mind that he never really had been—was too daunting an idea to take on. Katie would be gone in a couple of days. It wouldn't hurt anyone if she left under the assumption Nate wasn't going to die alone.

Nate looked at her curiously. She had exchanged the brittle anxiety of the last few days for an upbeat attitude and bright eyes. Some of it was probably the wine, but it was still a big change.

"Are you okay?" he asked.

Katie blinked owlishly. Maybe a bit more of it than Nate had thought was the wine. She sighed. "It was supposed to be perfect—the perfect day, the perfect dress, the perfect couple."

"I *am* sorry," Nate repeated earnestly.

The naked bow of Katie's lips folded in a rueful line. Before she could say anything, Bradley reached the end of his patience.

"For God's sake, Mam, will you give over?" he burst out. Sheila went red with temper and blustered something, but he just raised his voice to drown her out. "The last family wedding we went to, in that bloody drafty old hall, Auntie Glynnis tried to glass a man in the parking lot, and you said the only one there with a full set of teeth was the dog."

"That's not the point. I just want what's best for you. And she—"

Bradley interrupted her again, but he didn't yell. "I'm getting married tomorrow to Katie, and all this stuff is important to her, so it's important to me. If you don't like it, you don't have to be there, but either way, you have to shut up about it."

Sheila pressed her lips together into a tight line and swallowed hard. She still didn't look happy, but she stayed quiet. Bradley heaved out a long, tired sigh that puffed his cheeks. He turned to nod reassurance at Katie. She smiled back at him with eyes bright and watery, and then turned to Nate.

"I guess it can still be perfect, even if things go wrong," she said.

"Sometimes," Nate agreed.

He held the smile until Katie looked away. Then he felt it crack at the corners and slide off his face.

Sometimes when things went wrong, it all just went to hell.

CHAPTER TWENTY-TWO

"Look, I used to like Flynn well enough, but I've got kids now. I don't want them looking at him and thinking they can follow in his footsteps."

A COLD shower was his traditional cure for a hangover. In Flynn's experience a morning clamber up a cliff face was just as effective. He edged out along the narrow ledge, toward the little girl miserably stuck on the spur of rock that jutted out of the cliff. One of her arms was wrapped around a fat Jack Russell that dangled from its armpits, its back legs kicking as though it could swim to safety. Gulls swooped and screeched overhead in furious defense of their nests, even though no one was near them yet.

"Hey, Gwennie," he said. "What are you doing up here?"

She wiped her sleeve over her face and left a trail of snot and tears on the denim. "Bobby chased a bird," she said, her lower lip pouted out. "We got stuck."

"Oh," Flynn said. The wind came whistling in off the sea and shoved at him. It caught his T-shirt and belled it out behind him. The tug of it gave him a visceral jolt. He knew he wasn't going to fall, but for a second, he imagined what it would be like. That wasn't helpful. Flynn sucked in a breath and shook the chill off. "That happens. How's your puppy?"

Gwennie hugged her dog tighter.

"He's skeered."

"I bet."

The roar of a car engine made him check over his shoulder. A jeep skidded to a stop in the parking lot below, and Jessie scrambled out with a float gripped in one hand. Gwennie's mother, stuck in her wheelchair on the narrow concrete walk, pointed frantically up, away from the sea. Jessie tossed the float back in the jeep and ran. Flynn turned back and saw Gwennie shuffle her feet on the rock and lose her balance for a second. Her pink-jean-clad leg dipped precariously out into space, and the Jack Russell whined and squirmed as it slipped down an inch. She caught herself with the ease of one who is too young and unscarred to be afraid of the fall.

"Gwennie, just stay still," Flynn said around the sudden lump in his throat. They weren't that high. The cliffs stretched up a hundred feet overhead, and he'd had to drag kids off the crags in the middle of winter. It was only about twenty feet where they were, but it was high enough for a little girl. The tide was out, and the stretch of rocky sand below would be a bad place to land. "Stay where you are."

"I'm gonna be in trouble," she said. Her arms tightened around the dog and made it grunt and squirm. The thought started the tears again, and her cold-reddened face creased as she started to sob. "Mum's gonna be mad at me."

She shuffled nervously again, and her trainers slid on patches of bird shit and moss.

"Maybe," Flynn said. His mouth was dry, and his muscles itched with the need to just lunge out and grab her before she fell. "Or maybe she'll be so happy to see you back safe and sound that she won't be mad at all."

He glanced back to see where Jessie was. She had scrambled nearly three-quarters of the way up the cliff and dislodged shale from under her feet and onto the beach below. That Gwennie had managed to get up there was amazing, and Flynn had no idea how the fat little dog had managed it.

"I'm not supposed to go on the beach on my own," Gwennie said.

"We all do stuff we shouldn't," Flynn said. He jumped across a broken bit of ledge and caught the spur of rock. The sharp edges sliced his fingers, but he managed to hold on. "The people who love us? They might yell a bit, but they forgive us."

Gwennie shifted and frantically batted at the air with one hand. None of the gulls had actually swooped down on her, but the noise of them was intimidating on its own. She wiped her face again. "You sure?"

"I am."

"You gotta take Bobby first."

Flynn boosted himself up and grabbed the little dog by the scruff of the neck. It barked and twisted as it tried to get its teeth into him, but he swung it across the gap to Jessie, who shoved it under her arm and wrapped her fingers around its muzzle.

"Your turn, Gwennie," he said. "Come on."

She hiccuped out a sob and hesitated, suddenly scared of more than just her mother's anger. "I don't wanna fall!"

"I'll catch you," Flynn promised.

After a moment of scrunched-face doubt, Gwennie shuffled carefully to the edge of the rock, and he grabbed her. For a second she clung to him. Then the situation hit her, and she burst into tears and started to thrash.

"I want my mummy! I wanna go home!" she wailed.

Her heel nailed Flynn firmly in the stomach. He grimaced and oofed at the unexpected pain but kept his balance.

"You okay?" Jessie asked. Her mouth was pleated in an odd line that wasn't quite sure if it needed to be worried or amused.

"I'm fine." Apparently that meant Jessie could settle on amused. Her mouth tilted up into a silent snort of laughter at his pain. She didn't even know the half of it. Flynn gave her a sour look over Gwennie's flopping brown curls and then jerked his chin back to avoid an elbow to the face. He felt his weight shift and the tug of gravity catch in his stomach. "Gwennie, we're going down now. Your mum is waiting. You have to calm down."

She struggled a minute longer and then went limp. For a small child, there was a surprising amount of weight in her sniffling little frame. Flynn hitched her up onto his hip, and she wrapped her arms around his neck. She pressed her wet and snotty face against his shoulder.

"I want Mummy," she sobbed.

"Then why don't we go down to her?" Flynn patted her back and nodded to Jessie. She slipped the still-yapping dog into her windbreaker, left its head stuck out resentfully over the zipper, and started down ahead of him.

It was slower going back than it had been coming up. Flynn could feel the throb of the hangover that lingered at the base of his skull. It ached every time he had to put weight on his split and bruised knuckles. Responsibility always made mistakes feel heavier. That was why he'd always dodged it.

Gwennie's mother was crying nearly as hard as her daughter when they finally reached the ground. "Thank you," she said as he deposited Gwennie in her lap. "Oh God. Thank you so. Gwennie. Gwen, what were you doing? You know you're not meant to go up the cliffs. What if—"

Her voice cracked and she couldn't get the words out past the fear of how bad a "what if" could have been. She hugged Gwennie so tightly that it made her squeak and squirm, and she buried her face in her curls until she had her composure back. "What if these nice people hadn't been here to get you down?"

"It wasn't my fault," Gwennie said, her voice high in protest. "I told Bobby not to go, but he went anyhow. He never listens, Mum."

"You are in *so much* trouble," her mother said as she hugged her again. "I was so worried."

By the time they got Gwennie, her mother, and the troublemaking Jack Russell back to the trailer park down the road, it still wasn't quite eight o'clock. Apparently Gwennie liked to get started early. Flynn left the family to recuperate and gave Jessie a lift back to the cliff's edge.

"Did you hurt your hand?" she asked.

Flynn stretched his fingers out and grimaced at the spreading bruise. "Max St. John's got more chin than you'd expect from a spoiled brat."

She pulled a surprised face in the periphery of his vision. "Decided not to take Teddy's check, then?"

"Kinda the opposite," Flynn said. He paused and swallowed. The sour taste in his mouth could have been regret or the aftertaste of last night's whiskey. "Kinda didn't leave myself any other choice."

Despite what a massive fuckup it had been, it didn't actually take that long to fill Jessie in on what had happened the night before. He wrapped it up with letting Nate just walk away, and there was still a minute to go before he turned in toward the parking.

"Holy crap," Jessie said. "I wish I'd been there to see it. Damn. Teddy must have been… incandescent."

"I've seen him happier."

Jessie shook her head and chuckled at the scenario. Flynn supposed he should be glad someone could see the humor in it. He didn't bother to pull into one of the outlined bays, but just veered into the side and stopped to let her jump out. Her jeep was still sitting where she'd left it with the door hanging open and a gull perched on the roof. He waited, but Jessie didn't move.

"What?" he said.

"Look. You know I'd take the money and run," Jessie said. She shoved her hand through her hair and absently scratched the back of her neck. "But… you don't have to leave it like this with Nate."

Flynn grimaced ruefully. "I think he was pretty clear that he wants it left like this."

"And since when is he the boss of you?" she asked archly. "What was it you told Gwennie? We all fuck up, but the people we love deserve a chance to forgive us. Or not."

"That's not even close to what I said."

"It's the drift." Jessie popped the door open and swung one long leg out. "Do what you like, Flynn, but the guy makes you happy. Maybe it's not worth flushing that down the toilet just to avoid apologizing."

She jumped out before Flynn could answer and slammed the door behind her. Flynn scowled through the windshield as she walked away with her hand lifted in a casual goodbye. It wasn't as though she knew the full story, anyhow. The whole relationship that had made him so "happy" had been a con. There wasn't anything real to flush down the toilet.

If there had been….

Flynn rubbed his hand roughly over his face. Who was he kidding? Because it hadn't fooled Jessie, and it wasn't fooling him. Sure it had started off as a lie—a fingers up to the island that was only too happy to think the worst of him—but who had they been lying for when they were alone? Who was supposed to disapprove of Nate's smirk under Flynn's kiss or of his body tucked against Flynn's as he slept?

Yeah. It might not be real enough to last, but did Flynn really want to end things like that—like he had with his dad all those years ago, with punches thrown and everything unsaid festering until it was too late? The old man died without ever answering the questions Flynn had been afraid to ask—before either of them had been able to say "sorry."

And after last night, Flynn supposed he owed Nate a "sorry."

FLYNN REGULARLY threw himself into ice-cold, raging seas and down cliff faces without a second thought. He used to run *into* burning buildings, so it was particularly pathetic to have lost his courage on his... on Nate's doorstep. He stood for a moment with his wrist cocked back to knock on the door, but his chest was squeezed tight with nerves, and he did nothing.

He finally dropped his arm and muttered, "Fuck."

What was he going to even say? "I know everyone on the island hates me, and I punched your boss's son in the face and put your job at risk, but no hard feelings, eh?" Because no matter what it had been like in the light-house the other night, there was the rest of the world to deal with.

Maybe the apology could wait for later, once things had settled down. Flynn grimaced to himself. He was too sober for that. He couldn't get away with lying to himself. If he didn't do it, he'd let it slide until he could convince himself there was no more point in apologizing at all.

He didn't give himself time to think further. He reached up and rapped his knuckles harshly against the door.

Through the wood and double glazing he heard a muffled voice yell "I'll get it."

The door swung open and a half-naked Max St. John leaned out. He was barefoot and shirtless, a pair of old jeans slung low around his hips. His expression turned sour when he saw Flynn, and his eyes narrowed.

"What do you want?"

"Is Nate here?"

Max leaned his shoulder against the jamb and crossed his arms. He dabbed his tongue out at the scab that stitched his lower lip together.

"I thought he made it pretty clear last night that he's through with you," he said.

"Is he here or not?"

There was a pause while Max looked him up and down. After a second he hitched one shoulder in a dismissive shrug.

"You just missed him," he said. "He went up to the Granshire to smooth things over with Dad. Well, try to. I haven't seen the old man that pissed in years. Not since…. Huh, it was the last time you were there, wasn't it? I wonder what the connection is."

Flynn rubbed his eyes and pressed down with his fingertips hard enough to see whorls of color pop behind the lids. The last thing he wanted was to get into a slagging match with Max at Nate's front door, but it would be *so* easy.

"Just tell him I called."

He turned to leave and got three steps toward the curb before Max answered him.

"You know what? I don't think I will."

Flynn stopped dead. He could feel the old black temper claw at the back of his throat, eager to get away from him again. There had been a time when it had free rein more often than not, and Flynn had rarely gone a weekend without battered knuckles or a black eye. That was years before, though, when he thought every snicker in a pub was aimed at him and he had to answer them with a punch. Before last night he hadn't lost his temper in years, but it apparently wasn't eager to get leashed back in.

Either that or Max just had a unique talent for pissing him off.

"This isn't your business, Max," Flynn said flatly as he turned around. "Just tell Nate I was here."

Max stepped out onto the pavement and pulled the door shut behind him. He shoved his hands in the back pockets of his jeans and lifted his chin.

"Look, we both know Nate's worth it," he said. "Do you really think you are?"

Flynn clenched his jaw and swallowed the bitter taste in his throat. "I think this is none of your business," he said.

"That's where you're wrong," Max said. He stepped forward and smirked at Flynn. "Last night Nate was upset. I was there for him, like I always am, and, well, he upgraded."

"I don't believe you," Flynn said. They both knew he was lying. The only unbelievable thing about Nate and Max was that it hadn't happened before. He twisted his mouth into a mirror of Max's smirk. "Besides, what's the problem? Are you scared he's going to realize you're not his only choice?"

"Hardly. See, the thing is, Nate's a soft touch. You come around and act all sorry, he's going to look at you—old, beat-up, past it—and feel bad. That's going to put a cramp in my life, so why don't you do us both a favor?" He stretched to make up the difference in height between them and leaned in to murmur in Flynn's ear. "Take the money and go. No one wants you here. Hell, no one wants you."

Max leaned back. He looked pleased with himself, and there was still a smirk on his bruised mouth. The ache of his knuckles clued Flynn in that he'd clenched his hands into fists. Maybe he just hadn't punched Max hard *enough*? If he tried again, he might knock the smug out of the entitled prick.

Probably not, though, and it would just upset Nate. About the only other thing that Max and Flynn had in common was that they didn't want that. He took a deep breath and smiled tightly.

"Thing is, Max," Flynn said. "You're a rich kid who's boasting about a guy finally sleeping with him after twenty years. So who is it that wants you around?"

Max's eyes narrowed. His lip curled as he said, "Nate."

"Naw," Flynn said. "Twenty years. That's not want. That's settling."

He turned to walk away. Max grabbed his arm.

"My father—"

"Your father?" Flynn snorted. "I laid you on the floor of your own home, and Teddy's only worry was that I'd damaged the business. You think that's what Nate's mum would be worried about in the same situation?"

They both knew the answer was no. Flynn took his arm back.

"Teddy is paying me to get off the island," he said. "But he doesn't care whether you're here or not. If you really think that's better, that's pathetic."

It was obvious from Max's face—the twist of his mouth and the evasive flicker of his eyes—that Flynn's jab had drawn blood. Somehow that didn't make Flynn feel any better. Max was a lot of things, but he wasn't to blame for any of it. He was just there to take advantage of it. Part of Flynn couldn't blame him for that. If he'd had the chance to take Nate from Max, he would have done it. He still would probably.

With a disgusted noise that might have been for Max or for himself, Flynn headed for the car. He drove away without looking back. Nate still deserved an apology, but it didn't look like he needed one.

Kenny was waiting for him on the narrow seawall at the garage as gulls squabbled within feet of him. He hopped off when he saw Flynn, shoved his hands into the pockets of his overalls, and stood in front of the garage.

The *Delaney and Son* sign hung over his head. Flynn pulled in to the end of the road and stared through the dusty, bug-splattered windshield at the sign mounted over the peeling doors. He wondered how many times his dad had done the same thing and whether the lie of it had made him bitter or if he'd hung on to it in the hope that Flynn would come back one day.

Flynn wrenched the keys out of the ignition and scrambled out of the car. He could taste the salt on the air and the old grease from last night's chips still waiting to be changed. In his head he could see himself there five or ten years down the line. The Granshire cars would roll through whenever they needed a service or an oil change, and every few months he'd see Nate or Max around the town. They'd have a kid together, maybe, or Teddy would have died and Nate would support Max as they took over the Granshire.

It would be a life, whatever it was, and Flynn would just be there. He'd be too old to do rescue eventually, and all he'd have would be cars and a lighthouse no one ever came to. Would he get bitter, he wondered, or would he still hope that Nate would change his mind and come back?

He didn't know which would be worse.

"Fuck it," he said flatly. The sea wind caught his voice and blew it away from his lips.

"Boss?" Kenny said.

Flynn twisted the key to the garage off his key ring and tossed it. Kenny grabbed it out of the air and squinted at it as though he'd never seen it before. He looked back up at Flynn with a baffled expression on his face.

"Finish up on the cars we've already booked in," Flynn said. "Don't take on any more. Once you're done, lock the place up. I'll mail you your last paycheck."

Dismay pulled Kenny's face down. "I'm fired?"

Flynn shrugged. "I'm closing up shop," he said. "I'll give you a good reference. Someone will have to open up here again. Just wrap up existing business, and I'll pay you through to the end of the month."

He could afford it with Teddy's payoff burning a hole in his pocket. Kenny spluttered something about "what, when, why," but Flynn didn't feel like answering. He gave the garage one last look and wondered if he'd miss it.

It felt like he should, but he didn't think he would.

"There's a set of spare keys in my desk," he told Kenny as he climbed back into the driver's seat. "If you want, go up to the lighthouse tomorrow and grab anything you want before St. John chucks it all in the sea."

He left Kenny to gawp after him and turned the car toward the coast. It wouldn't take long to pack up what he needed—a couple of bags of clothes and a box of paperwork—but he'd made up his mind. The last thing he needed was a reason to spend one more day on the island.

It could easily turn into two days. A week. Longer.

Not this time.

CHAPTER TWENTY-THREE

*"You know, your problem is you're too picky.
Maybe if you'd settle for what you can get, you'd be
happier."*

ONCE AROUND the tree the fox chased the rabbit.
Nate pulled a face at his reflection in the mirror
on the back of the door. Nearly forty, and every time
he had to put on a tie, he heard the rhyme his mother
used when she helped him put on his school uniform
for the first time. He finished the knot and smoothed
the tongue down over his chest.

It was his event suit. Professionally unremarkable,
except for the shoes of course. Nate glanced down at
his black rubber toes and let Flynn into his head. The
dry humor and oddly easy laugh. He'd thought a lot
about Flynn Delaney over the years—mostly over the
first twenty-five or so—and he got some things right.

He *did* prefer to top. He cuddled after. That ass was ridiculously good.

But he'd never imagined Flynn having a low, easygoing laugh or that he'd be so earnestly open about who he was.

With a twist of misery in his gut, he wondered what the hell had happened between the steamy intimacy of the morning shower and the prickly anger of the rehearsal dinner. It didn't make any sense, and he didn't have time to puzzle it out.

Nate swallowed the lump in his throat and leaned in toward the mirror. He pulled his hair back from his forehead with one hand and frowned at his temples. Did they go back further than last week? Could he see more skin through the hair? It was an old paranoia—he'd been gray as a teenager and petrified he'd go bald in his twenties—and a fairly good distraction.

He still felt miserable, but it had sunk to the bottom of his brain. Under his vanity, the to-do list for the day, and the fact that he hadn't had coffee yet. By the time it worked its way back up to the top of his priorities, the wedding would be over. He could, with a clear conscience, hole up on the sofa, put on something gory, and debate whether it was too pathetic to let his recuperating mother make him s'mores.

It was, but he was tempted.

Nate let his hair fall back into place, buttoned his jacket, and went downstairs. "Who was that at the door?" He ducked around Max in the kitchen and grabbed a mug from the draining board. The coffee was already brewed and black in the coffee maker, and he poured himself a generous measure. "I was in the shower or I'd have gotten it."

"Nobody," Max said. He shrugged when Nate gave him a skeptical look. "Just the postman. He wanted you to take a package for next door."

"You didn't take it, did you?" Nate asked. He dumped an unhealthy amount of sugar in his cup and avoided looking directly at his mother's disapproving face as he leaned back against the counter. "Last time she called the police on me because I'd been working late and hadn't a chance to drop it off."

Max smirked at him. "You know me and responsibility. They'll try again tomorrow."

He sat down at the table and added a handful of dried figs to the steel-cut oat porridge and a dipper of weird red honey to his tea.

On the other side of the table, Ally put her toast down and gave Nate a concerned look. "Are you okay, sweetheart?" she asked.

"I will be," Nate said. It wasn't as though there were any other option. He slid around the table and leaned down to kiss her cheek. "How are you?"

She flapped her hand. "Fine. I'm fine," she said. "Don't worry about me. I know you liked him."

"We don't know why," Max said. His spoon rattled against the bowl as he stirred the figs in. He shoved a spoonful in his mouth and talked around it. "But we know you liked him."

"Go to hell," Nate said.

"Don't talk with your mouth full," Ally chided at the same time. She picked up a napkin and tossed it across the table. "Wipe your mouth. Your lip's bleeding. I can't believe Flynn just attacked you like that. He seemed like such a nice young man."

Max snorted around the wadded-up napkin pressed to his lip. "Young? Do you need glasses now too, Ally?"

"Don't be cheeky."

Max snorted but subsided. He took the napkin off his lip and checked for blood.

"It's not as though Max didn't start it," Nate said. He shrugged at Max's offended look. "Nobody asked you to get involved, Max."

"I was standing up for you," Max muttered. "You don't know what he's really like. What he's really after."

"If what he's really after is supposed to be you, I'll pour my coffee over you," Nate said. He leaned over the table and stole the bowl of oatmeal from in front of Max. "Go get dressed. I need to check that the hall is ready for the reception before I go up to the folly, so I'll give you a lift."

Max looked grouchy, but he drained his tea and got up from the table. "Trust me. Him dumping you is the best thing that could have happened. Give it a couple of weeks, and you'll see that too."

He stretched, and his shoulder joints popped loudly as he padded into the hall. Nate scowled after him and tossed the bowl in the sink. Oatmeal splattered the stainless steel.

"Don't be mad at Max, love," Ally said. "He means well, and he's your best friend."

"I'm not," Nate said. He looked around at her and found the skeptical expression he expected. "Not really. It's just…."

Ally finished the sentence for him. "Not how you planned it to go with Flynn?"

Actually Nate supposed it was exactly what he'd planned. He sighed and turned the tap on.

"Not how I wanted it to go," he hedged. "But it's not the first time I've been dumped."

"Idiots," Ally said staunchly. "All of them. Max is right. You're better off without him."

It was the sort of thing that mothers always said, and you did your best to believe because it was a lot better than the truth. But it didn't ring true. Without Flynn he just felt... deflated, not better.

"I liked him," he admitted. "It was nice, but I guess it was never going to work out. Max can't stand him, he can't stand Max, and Max has been my best friend since we beat up Michael Frances."

"I remember that," Ally said dryly. "His mother wanted you both sent to therapy."

"She should have sent him to therapy. He ate a frog. It was disturbing." Nate traded his mug for an insulated Granshire travel cup full of black coffee. Best friend or not, he abruptly couldn't stomach the thought of thirty minutes listening to Max say "I told you so." He popped the lid on the cup. "Tell Max I got a call, Mum. I have to go. Love you."

He leaned over and gave her a quick, one-armed hug on his way to the door. Ally caught his arm before he could make his escape and tilted her head back to look up at him.

"No fashion show?" she asked.

Nate glanced down at his suit and realized he didn't particularly care. "Eh, it's just work. This'll do. See you later."

He escaped before Max could catch up with him.

SUNLIGHT STREAMED through the broken stones of the folly and made the swagged lengths of silver fabric glow. Wildflowers spread up the walls in thick, bright ropes of soft color and greenery and dangled from a bower of twisted willow branches that hovered over the structure.

If it had been planned for months, it would have been stunning. For a makeshift design thrown together in a couple of days, it was astonishing. Nate made a mental note—his phone was on theater mode in his pocket and his clipboard tucked under his arm—to send Mahdi some token of appreciation. The man really could do magic with flowers.

Bradley had nearly sweat the starch out of his collar.

"What if she doesn't come?" He stood at the top of the stairs and squinted anxiously down into the parking lot. "What if she's changed her mind?"

Nate tugged Bradley back so he could straighten his collar.

"She's not going to do that."

"My mother—"

"Was your mother when Katie agreed to marry you."

An hour of nervous fiddling had left the silver tie pin grubby with fingerprints. Nate pulled his handkerchief out of his pocket and polished it up quickly. There was a click in the background, and he glanced around. Dale lowered the camera from in front of his face. He'd replaced his surfer-boy shades with blue-tinted glasses that suggested some artistic method was going on. The tint smeared the edges of his black eye enough that Nate wondered how often he'd had to do that.

"Candid shots," Dale explained.

"What if she *has* changed her mind, though?" Bradley insisted.

Nate glanced at his watch. "Someone would have called me by now," he said. "Since they haven't, everything is still on schedule."

It was the truth, but it didn't seem to convince Bradley.

"She loves you," Nate reminded him.

That dragged a sigh out of Bradley. The tension seeped out of him, and before he could work himself up again, the best man stuck his head out the door.

"Time to go," he said.

Nate gave Bradley a friendly pat on the shoulder and watched him disappear inside. He stayed where he was and checked his watch again.

The click made him shoot an annoyed glance at Dale. "I'm not in the wedding party."

Dale shrugged. "You're photogenic, mate. It's the hair."

Nate gave him the finger, which made Dale laugh and lower the camera to hang around his neck. He wandered over to join Nate at the top of the stairs.

"Not so sure she's really going to turn up?" he asked.

Nate gestured for him to lower his voice. "This has not been the smoothest wedding of my career," he muttered back. "If there was ever a day the car would get a flat or attacked by gulls, it's today."

Dale chuckled and wandered into the folly to take pictures of the groom and guests, but he was back by the time the big Granshire estate car pulled into the parking lot. The camera clicked steadily as Katie's dad offered his daughter an arm out of the car. Slight and glowing, she slid out in a cascade of ivory silk and delicate lace. She held a bouquet of wildflowers in one hand, and matching flowers were woven into her veil.

All the disasters that had given Nate the start of an ulcer? None of them dimmed the glowing expression on Katie's face as she climbed the stairs. She paused at the top and took a deep breath with a huge smile on her face as she looked at Nate.

"I'm getting married."

He nodded and waited until she'd gone into the folly and Dale had ducked in discreetly behind her to capture the ceremony. Nate waited until he saw her reach the altar and stand in front of the tall, gray-haired Canon Paisley. As his booming voice filled the space, Nate slipped away and jogged down the steps to head back to the Granshire.

THE CAKE looked elegant but deceptively simple from the outside—three stacked layers of sleek iced tiers decorated with a scatter of effervescent bubble pearls. It sat on a copper platter in the middle of the hall, and Star had promised Nate that it would be stunning when it was cut open. The chef had assured him that everything in the kitchen was in order, and all that was left was for Nate to check the place settings.

He had just sent one of the staff off to calligraph an extra *e* onto a bridesmaid's *Ann* when Max caught up with him.

"I'm sorry," Nate said. He glanced up from his clipboard and shrugged apologetically. "I didn't mean to ditch you this morning, but I just needed some time. You know?"

The bruise on Max's jaw had flowered since the morning. Max rubbed at it with his thumb and shuffled his feet over the polished wooden floor. He'd looked miserable when he came in, and somehow more miserable since he'd gotten an apology.

"Yeah. That's okay," he said. "I had a chat with your mum. Look, about Flynn—"

Nate heaved a sigh. "If this is an 'I told you so,' I don't need to hear it."

"Look, you wanted to know why I hate Flynn, right?" Max asked. "Well, there's something I didn't tell you about that night. You know, when he dragged me back here."

A bad taste scalded the back of Nate's throat. He put his clipboard down on the edge of the table and looked at Max. The question on his tongue wasn't one he wanted to ask, but he had to.

"Did he... did he touch you or something?" he asked. It was strange. Nate remembered how sure he'd been back then that he was old enough, ready for a full sexual relationship. Now, looking back, he'd been an idiot kid. "If he did, I'll—"

"No!" Max blurted out. He shook his head and held both hands up in denial. "God, no. He never. It was what happened after we got back. Dad got called down and I've never seen him so angry, Nate. He hit me."

That caught Nate off guard. Even though he got on fine with Teddy, he knew there'd been tension between Max and his dad over the years. He'd never seen Teddy ever raise his hand to Max, though.

"Why? Because, because you were gay?"

"No. I—" A door opened in the back of the hall and one of the waitstaff dragged in a stack of high-chairs. Max clammed up until the chairs were set out and the guy had left again. Then he took a deep breath and huffed it out. "No. I thought so too, maybe. He dragged me up to my room and locked me in, refused to talk about it, and you know he paid Flynn off to leave."

That had been the gossip. Nate supposed that it had to be right sometimes. He remembered the accusation Dani had spitefully dripped in his ear the other day and wrinkled his nose. It wasn't as bad as taking advantage of a fifteen-year-old boy, but it wasn't a pleasant image.

"You think Teddy fucked Flynn?" he asked.

Max grimaced sourly. "Please stop guessing, Nate."

"Then just tell me."

"Dad wasn't mad because I'd tried to pick up a guy," Max said. He took a deep breath and twisted his mouth like it tasted bad. "He was mad because I'd tried to pick up my brother."

That made no sense at all. For a second. Then Nate's idea of the world twisted twenty degrees and suddenly a lot of things fell into place. Half-heard fragments of gossip that people never finished once they realized he was in the room, the way people had tutted knowingly over the *Delaney and Son* sign, and the vague memory of an unhappy, beautiful mother before she died.

"Oh," He breathed out the word. "That's—"

"Fucked up?" Max said. "Yeah."

Nate bit the side of his lip and hesitated. "You think Flynn knew?"

"Maybe," Max spat out. His mouth twitched and he looked down at his shoes. "I don't know. If he did know, then it's his fault, you know. Not mine."

"Not Teddy's."

Max huffed out a dry laugh and shrugged that off. Just like he always did. He'd always found it easier to just lean into being the fuckup, rather than risk getting mad with his dad. Nate supposed it was a lot easier to judge from the outside, when you didn't get a couple of grand a month in "letting it go" allowance.

"Why are you telling me this now?" he asked.

The silence dragged out for a second as Max licked his lips. "There was no postman this morning," he said. "It was Flynn. I might have told him we fucked."

Nate punched him. He'd not really planned it out. There was just a hot, breathless ball of anger in his chest and he couldn't come up with the words to get it out. His fist caught Max on the cheekbone. The impact rocked Max back on his heels and jabbed a sharp pain through Nate's wrist.

"Fuck." They both said it at the same time. Nate shook his hand out, the pain in his wrist a dull throb, and Max rubbed his eye gingerly.

"Why do people keep hitting me?" Max asked.

"Because you're a dick."

"Still. Use your words."

The "sorry" caught on the tip of Nate's tongue. It was almost genuine—Nate didn't want to fight with his best friend—but not quite. He choked it back and picked up the clipboard instead. It gave his hands something to do other than punching Max again.

"In future, Max, stay right out of my sex life," he said.

Nate angrily ticked one of the to-do boxes and nearly tore through the paper. Max shifted awkwardly in the corner of his eye. He shoved one hand through his thick dark hair and left it stuck up on end.

"You not going to call him?" he asked.

Nate waved the clipboard at him. "I'm working. I can call Flynn later, if I decide I want to."

"That might be too late." Max reached around and shoved his hands into his back pockets. His shirt pulled tight over his shoulders as he rocked back on his heels. It looked cocky, and Nate had known Max long enough to know it was the exact opposite.

"What did you do?"

"… I thought if I called Flynn and told him I'd lied about having sex last night, I'd not have to tell you," Max said quickly. "I called the garage. Apparently he's quit."

"It's his business."

"He's closing up," Max said. He took a deep breath. "The kid that works there said he's leaving the island. Today."

Nate swallowed and looked down at his hands, his fingers tight around the clipboard. He felt a sodden mixture of regret, fear, and denial that wedged up behind his rib cage like papier mache. For the second time that day he didn't know what to say.

"Okay. Well, that's up to him."

"Don't be an idiot." Max yanked the clipboard off him. "Go. Talk to him."

"If he doesn't want to stay—"

"Then say goodbye. Get his number. Sext him. Whatever." Max grimaced at the words he'd said. "Don't just let go. You'll regret it."

"You don't know that."

Max grabbed his shoulder. "I've let a lot of things go." He turned Nate around and gave him a shove toward the door. "I regret most of them. Don't be like me."

"The wedding," Nate protested halfheartedly. He wanted to go—in his mind he was already halfway to the door—but he gestured helplessly at the finery surrounding them. "What if something else goes wrong? Teddy is already angry with me over the other night."

"Do you trust me?" Max asked. Nate gave him a wry look as an answer. It was a stupid question to ask under the circumstances. "I know, I know, you shouldn't. Do you?"

"… yes," Nate admitted.

"Then go. I'll make sure this is the best wedding reception ever. I'll get everyone laid." That stopped Nate in his tracks. He turned to protest, but Max rolled his eyes and hustled him toward the door. "I'm joking. Go. Before I decide my brother is too good for you."

It might have been a mistake, but Nate went anyhow. He reached the pier just in time to see the ferry pulling away.

Fuck.

Nate swung the car into a parking space and scrambled out. He left the keys in the ignition and the door hanging open as he hopped the low wall and ran toward the edge of the pier. The man who'd unhooked the mooring line stood on the back of the ferry, the rope half-wound in his hands, and watched Nate incuriously as he drifted away.

He *could* jump. The idea popped into Nate's head like it was a good one. The ferry had pulled out *that* far and he could probably make it. Even if he didn't, the water would break his fall. On the ferry the deckhand's face brightened with a dark fascination.

Nate chickened out at the last minute and stumbled to a halt at the peeling yellow edge of the pier. The deckhand, who'd apparently been looking forward to him taking a bath, looked disappointed. Sweaty and breathless, Nate doubled over and braced his hands against his knees. He could feel his heart in his throat.

"Fuck," he muttered. Disappointment dragged at him like a weight and he sank down into his haunches. He could call Flynn, but that was too easy to dodge. For both of them.

A slow clap interrupted Nate's mope. He scowled and twisted around to see who'd witnessed his humiliation.

Flynn stood behind him, a wry smirk on his face. "For what it's worth," he said. "I thought you'd make it."

CHAPTER TWENTY-FOUR

"Of course, I knew all about it from the beginning, but I'd not want to gossip."

WHATEVER REACTION Flynn had expected from Nate, he didn't get it.

"You shit!" Nate spluttered as he scrambled back up to his feet. He stalked over to Flynn and jabbed a finger in his chest. "You're supposed to be doing a midday flit. Why aren't you on the ferry?"

There was something oddly endearing about irascible Nate. He was like a cat that had taken offense at its own reflection. Or maybe that was just a side effect of how ridiculously, buoyantly happy Flynn felt right now. It was stupid—for all he knew Nate had just left something in his car—but he couldn't help it.

"I changed my mind."

Nate shoved him. "You're a dick."

"Yeah," Flynn agreed. "I'm your dick, though."

Once, in a bad winter storm, Flynn had dropped out of a helicopter into an ice-cold sea in the hopes he'd find a missing girl. He could have died, or been seriously injured, but he'd never been afraid. The risks had been weighed and accepted before he'd even gotten on the copter. This, a halfhearted, still deniable admission of feelings—maybe—was unknown territory, and he held his breath as he waited for Nate's response.

"Who else would have you?" Nate groused. Then he grinned and pulled Flynn into an eager, clumsy kiss that mashed lips and banged their teeth together. His hand cupped Flynn's jaw and then slid backward so he could twist his fingers in Flynn's hair.

Flynn dragged him closer. He bit the curve of Nate's lower lip and slid his tongue through the gasp into the wet heat of Nate's mouth. The easy way that Nate's body fit against him ran hunger through Flynn, an eager tickle of interest in his balls.

Someone whooped.

In his arms Nate flinched and started to draw back. Flynn didn't let him. "Fuck 'em," he mouthed against Nate's lips and dipped Nate back over his arm. A gurgle of startled laughter escaped Nate and he grabbed Flynn's shoulders for support, his fingers twisted into his T-shirt, but he went back to kissing.

Finally, breathless and hard under his jeans, Flynn had to put Nate back on his feet. Or tried to. Nate sprawled against him, his arms draped over Flynn's shoulder and his face buried in the side of his throat. He was laughing.

"What?" Flynn asked as he slid his fingers through Nate's hair in a lazy caress. He felt Nate's smile against his neck.

"Just wondering what you'd have done if I'd jumped."

"Jumped in after you and fished you out of the water."

"Hey!" Nate lifted his head to frown at Flynn. "I could have made it."

Flynn raised his eyebrows skeptically, but gave in to the notion. "I'd have fucking swum after you," he said. It started out as a joke, but he realized he meant it. Maybe not literally, but... "I'm done playing stupid games."

His stomach dropped for a second as Nate stepped back from him. What if Nate wasn't? What if he'd run down to the pier and chased after the ferry to tell Flynn he wanted to keep things casual? Nate tilted his head to the side, one hand raised to shade his eyes against the sun.

"I didn't fuck Max," he said.

Flynn let out a relieved sigh. He'd not been going to ask, convinced that he didn't want to know the answer. It turned out he did.

"It wouldn't matter if you had," he said. That was true, but so was what he said next. "I'm glad you didn't, though. Come home with me."

He could see the "yes" curve over Nate's lips, but it didn't quite make it out. Nate bit his lower lip and pulled a reluctant face.

"We need to talk."

"I know." Flynn put his fingers under Nate's chin and tilted his head back for another kiss. This one was soft, his lips just brushed against Nate's. "We can talk in bed."

Nate tried not to smile, Flynn could actually see him fight the curve of his lips, but he couldn't help it. He hooked his fingers into the waistband of Flynn's jeans, the brush of his knuckles against bare skin doing all sorts of things to Flynn.

"I suppose we could," he said. "Later."

The cramp of want that hit Flynn's groin made the whole bed idea a bit more pressing. He took a deep breath, reminded himself he wasn't twenty anymore, and stepped back.

"Go lock your car up," he said. "I'll drive."

Nate snorted. "I could just follow you."

"With our luck?" Flynn said as he slung an arm over Nate's shoulder. "You'd run into a misplaced bride on the moors, and I'd find a lost hiker on the cliff while I was waiting for you. No, we'll take my car."

After a second Nate rolled his eyes. "Maybe you have a point," he admitted.

A SLICK film of sweat cooled between their bodies. It was salty against Flynn's tongue as he kissed Nate's bony shoulder. He sprawled on top of Nate, sated, smug, and a little too lazy to move just yet. His cock was still in Nate's ass. The twitched aftershocks of orgasm sent electric shocks of pleasure/pain through him.

Nate reached back and curled his hand around the nape of Flynn's neck. "I had a whole speech."

"Hmm?"

This time when Nate shifted under him the prickle shock down his overstimulated cock was closer to pain than pleasure. Nate propped himself up on one elbow and looked around at Flynn.

"On the ferry," he said. "I had a whole speech ready."

"It's a twenty minute trip. What would you have done if I'd said thanks but no thanks?"

"… pretend to have been sleepwalking."

Flynn snorted and dropped a kiss on the corner of Nate's mouth. "I had a speech too, you know."

He lifted his weight off Nate and his soft cock, the shaft slick with come and lube, slid out of him. Once he wasn't pinned down anymore Nate stretched, all bones and elegance, and rolled over. He sat up and grinned at Flynn.

"Go on, then," he said. "Let's hear it."

Flynn leaned back against the pillows. Out on the balcony Nate the seagull was a fluffy ball with a resentful, beady eye trained on them. It probably wasn't the time to introduce Nate to his namesake, Flynn decided.

"Nate," he said earnestly as he held out a hand. Nate took it and crawled onto his lap, his cock pressed soft and heavy against Flynn's stomach. "Do you want me to stay?"

Nate braced his hands against the headboard and leaned in to kiss Flynn. His lips moved in a "yes." Then he leaned back and smirked. "Mine was better."

"Prove it."

"The moment's passed," Nate said loftily.

"Paraphrase," Flynn told him.

Nate paused for a second and then sat back against Flynn's legs. He felt the hard line of scar tissue against his inner thigh and started to lift his weight back off. Flynn caught his hips and pulled him back down.

"It's okay. It doesn't hurt."

That wasn't entirely true. He could feel Nate's weight through the scar tissue like pins and needles, but he liked the view enough to put up with it.

"Okay. Well, you're rubbish at being a bad boyfriend," Nate said. He ran his fingers over Flynn's stomach as he talked, patterns that made the ridges of muscle twitch. "So maybe you could just... drop the bad?"

Flynn sat up and wrapped his arms around Nate's waist. His hands cupped Nate's ass. "You want me to be your boyfriend?"

"I guess."

Flynn picked Nate up and dumped him onto the bed. He grinned at Nate's startled, indignant squawk as he hit the sheets. "I'll think about it."

He left Nate halfheartedly cursing him on the bed and went into the shower. A flick of the taps turned them on and he stood under the water, his head tilted back so it hit his face like rain. He waited it for it to wash the stupid happy away with the sweat and the sex.

No such luck.

It felt strange. Flynn wasn't used to being happy. It wasn't that he'd spent his life as a miserable bastard; he'd been fulfilled, content, smug, and frequently sated. Happy sometimes, on afternoons spent in bed or in the first flush of a relationship when the world seemed possible. He'd always known it wouldn't last, though. His dad's gruff misery in the back of his head always there to weigh him down.

Life's not about being happy.

This felt different. He felt....

"What the fuck!"

The blurted exclamation from the bedroom punctured Flynn's mood. He could feel it sink down into his gut, almost hear his dad's "told ya" in his ear, as the water circled the drain between his feet. It had been nice, Flynn supposed, while it lasted. He turned the water off, grabbed a towel, and went back into the bedroom.

Nate waved Teddy's creased check at him. Ah, that. Flynn grimaced. He should have known Teddy would manage to screw this up for him.

"I didn't go," Flynn said. He wiped the towel over his head and hung it around his shoulder. "I'm not taking his money."

"Are you mad?" Nate asked. "Did you misread the zeros?"

Flynn started to laugh. He had to sit down on the bed, and laughed until his stomach hurt. Once he could stop he sprawled backward into the sheets. It pretty much undid the bath, but he didn't mind the smell of sex and Nate and sweat that surrounded him.

"I figured you'd be mad I even thought about taking money to leave."

Nate snorted. "It's a lot of money," he said. The bed shifted under Flynn. Without looking up he could tell that Nate had sat down on the bed. "Did you turn this down for me? Because I don't know if I'm worth it."

He was. Flynn grinned at the thought, at how sure he was of it, but kept it to himself. That would just freak Nate out, and it wasn't the only reason he'd driven back off the ferry. He reached out and found Nate's arm, his skin warm against Flynn's wet fingers.

"C'mere." Nate resisted for a second and then crawled over to lie next to Flynn. The usual charm was gone from his face and he looked worried. "Do you remember my dad?"

Nate wrinkled his nose. "I don't—"

"Do you?"

"Yes."

"What did you think of him?"

"He was an adult. I didn't…." Nate trailed off and shrugged.

"Yeah, well, he was a miserable bastard," Flynn said. Guilt pinched. It was a familiar jab, in an old sore spot. He took a deep breath. "Dad wasn't a bad man. He made sure I had clothes, food, a roof over my head. He never beat me."

Nate rested his chin on Flynn's shoulder. "Did he know?" Flynn couldn't help the sudden tension that went through him. Nate must have felt it too, because he smoothed a hand over Flynn's chest. "Max told me. Today. I didn't know before."

"Dad did. I think sometimes he almost forgot." He paused for a second as he remembered his dad nodding approval of a haircut and the patience he'd shown when he taught Flynn how to fix his first engine. It had never lasted long, though. "Then he'd look at something he bought with Teddy's hush money and he had to remember. The money's tempting, but I'm not going to live like that."

Nate tugged at his chest hair. "So even if I'd not come to find you, you'd have stayed?"

"I'd have come to find you," Flynn said. He wove his fingers through Nate's and admitted, "Might not have hung around if you weren't interested. I'd still have wiped my ass on Teddy's check, though."

Nate laughed, and then winced. "You might want to rethink that," he said as he turned his face into Flynn's neck. His breath felt cold against Flynn's wet skin. "Between us and all the screwups last week, I might not have a job next week."

"Don't worry about it," Flynn said. He stared up into the peak of the sloped roof. "Teddy isn't going to take his problems with me out on you."

"I hope not," Nate said.

He seemed to think it was a prediction, not a promise.

YOU COULD see the lighthouse from Teddy's office. Flynn stood in front of the window with his arms crossed and watched clouds scud across the stark blue sky. He heard the door open behind him but didn't bother to look around.

"Mr. Delaney."

"I've got a name."

"I know."

Flynn turned away from the window. He got out of the way as Teddy walked around the desk and lowered himself carefully into the large, well-padded office chair. In an office that was all shelves of hard-backed books and big, dark pieces of furniture that glowed with wax polish, the space-age looking chair was out of place. Flynn supposed it was easier on old bones.

"What do you want?" Teddy asked. His back was very straight as he looked across the desk at Flynn. He couldn't have missed the check, set neatly in the middle of the expanse of green leather, but he didn't acknowledge it with even a twitch of his eye.

"You left something at mine. I thought I'd bring it back."

Teddy finally acknowledged the check with a brief downward glance. "You should reconsider."

The corner of Flynn's mouth twitched. He rubbed the taut muscle with his thumb and nodded over Teddy's shoulder to the window. "That lighthouse was my dad's middle finger to you, you know." He shook his head ruefully. "Everything he did was, I think. His whole life revolved around him hating you."

"Because of you."

"No. It was the money," Flynn said. "You bought and paid for him. He could never forget that, and he didn't want you to, either. Not that you gave a damn."

Teddy reached for the slip of paper, thought better of it, and drew his hand back. "I don't see why this has suddenly become relevant."

"Your money's poison," Flynn said. "I'm not taking it."

"Fine. Show yourself out. Tell Nathan to see me on Monday."

"Are you going to fire him?"

Under hooded lids, Teddy's eyes flashed angrily and his nostrils flared around a snort. "How is that your business?"

"I just wanted to let you know, I don't care," Flynn said. "Fire him if you want. It won't change anything, I make good enough money. He's smart."

The chair creaked as Teddy leaned back. He considered Flynn with something like interest. The first he'd even shown. His finger tapped idly against the desk.

"I could blackball your business. Make sure no one on the island would let you touch their car."

"I'm a mechanic, I can work anywhere," Flynn said. "It would probably be easier for Nate to get another job if we did leave Ceremony. You're the one whose life would come apart, Teddy."

The snort of laughter was incredulous. "I'm fond of the boy," he said. "But he's just another employee, in the end."

"Liar."

"I beg your pardon?"

"You heard me." Flynn crossed his arms. "Do you think I'm the only person in this room the gossips turn over, Teddy? I've heard it all. So think about it, before you do anything stupid. If I go, Nate goes. That means Ally goes too, and who will keep you company at Christmas then? Oh, and do you think Max would be far behind? I might think he's an idiot, but he loves Nate and you're not exactly a good father."

The finger had stopped tapping. "Max knows what side his bread is buttered."

"We'll see won't we, if you fire Nate." Flynn nodded briskly. "Good night, Mr. St. John."

He turned to go.

"That's it?" Teddy asked his back suspiciously. "No threats? No blackmail? No gloating?"

Flynn paused and looked down at his feet, scarred work boots battered and grubby against the rich carpet.

"I don't like you, and I resent the hell out of you," Flynn admitted. "But I'm done playing my dad's game. I don't know what your problem with me is, it's not like anyone would care about your bastard, but if you stay out of my life? I'll stay out of yours."

He waited. When there was no answer he shrugged and headed for the door. Teddy's voice stopped him on the threshold.

"Do you want to know what my problem is?"

Flynn looked back. "Knock yourself out."

The check was gone. Teddy had half turned in his chair so he could stare toward the mute, one-fingered accusation of the lighthouse.

"You're an eternal reminder I behaved badly," Teddy said quietly. "And I am a petty enough man to resent you for it."

It was a statement that invited an answer, a discussion of their problems. Flynn took a deep breath and licked his lips.

"Get over it," he said.

NATE THE seagull was eating chips off the grass when Flynn got back to the lighthouse. He gave Flynn the accusing, beady eye of a gull that had missed breakfast and flapped off to a rock to finish his greasy largesse. Flynn left him to it and followed the trail around to the strip of land behind the lighthouse.

"Teddy was fine," he said.

Nate glanced up at him. He'd left the jacket off and not bothered to tuck his shirt in, or put the tie back on. He looked like a groom's man that had gotten lucky.

"Are you sure about this?" he asked. "It really is a lot of money."

Flynn sat down next to him and slung an arm over his shoulder. "Well, you *are* officially my most expensive boyfriend ever," he said. Nate groaned and dropped his head back against Flynn's arm. "I figure if I let you Airbnb this place to bridal parties we can make it back, though."

It was somewhere between funny and insulting how quickly that prospect perked Nate up. "Really?" he said.

"Why not?" Flynn shrugged. "Of course, it means I'll need somewhere to stay when it's in use."

The smile that slid over Nate's face was that sly, foxy one that had lured Flynn into his misbegotten bad-boyfriend plot in the first place. He thought he might love that smile.

"My neighbor is going to hate you," Nate said wickedly. "With any luck she'll move."

Flynn curled his arm around Nate's neck and dragged him closer. He slanted a kiss over his jaw, the stubble rough against his lips, and up to the corner of Nate's mouth.

"No more bad boyfriend," he said.

Nate paused for a second and then leaned into the kiss. He cupped the side of Flynn's face in one hand. "I can live with that."

Just another day at the office.

For some people that means spreadsheets, and for others it's stitching endless hems. For Jacob Archer a day at the office is stealing proprietary information from a bioengineering firm for a paranoid software billionaire. He's a liar and a thief, parlaying a glib tongue and a facile conscience into a lucrative career. He just has one rule—never get involved with a mark.

Well, had one rule. To be fair, though, Simon Ramsey is dark, dangerous, and has shoulders like a Greek statue. Besides, it's not as though Jacob's even really stealing from Simon... just his boss and his brother-in-law. Simon didn't buy that excuse either after he caught Jacob breaking into the company's computer network.

That would have been that—one messy breakup, one ticket to Bali booked—but it turns out that the stolen information is worth more than Jacob thought. With his life—and his ribs—threatened, Jacob needs Simon to help him out. Or maybe he just needs Simon.

www.dreamspinnerpress.com

CHAPTER ONE

IT WAS past midnight when the small fleet of black vans bumped over the tire shredders and pulled up to the security booth. The bored security guard glanced up, back down at his graphic novel, and waved them through.

Syntech was Dyno-clean's biggest company, so they scheduled them in for a double-shift booking at the end of the night. Twice a month they doubled up the crew to make sure everything was spit polished and shipshape. It was as tightly organized as a military campaign.

Down in the parking garage, Jacob hopped out of the back of the van. He yawned until his jaw cracked, blinked back tears, and stretched his arms to work the kinks out of his spine. They'd been working eight hours already—four office buildings and the renovated dorm at the university—and the smell of disinfectant felt like it had soaked into his pores.

It had worn on the rest of the cleaning crew as well, especially with Jacob doing his bit to stir up existing tensions. So far there had been one accusation of sexism, a fight bad enough that the two cleaners couldn't be assigned the same floor, and everyone was quietly resentful toward the student who'd been caught reading his textbook instead of working. It had been two jobs since anyone had said a casual word or cracked a joke.

"Jacob!" the crew supervisor snapped, crooking a finger at him. He sauntered over, and she shoved a work order against his chest with stiff fingers. "You're doing the floors on the executive levels. Do a good job this time. You're still on a warning after what happened at the university last month, and if your next performance review doesn't improve…."

"I remember. I'm out of a job," he said. "Don't worry. I'll be on the top of my game tonight."

She squinted at him dourly, but he gave her his best trustworthy look. After a second she hmphed and stepped backward.

"I'm keeping my eye on you," she said. "Now get back to work."

He hummed contentedly to himself as he did what he was told. Everything was going according to plan.

THE HUMMING had turned into a tuneless whistle as Jacob stepped off the lift, dragging the buffer with him. He unwound the cord, snapped it to make it snake over the floor, and plugged it in next to one of the sullenly growing potted plants. The buffer juddered to life and skidded over the floor. He grabbed it by one hand and dragged it down the hall behind him, letting it swing carelessly back and forth over the floor. As he walked he bit the coating of glue and paint from his hand. The peeled-off strips of it went into his pocket.

The top floors were usually Naya's realm. She was presentable and polite, in case anyone was working late and she ran into them. And she spent all her time day-dreaming about her wedding, so she didn't mind the boring jobs. The last few weeks, though, Jacob had noticed her creaming her hands every time she got into the van. Not with the cheap, greasy stuff the rest of them used either. Something from a department store.

She wanted nice hands for the big day. Not the raw, peeling mess of contact dermatitis she saw every time Jacob peeled his gloves off.

Jacob dropped the buffer off outside Nora Clayton's office and kept walking. He unzipped the top of his boiler suit, squirmed out of it, and let the sleeves dangle. It had been a while since he'd had to actually work on-site, but luckily it looked like he hadn't become any less of an asshole.

His brain ticked through how long his manipulation of the cleaning crew's various resentments and tensions would buy him before someone came to check on how he was doing up here. Gun would be slacking, trying to steal five minutes to read his textbook, Anna would be crying in the toilet, and Jim would be trying to run interference with Ella. Add twenty minutes to the hour it usually took Ella to get up there and subtract ten because she didn't trust Jacob to do a good job.

He pulled his T-shirt up and untaped the stripped-down electronics from his stomach. Plenty of time for what he needed to do.

Something jabbed at the back of his brain—a nasty little squirm of doubt that he couldn't quite pin down. He hastily flipped through the plan in his head to see if he'd missed anything. It seemed solid, but that bastard qualm kept squirming. With nothing to pin it on, he squelched the thought and loped down the tiled floor to the president's office.

The door wasn't locked, which was sweet. It was cold inside and the heat that built over the day had leeched out through the span of glass that took up the external wall.

Jacob let himself in, nudged the door shut behind him, and headed to the desk. It was slick, polished glass, and the keyboard flickered to life in squares of light on the surface as he touched it. Folding one leg under him as he sat down, his heel pressing against the back of his knee, he strung the code breaker together with confident fingers.

He couldn't make one himself—social programming was his specialty—but he understood how they worked. Once it was hooked up, the touchpad flickered dimly to life. He reached under the desk and plugged it into the hard drive.

While it worked he sat back in the chair. The leather settled under him as he chewed absently at the skin around his thumb. He'd had to get himself an honest job because security at Syntech was good enough to have plugged his usual sources of information—the careless e-mails, the social network logins, the chatty tech in the coffee queue.

If the computer security was that watertight….

He took a deep breath that tasted of ozone and Amouage and swiveled the chair around to face the glass. There were marks that shouldn't be on that sort of conspicuous display of prestige—linen-weft smudges and a few smears of hair gel stickiness where Porter had forgotten it wasn't the sort of wall you leaned against.

If gut instinct had been enough, Jacob would have been out of work a month before. Porter was cutthroat, but he didn't play games, and industrial espionage was all about games. Besides, Porter was arrogant. He listened to maybe two people in the company. Not the sort who'd admit they needed to steal someone else's idea.

Jacob stretched his legs out in front of him and watched the reflection of his sneakers move in the glass. Or he was wrong and Porter was a thief. Either way Jacob got paid.

It was Christmas out there in the dark. Jacob could see the red and green glitter of lights strung in the street and bright in the windows of office buildings. The feeling in the back of his brain poked at him again, but he shoved it down firmly and bit through the tag of skin he'd been worrying. The copper tang of blood was sharp against his tongue, and he pulled a face.

Bad old habit. He thought he'd broken it years ago.

The stop clock in his head ticked down the minutes as he waited. He wasn't at the panic point, but he was just about to start fidgeting when the code breaker hiccuped behind him. He dug his heel into the carpet and swung around, and his mouth quirked with satisfaction as the narrow monitor flickered to life.

"There you go," he said approvingly. He laced his fingers together and bent them back to pop his knuckles—another bad habit, but not one he'd ever bothered to try to break. He tapped quickly on the glass, and his knuckles broke the beams of light as he typed in commands. "Now let's see what we've got."

On the floors below, thirty-two machines obediently allowed Porter's computer to access their hard drives and the thirty-two trojans that Jacob had spent the last two months installing handed over the data they'd mined. The packets streamed onto Porter's computer and immediately bounced to Jacob's private server as the percentage bars flickered over the screen.

Jacob watched the flickering data intently and occasionally moved his gaze up to the door as he heard a noise in the hall. His foot juddered nervously, heel twitching, as the waiting started to work at his nerves with all the things that could go wrong.

The final byte disappeared off Porter's monitor. Jacob hissed out a sigh of relief between his teeth and stripped his equipment out of the computer system. The trojans went first, politely self-destructing with a minimum of damage, and then he wiped the current session from the computer menu.

He yanked the code breaker out of the computer as it shut down, broke it apart, and shoved it into the pockets on his boiler suit. No point in wasting time taping it back to his stomach. They'd never been searched on their way out.

The computer shut itself down, the soft glow on the monitor cut off, and Jacob tugged a ragged, bright-orange cloth out of his pocket. He scuffed his fingerprints off the glass. Not that they'd help anyone find him. His prints weren't on any database out there, as far as he knew. He'd just prefer to keep it that way.

A shrill rattle made him flinch and taste his heart in the back of his throat. He pushed back from the desk and his hip hit the chair. Then he realized it was his phone.

"Shit," he muttered.

Jacob took a deep breath, exhaled the panic, and grabbed the phone out of his pocket. He slid the chair back into place as he answered it.

"Hey."

"Hey, babe," Simon's familiar, rough voice drawled in his ear. He was gorgeous in person—all dark, controlled male beauty and long, muscled lines—but his voice hinted at how dangerous he was. "You free tomorrow?"

Liquid heat spread through Jacob's muscles, a cramp of want squeezed his balls like a hand, and that bastard itch popped back into his brain. There it was—what he'd forgotten about, or what he should have forgotten about by then.

"I thought you were busy?" he stalled.

Simon laughed—a short, cat-rough rub of sound. "Playing hard to get?"

"Doesn't sound like me," Jacob said. He should have started a fight and hammered in the crack that he could blame the breakup on. Not that he'd ever actually broken up with anyone—the last relationship he had that lasted longer than a week was his short experiment in being straight with his third-grade girlfriend—but he understood the principle. Except what came out of his mouth was "I've got a few things to clear up in the morning, but I'm all yours from eleven. I thought you were going to look at buying another rusty ornament for your drive?"

He shoved the door open and stepped out into the hall as he tucked the phone against his shoulder and gave the handle a quick polish. Better to break up in person. Easier to salt the ground so Simon would never want to think about him again. It was a smooth excuse—good enough that he felt a pinch of regret at Simon's hate—but he'd never been any good at lying to himself.

Professional liars never were. That itch was a smug little shit when you got right down to it. Jacob tried to ignore it as he headed back toward the abandoned buffer.

"Nora said they had a '69 Firebird," Simon said. "I asked them to send me pictures, though, and it wasn't. So I canceled, and I'm going to have to take Nora to the Cars-and-Coffee cruise in Austin so she knows what a Firebird looks like."

The elevator dinged. Jacob cursed to himself. They weren't meant to have phones, and recently fired employees *did* get searched.

"Simon, I gotta—"

"What the fuck?" Simon's mutter interrupted him. At the same moment, Jacob saw the buffer jerk backward as someone got hold of the lead and tugged on it. His stomach knotted with a sick premonition.

"I'm sorry." It was probably the most honest thing he'd said in a year.

"Sorry?" Simon said. He sounded distracted already. "What for? Look if you can't make it—"

The lead dropped, and Simon stalked around the corner, jacket tucked back behind the holster of his gun. He looked good, even under the lights that sapped the color from his tan, and then he saw Jacob, and he just looked… confused.

"This," Jacob said.

He turned on his heel and ran. The rubber soles of his sneakers squeaked on the tiles, and panic scattered his thoughts as he tried to plan on the run. He could hear Simon sprint after him, his boots heavy on the tiles and getting closer.

"Jacob!"

The first time they met, Jacob had seen Simon beat three men bloody. It had been hot at the time—and it wasn't like the gay-bashing assholes hadn't deserved it—but not so much right now. Legs burning, Jacob pushed himself to keep moving—hard enough that he nearly overshot the door to the janitor's closet. He swung himself to a stop and grabbed at the door to get it open. It was metal and heavy enough that Jacob could feel the weight of it in his shoulder. Out of the corner of his eye, he could see Simon grab for him.

Shoving the door open, Jacob fell through—just dodging Simon's grab—and kicked it shut. He put his shoulder to it and braced his feet on the ground. Simon hit it hard enough to make Jacob slide on the floor and shoved the door open an inch. His sharp, handsome face was bleak with rage. Jacob managed to get it shut again.

"You think you can hide?" Simon snarled and bashed his fist against the door. "Who do you work for?"

Jacob fumbled a screwdriver out of his pocket and wedged it under the door as a block.

"That's confidential," he panted. "Simon, fuck, this wasn't meant to happen."

"No. I'm sure you meant to rob us and go, not get caught." There was something thin as a razor in Simon's voice. It made Jacob flinch. He felt an odd ache in his stomach that wasn't exactly fear or exertion. Whatever it was, it wasn't useful.

"Well, yeah," he said. "But I meant, you… and me."

The door jolted against Jacob's shoulder and made him flinch.

"You lying little fucker." There was the thump of a fist hitting the door. "There's nowhere to go. Come out, stay in. It's not going to change anything."

Jacob wedged the screwdriver that bit farther in and scrambled to his feet. He still couldn't breathe, and there was a stitch cutting into his ribs. Fuck, he really needed to start working out.

"Good to know."

He could hear Simon on the phone outside, snarling orders and demanding answers. While he was busy doing that, Jacob stripped out of his boiler suit. Simon was probably right. After all if anyone knew the security weakness of the building, or lack thereof, it would be the security consultant.

Shit.

As he dropped into a squat and worn denim stretched over his knees, Jacob shoved his hands into his hair and tried to think. There was a freight elevator shaft behind the wall of the closet. If he had a crowbar, he could pull the bricks out of the wall, crawl through, and... fall to his death, probably. He wasn't Tom Cruise.

"Damn it, damn it, damn it." Jacob clenched his fist in his hair as though he could pull an idea out of his head through his scalp. Why did everything *always* go wrong for him?

Outside he heard Simon yell at someone to "get a goddamn Masterkey to breach the door if you need it." Jacob lifted his head and bit his lower lip. It wasn't necessarily a *good* idea, but it was the only one he had, and there wasn't time to wait for inspiration.

He gave himself a second and squeezed his eyes shut as he waited for some—for any—other idea.

His phone was still lying where he'd dropped it as he fell through the door. He picked it up, wiped the dust on his sleeve, and tapped the screen with his thumb. It rang twice, and then the operator picked up.

"Hello, could you please state the nature of your emergency," a light, faintly accented voice—Wisconsin, Jacob guessed—said.

"I… look… this is embarrassing," Jacob muttered. He shifted away from the door to mute his voice. "I've had an argument with my boyfriend, and he's *really* angry. I've locked myself in an office and…."

He didn't deliberately put the accent on. He just picked up the inflections as she dropped them. Instinct or habit.

"We're at work." He answered the operator's questions quickly. At the same time, he'd pulled the code breaker out of his pocket, tore it apart, and ground the pieces underfoot. The waste made him twitch. "In Syntech. It's just off Beagle Road? He found out I lied to him about something, and I've never seen him like this."

Outside the door Simon hammered against the metal and cursed flatly. The operator murmured reassuringly and promised they'd be there soon. Jacob hung up on her, called his lawyer, and sat down on the floor with his back against the boast wall that butted onto the elevator shaft.

Leaning his head back against the dusty plaster, he listened to the ringtone and the bang of Simon's fist on the door. It had been *one* stupid decision in the middle of a well-planned job, and look where it got him. The minute it started to get tangled, he should have ditched.

Too cocky for that, or too greedy, and look what it got him.

Someone lifted the phone and mumbled something down the line.

"Hey, Allison," Jacob said. "I might need you to get me out of jail. In about half an hour."

CHAPTER TWO

TWO POLICE officers walked Jacob off Syntech property to a waiting taxi. Apparently, without evidence of wrongdoing, that was the most they could do. Simon stood in the window of his office, jaw clenched until his skull ached, and watched through the smoked glass as they crossed the carpark.

At the fence the blonde policewoman handed over Jacob's shabby, searched backpack and said something to him. Then she and her partner turned and headed back toward the building. Left on the property line, Jacob hitched his bag over his shoulder and looked up at the window. Simon had never brought him there, but apparently Jacob did better background checks than he did.

After a second, Jacob shrugged one shoulder and got into the taxi.

Simon pulled his phone out of his pocket, flicked it on, and speed dialed the security team.

"Murtagh? Keep a detail on him," he said. "I want to know where he goes, who he speaks to, and for how long. I don't want him without eyes on him from now until I tell you different."

He got a grunt in answer, and then Murtagh hung up. The taxi pulled away from the curb, and five minutes later, a Toyota pulled out of a nearby street and fell in behind them.

Simon dropped the phone back in his pocket.

His stomach was in a knot of closely collared rage, and the familiar itch of frustrated self-loathing crawled down his back. He should have known better. The minute he risked trusting someone—something— outside of the few family and friends he still had, it was just a matter of time until they let him down, or he let them down.

The anger slipped his leash, and he turned around, kicked the chair, and sent it spinning over the office. It hit the wall, bounced, and landed on its side. Still fuming he sent the bin flying after it. The thin metal canister buckled against the wall and spilled out crumpled paper and a Red Bull can.

It didn't really help. He wanted the solid pain of broken bones and split knuckles, the satisfaction of turning his feelings into blood and bruises. Not Jacob. The fucker might deserve it, but Simon couldn't bring himself to imagine it. Just a nonspecific face and nonspecific fists—the sort he never had trouble finding.

"I didn't know you were seeing anyone," Devon said from the door. He'd been polite enough to wait for the tantrum to be over, even though, as CEO of Syntech and Simon's brother-in-law—or whatever you called someone after their wife, your sister, died—he had grounds to interrupt.

Simon gave Dev an impatient look. "That's your takeaway? We've either had a thief with free rein of your office, or your security consultant locked a cleaner in the janitor's closet. And you want to ask about my dating life?"

Dev shrugged, straightened a chair, and spun it around so he could straddle it backward. His heavy shoulders bulked under his shabby band shirt as he crossed his arms over the back of the chair. The watch on his wrist was classy. The scars on his knuckles weren't.

"One is related to the next, isn't it?" he said. "According to Dyno-clean, Jacob Archer has been working with them the last seven months. Five months ago one of their cleaners quit, and they moved him onto our rotation. He passed their background checks, never raised a flag until tonight. Maybe he just didn't want to tell you he scrubbed our toilets for a living?"

"You think that's something I'd care about?"

"Not the right question. Do you think he cared about it?"

Simon made himself slouch and tried to fool his wire-twitching nerves into thinking he was relaxed. Despite his best efforts, his fingers drummed nervously against the desk.

"I don't think Jacob would know shame if someone express shipped him a packet of it," he said. An odd pop of inappropriate fondness made its way into his voice. He swallowed it and shook his head. "Under the circumstances I know it's a lot to ask. But trust me, we need to find out what he's done."

Devon waved his hand. "Don't be an idiot," he said. "Of course I trust you. I've already got people stripping my computer, and I assume you've got a team on Jacob?"

A bit of the raw tension in Simon's spine eased. After he came back from Afghanistan the last time, he was a mess. He wouldn't have taken a risk on himself if he'd been Devon, and with Becca a year dead, Devon didn't owe him anything. The last thing he wanted to do was let the man down.

It was a weird thought, considering how much they'd hated each other back in their hometown.

"Did he ever ask you anything that seemed suspicious?" Dev asked. "Even if only in hindsight."

Simon snorted and pushed himself up out of the chair. Energy itched under his skin. His body was convinced that being *this* angry meant a fight.

"I know how not to talk about my work," he said. "And he never asked me anything about here, not even if I'd be leaving for the night. He was in my house, though. I'll need to sterilize, see if there was anything he could have accessed."

Dev scratched his jaw and rasped his nails through dirty-blond stubble. "Okay," he said. "There's nothing we can do until we find out what he actually did. Go home, check the house, let me know if you find *anything*. And get some sleep."

The suggestion riled Simon's temper and dragged a snarl out of him. "I'm fine."

"Well, I'm your employer," Dev said as he stood up. He wasn't short—although the seventeen-year-old prick Simon had been insisted on snarking that he was short*er*—but the muscle made him look it. "And when there's something we can do, I want you in a state to do it."

It went against the grain to admit it, but that made some sense. Simon pinched his nose between his thumb and forefinger. He could feel the tug of the whiskey in the drawer. It promised a dreamless sleep if he just took a swig. Or two. Or more, since he'd never been a quitter.

"Fine," he said flatly. "I do need to strip the house down, anyhow. Make sure he didn't plant anything. What about you?"

Dev gave a tight grin that crinkled the corners of his eyes. "Like I tell Callie, do as I say not as I do. And you're not my kid, so you don't even get to argue with me for three hours and call me a hypocrite."

"She could be worse," Simon defended his niece out of habit. He was the uncle she'd seen at Christmas every other year before her mother died. So he curried favor by always being on Callie's side. "My sister would have just climbed out a window and gone to do whatever it was anyhow."

"Callie wouldn't let me off that easy. She wants me to admit I'm wrong," Dev said. The digression was a welcome distraction, but it couldn't last long. The smile faded from Dev's face, and he glanced down at himself. There was a smear of something tomato based on his T-shirt, and he picked at it with his thumbnail. "Speaking of Callie, could you sort out an Uber to go and pick up one of my shirts from her? I'm going to need to call the board."

Dev never sounded enthusiastic about talking to the board, and he sounded less enthusiastic than usual. Guilt hooked its claws into Simon's gut and shredded what should have been numb scar tissue by then if the world were just. He jerked his chin down in a short, hard acknowledgment of the request and pulled the door open.

"I am sorry." He ground the word out past a clenched jaw as Dev crossed the threshold. "If you want to me to resign…."

Dev thumped him in the arm with a loosely closed fist. "Shut up, Saint Simon," he said. The decades-old nickname—it predated Dev dating Becca, back when they'd been allowed to hate each other—made Simon scowl, despite his best efforts to look repentant. "Look, I'm not the security expert, and if they tell me different, I'll be happy to string you up like a piñata, but from what I can tell, the *only* thing that Archer could have gotten from you was dick and your schedule. Neither of those seems vital to his infiltration. So no throwing yourself on your sword. Okay? Not until I tell you to."

It was sort of a "get out of jail free" card, but it sat uneasily on Simon. He shifted his shoulders and leaned into it like forgiveness had a physical weight he could stop in its tracks. "I still fucked up. I should have known better."

Dev shoved his hand through his hair. "Yeah, you did. Maybe you should. So?"

"So?" Simon repeated, more exasperated than he meant to sound.

"So."

Dev walked away, and Simon slouched back against the doorjamb and shook his head. Fuck up in the military, and a dressing-down was the least you could expect, the *best* you could expect. More likely you'd get yourself, or someone else, killed.

A fuckup had ended his career in the military—dropped him back in his hometown with a messed-up shoulder and nightmares—and it hadn't even been *his* fuckup.

This mess deserved a more savage payback than a "so." Simon peeled his long body off the door. Not sleeping—despite Dev's veiled order—would do.

THE APARTMENT was huge and stylishly empty—all dull golden wood and heavy black furniture. Simon had bought it furnished and lived there for two years, and it was becoming clear that the only significant change he'd made in that time was Jacob. He had a boyfriend when he was discharged, but that crashed and burned because Dean was career military and Simon was actively fucked up. That was long before Simon moved in here.

There'd been a couple of one-night stands, a couple relationships that were just three one-night stands strung together by texts, and the month he'd spent dating Julie—because pretending to be straight and dating your AA sponsor was totally a good idea.

None of them had changed anything. Jacob's handwriting was all over the whiteboard, scrawled in red pen and decorated with exclamation points. His spare phone charger was plugged in next to the bed, and three bottles of that disgusting sugar syrup he had in his coffee sat in the cupboard, since Simon would rather keep him in bed than lose him to a Starbucks run.

Simon stood on tables and unscrewed light fittings, dismantled picture frames, and scanned the rooms for bugs hidden under plaster. There wasn't even a spider. He took his computer apart and broke the plastic down to circuits and wire, but there were no extraneous components.

He stared down at the dismantled Toshiba and chewed on the inside of his lip until he tasted salt. With nothing to aim it at, his temper was just a restless weight in his gut. It was like sourdough—wet, heavy, and feeding on itself to get bigger.

If he'd found some evidence of Jacob spying on him, of collecting information, at least it would make sense.

In a burst of frustration, he swiped his arm over the table and sent the components and plastic casing flying onto the floor. The single jolt of anger got him moving, and he supposed he might as well use the momentum. He stalked across the room, grabbed the few souvenirs of Jacob, and shoved the syrups, dog-eared magazines, and odds and ends into a bag. Glass rattled as he tied it shut, the plastic stretched under his fingers, and he tossed it in the garbage. Then he soaked a handful of paper towels under the tap and scrubbed the whiteboard. Jacob's crooked scrawl disappeared in a smear of red.

It took under an hour to wipe away any trace that Jacob had been in the apartment. All that was left was the realization that the only person who could stand to spend time with him had been lying about it.

Simon paced the apartment restlessly and texted orders to the security teams until the sun came up and fatigue finally hit. From experience he knew he could keep going, but there was no point in pushing the limits until he had to. The bed in the other room tempted him, but he resisted the thought of its comfort. Instead he folded himself down on the couch, closed his eyes, and willed himself to unconsciousness.

He slept hard, and if he dreamed, it wasn't anyone's business. By five thirty the next morning, he was back at Syntech, sitting on the opposite side of Dev's desk with Nora Reyes, his brother-in-law's slick, professional second-in-command and computer expert. She'd been Becca's best friend too. It wasn't nepotism. Exceptional people just liked Simon's sister. Always had.

One thing Nora wasn't, though, was lenient. Simon wondered bleakly if he should have packed up his office before he came.

"Here's my report," Nora said as she tossed a folder onto the polished desk. She sat down, took her glasses off, and pressed her fingertips against her tear ducts. "It's all in there, but I can tell you the short version. He cleaned us out. Last night a huge packet of data was uploaded to a secure location. The details of the transaction were wiped, so we don't know what data he was after. However, the cyber forensic team was able to pinpoint the targeted computers, and they're going to autopsy their hard drives."

Simon forced his jaw to unclench long enough to ask, "Do you want to fire me, Dev? Or would you prefer my resignation?"

"Stop trying to quit." Dev leaned back in his chair. Carrie had gotten the Uber driver and a clean shirt to him the night before, and Dev had already managed to make the stiff designer linen look crumpled and sweaty. He hooked a finger into his collar and absently tugged at it. "I'm not dealing with this without my chief of security."

Nora cleared her throat. "Your chief of security got you into this," she said. She shot Simon a quick apologetic look with a twist of glossy lips and a shrug. They were friends too—enough that she'd pass on a tip about a car she thought he'd like, not enough that he talked to her about his love life—but that just made her judge him to a higher standard. "The board will not be happy that he's still on the payroll."

"The board will be happy with what I tell them," Dev said, and that old sullen scowl settled on his brow. He'd always been that guy, the one who would cut his nose off just to spite whoever had told him not to. Nora frowned and went to say something, but Dev stopped her. "Enough, Nora. The board isn't your problem anymore, remember? I'll deal with them, you find out what data was stolen, and Simon will find our Mr. Jacob Archer."

Of its own volition, Simon's hand clenched against his thigh. His knuckles showed bony and white through the callused skin. "And then?" he asked, his voice rough with frustration. At himself. "What will happen to him?"

"Do you care?"

"Yes," Simon said. "I want to see him punished."

That was true. But it maybe wasn't the whole truth, not yet, and Dev looked like he knew that. It didn't matter. By the time Simon caught up with Jacob, it *would* be the truth. He changed the subject.

"The team I had on him lost his trail on Riverside last night," he said. "I have them staking out his flat, but I don't think there's anything there he cares enough to go back for. The worry is that his client was from out of the city or the state, because as far as I can tell, he's got no family or long-term ties here. I have teams watching any mass transit, but it is a big place, and you're rich, but not *that* rich."

Dev leaned back in his chair and tapped his pen against his knee. It was the beat to some country song, but Simon couldn't place it.

"What if he just drives out?"

Simon shrugged. "He can't drive."

It took a second, but Nora finally voiced the question that Simon asked himself every time he thought about Jacob.

"Are you sure he wasn't lying?"

"I considered it," Simon told her. "Unless it was a very long inconvenient con, though, I think this one thing is true."

He didn't say *why* he was sure. Pretty sure, at least. The night at the Raceway had been reframed in his memory as turgidly sentimental now that he knew he'd been a mark, but that didn't mean he was going to vomit it up for anyone else to look at.

But there were bits that still felt authentic. It had been hot, packed, and noisy. Simon spent most of the day leaning against walls, envying people their cold beers. Jacob spent it talking to mechanics and betting on cars. But when Simon offered to hire a car so he could have a go, Jacob had gone gray.

"I couldn't leave you sitting here," he'd objected. It was warm, and Jacob had already been sweating, but he was sweating more. "Besides, I wanted you to have fun."

Consideration and modesty were not traits that Jacob pretended to have. Probably because they weren't qualities he prized. So yeah, Simon trusted that one thing.

Simon pushed himself back from the desk and stood up. He shot his cuffs and tugged his jacket straight over his shoulders. Dev wore his suits with the resentment of a kid on the first day of school, but Simon found their strict lines reassuring. It was almost like a uniform. To keep the proper lines required the same posture.

"I'll find him," he said.

Dev rocked back in his chair, and the hinge creaked under him. "I know," he said. "And just as important? Find out *who* hired him."

Nora put her glasses back on. "My money's on Bres Industries," she said. "With the court's ruling in our favor on the lawsuit, they're going to have to pull out of their Arctic projects. That will be a big loss, especially if our experiments bear fruit."

"They're going to appeal," Dev pointed out slowly, but Simon could tell he liked the idea. It wasn't like Dev was stupid or easily led. He was one of the leading voices in a scientific community that Simon, despite having it explained with small words by a twelve-year-old, didn't completely understand. But it was personality, not intellect. He liked his problems straightforward—something to fix, whether it was a carburetor or the ozone layer, and someone to hit.

Simon didn't think it was going to be that simple. Syntech was on the cutting edge of geo-engineering. *Everyone* had problems with them—from hippies who thought they were interfering with Mother Nature to competitors who thought they might have a head start on interfering with Mother Nature.

He said, "I'll check them out first." If he'd owed Dev before, he owed him even more after the other night. So if he wanted an easy answer, Simon would do his best to get it for him.

TA MOORE genuinely believed that she was a Cabbage Patch Kid when she was a small child. That was the start of a lifelong attachment to the weird and fantastic. These days she lives in a market town on the Northern Irish coast and her friends have a rule that she can only send them three weird and disturbing links a month—although she still holds that a DIY penis bifurcation guide is interesting, not disturbing. She believes that adding 'in space!' to anything makes it at least 40 percent cooler, will try to pet pretty much any animal she meets—this includes snakes, excludes bugs—and once lied to her friend that she had climbed all the way up to Tintagel Castle in Cornwall, when actually she'd only gotten to the beach, realized it was really high, and chickened out.

She aspires to be a cynical misanthrope, but is unfortunately held back by a sunny disposition and an inability to be mean to strangers. If TA Moore is mean to you, that means you're friends now.

Website: www.nevertobetold.co.uk
Facebook: www.facebook.com/TA.Moores
Twitter: @tammy_moore

BONE
TO PICK

TA MOORE

Cloister Witte is a man with a dark past and a cute dog. He's happy to talk about the dog all day, but after growing up in the shadow of a missing brother, a deadbeat dad, and a criminal stepfather, he'd rather leave the past back in Montana. These days he's a K-9 officer in the San Diego County Sheriff's Department and pays a tithe to his ghosts by doing what no one was able to do for his brother—find the missing and bring them home.

He's good at solving difficult mysteries. The dog is even better.

This time the missing person is a ten-year-old boy who walked into the woods in the middle of the night and didn't come back. With the antagonistic help of distractingly handsome FBI agent Javi Merlo, it quickly becomes clear that Drew Hartley didn't run away. He was taken, and the evidence implies he's not the kidnapper's first victim. As the search intensifies, old grudges and tragedies are pulled into the light of day. But with each clue they uncover, it looks less and less likely that Drew will be found alive.

www.dreamspinnerpress.com

TA MOORE

DOG DAYS

Wolf Winter: Book One

The world ends not with a bang, but with a downpour. Tornadoes spin through the heart of London, New York cooks in a heat wave that melts tarmac, and Russia freezes under an ever-thickening layer of permafrost. People rally at first—organizing aid drops and evacuating populations—but the weather is only getting worse.

In Durham, mild-mannered academic Danny Fennick has battened down to sit out the storm. He grew up in the Scottish Highlands, so he's seen harsh winters before. Besides, he has an advantage. He's a werewolf. Or, to be precise, a weredog. Less impressive, but still useful.

Except the other werewolves don't believe this is any ordinary winter, and they're coming down over the Wall to mark their new territory. Including Danny's ex, Jack—the Crown Prince Pup of the Numitor's pack—and the prince's brother, who wants to kill him.

A wolf winter isn't white. It's red as blood.

www.dreamspinnerpress.com

TA MOORE

STONE THE CROWS

Wolf Winter: Book Two

When the Winter arrives, the Wolves will come down over the walls and eat little boys in their beds.

Doctor Nicholas Blake might still be afraid of the dark, but the monsters his grandmother tormented him with as a child aren't real.

Or so he thought... until the sea freezes, the country grinds to a halt under the snow, and he finds a half-dead man bleeding out while a dead woman watches. Now his nightmares impinge on his waking life, and the only one who knows what's going on is his unexpected patient.

For Gregor it's simple. The treacherous prophets mutilated him and stole his brother Jack, and he's going to kill them for it. Without his wolf, it might be difficult, but he'll be damned if anyone else gets to kill Jack—even if he has to enlist the help of his distractingly attractive, but very human, doctor.

Except maybe the prophets want something worse than death, and maybe Nick is less human than Gregor believes. As the dead gather and the old stories come true, the two men will need each other if they're going to rescue Jack and stop the prophets' plan to loose something more terrible than the wolf winter.

www.dreamspinnerpress.com